Raymond Tolman

The Rise of the Serpents

Second Volume in
The Serpent Trilogy

SUNSTONE
PRESS

SANTA FE

Sunstone books may be purchased for educational, business, or sales promotional use. For information please write: Special Markets Department, Sunstone Press, P.O. Box 2321, Santa Fe, New Mexico 87504-2321.

Cover art by the author
Book and cover design › Vicki Ahl
Body typeface › Granjon LT Std
Printed on acid-free paper
∞
eBook 978-1-61139-536-5

Library of Congress Cataloging-in-Publication Data

Names: Tolman, Raymond, 1948- author.
Title: The rise of the serpents / by Raymond Tolman.
Description: Santa Fe : Sunstone Press, [2018] | Series: Serpent trilogy ; volume 2
Identifiers: LCCN 2018000438 (print) | LCCN 2018008483 (ebook) | ISBN 9781611395365 | ISBN 9781632932112 (softcover : alk. paper)
Subjects: LCSH: Indian mythology--Fiction. | Domestic fiction.
Classification: LCC PS3620.O3285 (ebook) | LCC PS3620.O3285 R57 2018 (print) | DDC 813/.6--dc23
LC record available at https://lccn.loc.gov/2018000438

WWW.SUNSTONEPRESS.COM
SUNSTONE PRESS / POST OFFICE BOX 2321 / SANTA FE, NM 87504-2321 /USA
(505) 988-4418 / ORDERS ONLY (800) 243-5644 / FAX (505) 988-1025

The Rise of the Serpents

Dedicated to

Richard Tolman,

My little brother who now climbs mountains
and runs rivers in heaven.

Preface

*V*olume two of *The Serpent Trilogy, The Rise of the Serpents* is based upon events and situations that are all too real. The intriguing storylines are enveloped within real historical events and settings. Unfortunately, the real world appears to be spiraling out of control. Currently the Doomsday clock is ticking ever closer to Armageddon. According to media such as television, the average person is lead to believe that as the clock ticks to finality, the cause will most likely be from an impact from an asteroid like the one that killed the dinosaurs, a nuclear exchange between the superpowers, or a down and dirty revolution between the divided political parties that govern countries. Indeed, this may be the case, but in truth there is something that is far more likely to occur that could end human dominance on this planet.

Here in the United States we are hardwired to resist social change. But as politics are forever changing, we fear uncertainty. We are conditioned from birth to fear the things that could end our lives. However, for the scientists who actually study the probabilities of death, the statistics clearly indicate that we rarely fear the things that most likely could actually kill us. For example, as a teacher, I was required to conduct drills with my students in case of a terrorist attack. In reality the real danger I perceived happened every afternoon as students in the bus loading area pushed each other and stepped in front of oncoming buses to be the first to board. In the parking lot, young people drove their pick-up trucks and cars as fast as they could to clear out at the end of the school day. It was a nightmare being on duty. Despite expressing concern to the school authorities, I was ignored. Far more students were hurt in those few moments than at any other time of the day.

Far more people die in automobile accidents than by guns and currently more people are dying from overdosing with opium based prescription drugs, than by automobile accidents. Yet where I am currently living, in East Tennessee, all my neighbors are armed to the teeth just in case a terrorist, a meth crazed addict, or a roaming band of agitators might come to our doors. Even silencers have been legalized here, with the excuse that our hunting dogs need ear protection. Yet we are in far more danger from a domestic argument going nuclear than any terrorist attack. I have found myself in many social situations where people actually take out their weapons and show them off to each other in a crowded restaurant or barber shop. Disagree with one of these characters, particularly over politics or religion and one risks the chance a gun toting and imbalanced character challenging you. I personally find all these situations to be unnerving. I know how to handle a gun but I don't know if they do. People do get shot, run over, and even killed by an occasional terrorist but they are local situations and even the terrorist are for the most part; homegrown.

By far, the one unknown danger that could dramatically change life on earth is a world-wide pandemic. Consider the Native Americans who lived in North America, in many instances an estimated ninety-five percent of many Indian populations perished after the first Europeans introduced smallpox, influenza, and many other European diseases to a population that had no biological resistance. The single most likely cause of a nightmare scenario is not the oft-discussed threat of asteroids, automobile wrecks, drug crazed addicts, and gun shootings we are conditioned to fear but rather an overlooked one; pandemic illness. Throughout all of history biological agents have been used as weapons of mass destruction. In laboratories throughout the world, including the United States, unscrupulous scientist experiment with biological agents that could on purpose or by accident escape the facility to infect millions of people. So far, we have been lucky, but given time, someone may succeed in allowing a pathogen to escape.

What is it that makes humans the most dangerous creatures to ever evolve on this planet? Is it in our nature to be killers as a species or have we been directed, taught and manipulated by an outside force to become the creatures we are?

Archeologists have discovered that serpents have been associated with human civilization, on every continent from the earliest of times. From dragons in China to Quetzalcoatl and Kukulkan in South America, they are an enigma to both the archeologists and historians who document such matters. Why do they have such a profound impact on human psychology even though they are thought to be products of fiction? Why are serpents, always found in association with cultures that adopt human sacrifice and blood rituals?

To the Native Americans who have lived in the Southwest for several millennia, these creatures are absolutely real. In *Rise of the Serpents*, an alien race of serpents is discovered that have been secretly manipulating humans but when they are discovered they sense a reprisal from the humans. They fear an upcoming attack and test their abilities to manipulate the minds of the civilian population in northern New Mexico in retaliation against the efforts of the governmental agency directed by General Armstrong. The scope and setting expands as Penny, Corey, and Hidalgo become much more than mere historical detectives, they become the key for the survival of the human race, drawn into the conflict as news of tragic events occur.

The team is dealing with an entirely new kind of mystery. They are dealing with a military that is a necessary evil in a world of terrorism and rogue nations that possess thermonuclear bombs or terrorists who would like to sneak dirty bombs into our borders. The real mysteries to solve are man-made and truly terrifying. They find themselves at odds against the military industrial complex in their efforts to eradicate the newly discovered enemies; the serpents.

Knowing the powers of the serpents, the historical detectives can only wait and advise the governmental agencies that request their assistance. But first, they must help some old friends; the Hopi people. The Hopi people are direct descendants of the Ancestral Puebloans that long ago settled in Aztlán. They are renowned for prophesies that are very accurate and respected. At the time this story was written, reports were just making the headlines of news agencies concerning the auctions of Hopi ceremonial objects that were being conducted in Paris, France. I felt it my duty to bring attention to this pervasive problem. These were not objects that were discarded and then later found, they were stolen from the Hopi people. I hope to shine further light on this pervasive problem. Antiquity thieves are only one of many modern problems indigenous Americans deal with.

In, *The Rise of the Serpents* an examination of the serpent's physiology and history is undertaken. They are intelligent, with a telepathic language which uses hieroglyphic symbols as a form of communication.

Stories in this novel are all lessons learned while experiencing the dynamics of human interactions, interactions that color our lives with both sadness and joy. They are also stories about facing great challenges, using critical thinking skills, and using a scientific approach to solving problems that to others seem mysterious and otherworldly. Traditionally, young girls have been discouraged from pursuing science and math careers. Penny, the young protagonist of this novel, is a model of what girls can accomplish while overcoming great personal difficulties. Putting myself in the mind of Penny has been a challenge for me. Thank heavens I have loved ones to draw ideas and insight from like my precocious young granddaughter, Jenna, who certainly speaks her mind. But there is one person to whom I am absolutely indebted to and for whom I would like to express my appreciation. Whenever possible my wife, Judy Duggins Tolman, has traveled down southwestern rivers, climbed mountains, explored caves and hiked many miles with me in search of an adventure. But far more important, she has offered me valuable academic assistance, encouragement and insights into the science of human interactions; and a women's point of view. After all, what would I know about a bridal party? Why would I know about baby breath flowers? She was always willing to make sacrifices and do her best to make an adventure possible for me despite severe health problems associated with diabetes. She is what is known in modern parlance as a soul mate. As they say, "Bless her heart!"

I would also like to express my appreciation to Jim Palmer who photographed my cover paintings and finally, I wish to express my appreciation to the fine people at Sunstone Press in Santa Fe, New Mexico. Without their help and understanding The Serpent Trilogy would likely have not been published.

Part 1

Declaring War

Quetzalcoatl is a primal idea of the duality of human nature. The serpent is the embodiment of Heaven and Earth. It scares people in many ways.

—Robert Graham

Bloomfield, New Mexico

With five people, all working together it only took a few minutes to load the canoes and gear onto the boat trailer, but it would take us all day long to drive home. We stopped in Wagon Mound for lunch and noticed in the local newspaper an article describing how four Navajo youth had been charged for the murder of a prominent businessman's son in Bloomfield. According to the newspaper it was pretty much a closed case with the boy's father demanding that justice be done. Sure enough, there was a picture of four young Navajo men including Alan Begay.

From Wagon Mound, we drove all the way to Serpiente in order to drop off the canoes and gear we didn't need. After a good night's sleep in real beds, followed the next morning with a great breakfast, we again began the long journey to Bernalillo where we turned north on route 44 past Chaco Canyon and made it to Bloomfield late in the evening.

Coming into Bloomfield we encountered a roadblock. Hidalgo, who was taking his turn at driving, took out his driver's license but was surprised when the policeman demanded to know why a Navajo was driving around in a new truck full of Anglos. Hidalgo was getting angry at the insinuation that was being made, but everyone sensed that there already was a certain amount of animosity building due to the murder that had occurred. Hidalgo explained to the officer that he was an employee and they were traveling to Shiprock on business on the reservation.

"Okay," answered the state policeman but what are these other people doing with you? Hidalgo knew that they would never understand if he answered that he was with his other family, adopted or not. "They are my employers; they are just dropping me off with my parents who called me for help."

The policeman shook his head in a negative response but started to walk away after waving us on. Turning he looked at Ken who was doing his best not to take out what he was thinking on the officer, and said. "As soon as you drop this fellow off I recommend that you leave the area as fast as possible."

"You bet," Ken answered. With that, they drove on in to Bloomfield in order to find a motel where they could all find a welcome respite from the monotonous drive. Ken and June walked in to pay for the rooms and all was well until Hidalgo walked up to the desk.

"Sorry, we are out of rooms," says the clerk to Hidalgo.

June looked at him and interjected, "Well, that's all right, we have already paid for this fellow's room. He is with us."

The helpless and flustered clerk handed over the keys to three rooms. Hidalgo had a room all to himself in an almost empty motel.

The Star People

The galaxy that would come to be known by humanoids as the Milky Way Galaxy was the home of the star people. Although there were billions of other galaxies that occupied the bubbles that made up the known universe, the galaxies that the star people would occupy, was a benign galaxy with few warring creatures living in it, certainly none that would worry the star people. Most planetary civilizations that the star people encountered were considered by them to be extremely primitive.

The creatures found on those planets were hardly able to lift themselves above the gravity of their own planet. A few creatures had just learned to split the atom, a feat that was child's play for the star people. The majority of the creatures that the star people encountered, those that were at the top of their food chains, were more like parasites than intelligent invading armies. The star people were usually unconcerned with planetary affairs. They did not live on planets anyway. They constructed their own homes in space. Large crystalline spheres that were so large they had their own gravity fields. Completely removed from the terrain environment, they had escaped disease and want millions of years ago.

Quetzalcoatl and Kukulkan were certainly not star people, but they were also from a distant place in the galaxy. They had long ago lost track of the genealogical line of creatures who always named their nest leaders Quetzalcoatl and Kukulkan. There had been thousands of generations of them. They remembered that distant place they had come from, located directly above the bright star Sirius, in the constellation Orion. Located there is a single nondescript star, invisible from where they now lived, which had two habitable planets which circled it. One of those planets was similar to the planet they were now on. The serpent's ancestors had been discovered on that far away planet millions of years ago by the star people.

The star people, whose powers were far greater than the serpent's powers, were composed of almost pure technology and energy. Traveling through space was normal for them; they had made peaceful contact with thousands of other creatures living on thousands of other planets. They didn't believe in interfering with other creatures preferring to let them live their own lives. They preferred to remain invisible, blending into the stars and not bothering any other beings, but over time, the serpents had learned too much from them. Some of the serpents had begun to make use of the dark energy that was available to them, greatly expanding their abilities. The star people had forbidden the serpents to use that energy, but they learned to use it anyway.

The serpents had lived among the star people for millennia, learning many of the secrets of the star people. The serpents were considered pets by some the star beings that were benevolent but far more evolved than the serpents. But the serpents were also very intelligent. They had a special intelligence, processing a collective consciousness, contriving their own ways of traveling through the vastness of space by traveling with the star people.

Simply by going into hibernation and ceasing all mental processes, they were able to hitch a ride to all manner of places in the universe. Then, when the star people visited a distant planet they would simply exit the landing craft in pairs and search for a place to build a nest. Unfortunately, the star people soon discovered what the serpents were up to and decided to round the serpents up. The star people then searched for a planet that had liquid water; an atmosphere of nitrogen and ample amounts of oxygen; dry land in order to build serpent nest; and local creatures they could use for nourishment.

The serpents would be banished to some insignificant planet where they would be unable to return to the stars and cause harm. They were then dropped off in various localities around those insignificant planets. One of those insignificant planets, which long ago had no intelligent terrestrial creatures, would later become known as Earth. Earth had become their prison.

The serpents never required much in the form of nourishment. Any small creature who would wander into their company could easily be bitten. Their venom was deadly and the small creature would crawl only a short distance until death occurred. The creature would then be swallowed whole and slowly absorbed. One small creature would suffice for several weeks at a time. Each serpentine creature could live for many hundreds of years, needing to reproduce only when the level of snakes in the nest dropped to a certain minimum population.

They drew most of their nourishment from the energy that was all around them. Energy that is everywhere there is matter, a universe full of energy. Within the very atoms that made the universe there were many forms of energy that would not be discovered by most terrestrials until they had evolved for millions of years. The serpents became known as Feathered Serpents, Dragons and in the area that would become the American Southwest, they were known as the Rattlesnake clan by the first early humanoids they encountered. Usually they would draw upon a positive energy, a life force that would nourish them and keep them well. But when encountering intelligent creatures, they would use negative energy and they would war upon those creatures.

They had great skills in concealing themselves and used energy to change their very appearance when necessary. They could shift the very molecules in their bodies. Using that energy they could alter their shape to assume the likeness of any creature they wanted to. Furthermore, they could control the minds of the primitive creatures around them and easily manipulate them.

Long ago, the star people cleaned their spaceships, disposing of the pesky parasites that had intrigued them for a while but now had become just so much extra baggage that was being cleaned out. The troublesome serpents were dropped off in isolated ecosystems where the star people knew they would probably survive yet do little harm to the indigenous populations.

Serpent clans in the Americas had lived in peace for thousands of seasons but with the retreating ice that had covered much of the planet, a new species of creatures arrived; humans. They were a large and dangerous species and to the serpents they were just another creature out there that was too large and dangerous to swallow. Yet the humans and the rattlesnake clans lived in peace for several thousand seasons until the population of humans became so large and skilled at hunting then the local creatures began to disappear.

When other creatures discovered the serpents, or made war on them, the serpents could read their minds through the energy that all living creatures possess. It was child's play for them to create envy and fear between them and the other creatures would war upon themselves. Mind manipulation was a skill the serpents had perfected millions of years ago and was particularly useful on the planet called Earth where the dominant species, called humans, were easily controlled. The humans would exterminate themselves, leaving the serpents in peace.

Then the humans who would come to be known as Anasazi became too numerous. The serpents now had to compete with them in order to obtain food and besides, they expected respect from all the creatures they shared the land with but the Anasazi had lost respect for the serpents, treating them as just a nuisance to be dealt with; to be exterminated.

Drawing upon the dark energy that was at their command, the serpents changed their forms. Sometimes they actually walked among the humans, studying them. They enjoyed playing their games with the humans. Soon, they coerced the superstitious humans into killing each other. Many of the humans moved to the north along a river that would come to be known as the San Juan, building their homes in inaccessible cliffs to avoid other warring humans. The humans thought that building their homes high on the hillsides would keep them safe, but it didn't matter, the serpents wanted them out. In time, the terrified Anasazi people who had no idea why they were warring upon themselves moved out, leaving their homes and all their belongings in place, just as if they just decided one day to walk away, which is exactly what they did.

The serpents became addicted and accustomed to the negative energy created by dealing with the humans. Following the humans, the serpents moved to the south and created a new nest to live in. Many generations of the serpents had come and gone and they had lived in peace. Then a thousand years ago, the Anasazi reappeared around their new nest. But this time things were very different. The humans had learned their lesson. Human clan had learned to live with the rattlesnakes by offering sacrifices, showing them the respect they expected. They would reciprocate by offering the humans pretty trinkets that they seemed to covet. For several hundred years all was fine but soon, other human clans had moved through their territory. The new intruders were not evil but brought with them a sickness which destroyed the Anasazi clan that had lived with the serpents for generations.

Soon there was an imbalance that caused the deaths of many of the serpents. Other creatures began to war with them. The Coyote clan was particularly proficient at finding serpents and then killing them. The balance of nature was again unbalanced. The serpents decided to make war on the humans and coyotes until finally three humans befriended them. Respect and peace was reestablished in their homelands that would be known as Serpiente. Then an evil pair of humans that coveted their small treasures that were being traded for sacrificed food came to their nest. Using deadly chemicals, they managed to kill all but two of the serpents.

Quetzalcoatl and Kukulkan, who were the leaders of the serpent clan, left the nest to seek privacy to mate that fateful day. After mating, Kukulkan would carry a dozen or so tiny serpents in her ovum which would be born alive. After they were born, unlike all native snake species on Earth the babies would be fed and pampered by their parents for several months. Just like their human counterparts, the more evolved, the longer the gestation and the longer it would take to raise the juvenile serpents until they could take care of themselves.

The two serpents then escaped from Serpiente, New Mexico. They changed their shape into ravens, flying to their former home along the San Juan River hoping to find it deserted as it had been when they had originally left.

Once they reestablished themselves back in San Juan country they continued to mate and started to build another nest shaped like a tiny volcano. Reclaiming dark energy, power from the universe that is held within atoms themselves, they made a comeback but fumed over the disrespect they had been shown and they looked forward to the vengeance they could enact with the humans. They felt like they had been double crossed by the arrogant humans and now they were seeking to punish the numerous human ants living in the region. They drew upon the dark power of the universe to create evil among the humans which generated even more energy for them. It became a positive feedback loop of negative energy. As the serpents gained more energy from the evil around them they taught their little ones how to shift their shapes and honed their abilities to wage war.

Two Weeks Earlier, Dalton and Jackson

Bloomfield, New Mexico is the home of Salmon Ruins. At one time an outlier settlement of the Chaco Canyon phenomenon, it is now the home to many who work in the oil and natural gas industry as well as people who make the daily drive over to Farmington to work at places like Jackson Auto Sales. It was also the home of Neil Jackson and Robert Dalton who were not typical high school students. They were cocky and arrogant, particularly Neil Jackson. Jackson, heir to Jackson Auto Sales, had grown up with well- developed muscles due to lifting weights which his father had encouraged since he had turned fourteen.

Robert Dalton was a follower. Without the wit or inclination to be a self-starter, he was a large bulky kid with a pot belly. He followed Jackson everywhere he went. They had been good friends ever since fourth grade when Jackson had managed to pour a chemical into the school's cafeteria dishwasher, turning everything a permanent blue in color. The chemical was not poisonous but the cafeteria trays and dishwasher had to be replaced anyway. Immediately they suspected that the school hooligan, Jackson, as the culprit. Dalton lied for him giving him an alibi. No one was punished but everyone had their suspicions and in the next few years Jackson did little to improve their suspicions and opinions.

The two boys had almost single handedly turned their school into a battle-ground. Grades meant nothing to them because Jackson assumed his future was already assured because his father was a well to do car dealer in Farmington with political connections and ambitions. He would inherit his father's fortune. He knew that even if he simply sold everything he could easily live the remainder of his life off the money.

On the other hand, Robert Dalton was overweight and lazy; his entire life was in the service to his friend Neil Jackson. Easily manipulated, he simply couldn't care less about the consequences of his actions. There rarely were consequences for his actions. Jackson saw to that. Because of that he was willing to do anything for his best friend, however when he was separated from Jackson, he lost all his bravado.

Already two teachers had crossed their paths. The teachers, expecting some degree of respect from all their students as well as the school administration had lost their jobs. Now any teacher would be shy about attempting to discipline the boys for anything, preferring to teach through Jackson's classroom interruptions or Dalton's snoring. Jackson had learned early on that having powerful connections meant that he and his friend would rarely be punished for their transgressions. Because of that, they relished the power and fear they could generate.

In high school both boys had tried out for the football team but only Jackson had made the team. Dalton loved a good street fight with Jackson backing him, but hated the discipline and effort it required for him to make the football team. Neil Jackson however, was good enough to compete as a quarterback but he had stiff competition. The best players, fearful of retribution, stepped aside and let Jackson have the position. Some of them even thought that if Jackson could exceed at football maybe he would accept other responsibilities, be more serious, perhaps be civil to them. All went fine until the first game when he was intercepted twice during the first quarter and then fumbled the ball. By halftime, with the score 34 to 0, the coach pulled him out and benched him. Jackson was infuriated. Even while he sat on the bench, Jackson would hatch a plan to dispose of the coach that had the audacity to put in another player.

Within a few days, the school board began receiving complaints from parents that the coach was making sexual advances to the high school girls. One girl in particular, who was infatuated with Neil Jackson, manipulated her mother into making several calls to the board of education to complain. The coach was dismissed and a new one was hired. It didn't matter; Jackson by then had lost all interest in playing on a football team where he couldn't be the star player. Football had become a game of little interest to him. The game was below him but in the Four Corners there is another game that many young boys became involved with, rodeo.

Rodeo was and is an important sport in the Four Corners area and even Dalton got involved. They fancied themselves modern day cowboys; rodeo stars although they had never competed except on a very local level. Often, in rodeo competition, they were beaten by the local Navajo youth from Shiprock, creating an untenable situation for them. It was Jackson who figured out a simple to way to eliminate the competition. Jackson stayed in the shadows while his friend, Dalton, walked up behind the Navajo youth and hit him in the back of the head as hard as he could. The young Native American hit the ground hard but immediately got back up and returned punch for punch eventually putting Dalton on the ground. Immediately a large crowd gathered around as the boys began screaming profanities at each other. Dalton got up and again they traded punches that were by now getting very ineffective due to their fatigue. Both boys were then separated by the local police, handcuffed and taken down to the juvenile facility and then, after several hours released.

Neil Jackson won his event that day when the only real competition, the Navajo youth, failed to show up to compete. Both Robert Dalton and the Navajo youth were disqualified from rodeo competition. Dalton could have cared less, but the Navajo boy was bitter about the whole event. He figured out what had happened when apparently, no one else could.

Being good street fighters, Jackson and Dalton took every opportunity to demonstrate their skill as bullies by picking as many fights as they could. When the police attempted to deal with them they were always stymied by the Jackson's family lawyer who was paid a generous fee to keep the two boys out of trouble. Rumors began to circulate around the town about their extracurricular activities.

At first, their activities had been harmless enough, really just childhood pranks, but soon they found themselves always needing to outdo each other. It was cheap entertainment, the only real entertainment in the small community. They toilet papered several houses, soaped several screens that belonged to elderly people. Then things began to get a little more serious. After disconnecting a trailer hitch, they relished watching a camping trailer, full of sleeping occupants roll down a steep ravine where it crashed. Several out of state cars belonging to tourist were destroyed when sugar was poured into their gas tanks. When law officers questioned them, the boys were again protected by lawyers. Besides, it meant more business for Jackson's car dealership.

Once, they found an elderly Navajo man who had passed out in an ally after drinking too much of the white man's poison; whiskey. They pulled the old man's pants down and pushed a fire cracker into the sleeping man's butt crack. They lit it and ran. They were unruly and arrogant, thinking that they had pulled a great stunt and no one would ever know. But what they didn't know was that they were seen doing their deed.

Then it all ended. As the cold winds of winter rolled into the southwest they seemed to lose interest in their activities. But when spring came and the air warmed, it all started again. Several of the more adventurous and rowdy teenagers found a private strip of beach alongside the San Juan River which flowed out of Navajo Reservoir. Being on private land, part of Jacksons father's estate, they would party, drinking beer and smoking marijuana but the main objective was in trying to get the girls to skinny dip with them. It wouldn't happen. In the early spring the water is ice cold but Jackson knew things would change as the water warmed. Jackson then had an idea.

It was all just a tease convincing Dalton to remove all his clothes to coerce everyone into the icy water. Dalton did just as he was expected to do, causing the girls to stare and giggle at the overweight boy as he waded into the cold water. Apparently, it never dawned on Dalton that no one would want to get into water that cold but with Jackson's prompting in Dalton went. Then Jackson did something unexpected. He gathered up all of Dalton's clothes and everyone left, leaving Dalton there, waist deep in cold water among the cottonwoods and newly hatched mosquitoes, contemplating how he would get home and wondering how his best friend could have double crossed him.

Dalton had never experienced anything like this in his life. It was one thing to be naked in the presence of several other persons but now he was alone with a mile walk out to the main road where hopefully he could hitchhike back into Bloomfield. Needless to say, it caused quite a stir when he finally walked out to the road. With one hand, he held a piece of cardboard over his more private parts and his other in a fist with his thumb up, he was the subject of a humiliating array of cars and trucks with people screaming profanities at him and blaring horns. He was actually thankful when the police car finally arrived. The local policeman wrapped him in a blanket and hauled him off to jail.

An hour later, Dalton's very embarrassed mother showed up at the jail with a set of clothes and took him home. Before he could leave the jail, he was informed that he would be required to appear in court for indecent exposure and would surely be required to pay a stiff fine. This time however, Jackson was not there to bail him out of his predicament.

Usually Dalton could live with almost any embarrassment but what had occurred to him was in a whole new realm of humiliation. How could his best friend have done this to him? Sitting in his room, listening to his parents scream at each other over which one of them was responsible for Dalton's lack of up-bringing and how they were going to pay his court cost and fine, he hatched a plan to get even with his ex- friend.

Tidbits of Human Flesh

The following day Dalton was lucky. He had followed his ex-friend all day before Jackson finally pulled onto one of the gravel roads that lead out into the countryside. Jackson was smart enough not to leave incriminating drug paraphernalia around his house so he had hidden several ounces of marijuana in an ammo box under a pile of rocks along the edge of a small ravine. Dalton knew Jackson's secret and followed him until he finally passed Jackson then slammed on his breaks. Both vehicles came to a sudden stop. Dalton jumped out of his car and ran over to the driver's side window. Jackson, believing that he could easily brush off the previous tease, rolled down his window and stuck his head out of it. His grin vanished as soon as he saw the gun in Dalton's hand. Dalton raised the gun up and pointed it directly at the center of Jackson's forehead. The gun went off. Dalton looked first at the barrel with the hot gases still coming out of it and then at his old friend's face which now had a tiny hole, right between the eyes.

Blood started to spurt out of the hole as the body slumped into the seat. Dalton had not intended to actually shoot Jackson, only to scare him. Pondering what to do, he stuffed the gun back into his car, and then thinking, he grabbed an old towel that was always lying on the floorboard. Turning the wheels sharply he then pushed Jackson's car off the road where it gained momentum and finally crashed into the shallow ravine. Dalton then wiped off his fingerprints and left the scene of the crime.

An oil worker discovered the car within an hour of the incident. Returning to town the worker drove directly to the Bloomfield Police Department to report what he thought was a car accident. The police quickly established that a murder had occurred as soon as the body was examined. Neil Jackson had been killed execution style in the face.

When leaving the scene of the crime, doubts and fears immediately began to consume Dalton. The Bloomfield police were not exactly known for their professionalism but they certainly were professional enough considering the budgetary restraints they were dealing with. What they couldn't accomplish was easily compensated for by a simple call to nearby districts. Teamwork could lead to solving the crime. What felon can run faster than the speed of a telephone call? Dalton knew he had to quickly establish an alibi for himself.

Despite the giggling girls and teasing he endured from the local boys who had all heard about his misadventure at the river, Dalton swallowed his pride blending in as best he could into the crowd of teenagers that he usually hung around with. In Dalton's mind, the only thing that really mattered was that everyone would see him hanging around providing him an alibi. For the first time in his life Dalton's mind went into overdrive.

While sitting with another student from school in a booth at Chad's Pizza and Game Room, four Navajos, high school seniors from Shiprock, soon entered the Pizzeria and ordered a pizza. Dalton causally walked out to the old truck he had been driving, pulled the 22 caliber pistol he had used to kill Jackson and slipped the gun under the car seat of the Navajo's car. He then returned to the inside of the Pizzeria and closing the door to a phone booth made an anonymous call to the police department. Dalton then left and drove just far enough away to see what would happen but not close enough to draw attention.

When the car was searched a 22-caliber pistol was indeed found under the seat. The boys claimed no knowledge of the pistol. They had heard of Jackson but did not know him personally nor did they have a grudge against him. It didn't matter, they were all four charged with murder and incarcerated pending ballistics test.

The ballistics test proved to be conclusive so they sat in jail, in limbo until further evidence was discovered. No one really believed the young Navajos had committed the murder. They had alibis themselves, having just driven down from Durango and a service station attendant remembered seeing them when they stopped for gas. The problem was the gun. No one could account for the gun in the car and certainly no one could explain the anonymous phone call.

Meanwhile, the occasional teasing that Dalton received caused him to think about himself in an entirely different way. As he thought to himself, once you have been embarrassed this bad, what else can they do? It really didn't matter anymore. He thought to himself; once your reputation has been ruined, then you have the freedom to do what you want to do. Dalton exercised that freedom but in an unexpected way. When others teased him he simply grinned or ignored them but his mind was always working. Two days later a house was consumed in fire where four local high school girls who had been particularly cruel to Dalton were sleeping over. They all died and arson was immediately established. The arsonist had left the empty five gallon can of kerosene on the wooden poach where the fire had started.

When news of the murders erupted through the fabric of not only the Bloomfield community but the entire Four Corners area, fear began to grip people. A killer was loose among them. Dalton was questioned by the police when investigators remembered the story of Dalton's altercation at the river and connected the two boys; however, everyone they talked to explained that they were really best of friends and Dalton did have friends who claimed to remember seeing him at the pizza place around the time when the murder was committed. In regards to the fire, Dalton's parents argued with the police that he was asleep in bed all night long providing him another alibi.

Dalton was lucky. In only a short time everyone had conveniently forgotten what a bully Jackson was and began to worry about their own safety. They felt that despite the fact that Jackson was a monster, he didn't deserve to be killed. The football coach was immediately questioned as well as anyone, and there were many, who had had an altercation with Jackson. No one could imagine the four girls having an enemy. Dalton simply muddled on through life as if nothing had happened but he was getting creative, his mind was constantly devising plans to cause havoc to those that had tortured him.

The local kids who attended the high school had ideas of their own. They immediately began to blame the Native Indian students. Fights began to break out on a daily basis as everyone looked for a scapegoat. Dalton, of course, thought this was all great fun. The more pain that was inflicted without his personal involvement the better.

As in most rural communities, baseball is the major spring sport and the players were the pride of the community. Bloomfield had a good team that year having won all but one game but when Shiprock High School came into town everything changed. It all started out as a typical game with the field announcer giving a play by play description of the game almost as well as the local radio announcer. With Shiprock up to bat during the bottom of the fourth inning, all was going well except for the large flock of ravens that had settled on the field behind second base. The announcer even made the comment; "Let's hope this young man from Shiprock doesn't take out one of our crows out there."

The Bloomfield pitcher, deciding that the batter was likely to hit his next pitch, slung a fast ball directly at the face of the batter hitting him squarely in the nose. As the batter's knees buckled and began to fall the Shiprock team, composed of young Navajos, all came charging out of the dugout, grabbed baseball bats and charged the other team. Within moments the entire field was full of young boys trying to beat each other to death. The problem was, once a player hit the ground the beating didn't stop. In all, the resulting melee resulted in numerous broken bones and concussions and the pitcher died from massive brain injuries.

Police were, of course, called in to assist the resource policeman who had been assigned to police the spectators but was overwhelmed as the spectators spilled into the melee. Forty-three people were arrested and the season was suspended. As the field was evacuated the ravens moved in to pick at the tidbits of human flesh and blood that were evident around the field. Curiously, the birds ignored the popcorn and trash that all humans leave behind them at a sporting event.

Working Undercover

Ken and June had friends who owned a vacant house in nearby Flora Vista which was used as a staging area to investigate the crimes. They allowed Corey and me to set up house there. I looked very young, despite my age. I immediately enrolled as an undercover student at Bloomfield High School under the pretext that I had gotten into trouble in Albuquerque and my parents wanted me to stay in a small community where I could stay out of trouble.

Corey worked himself into a job at the Pizza place which was always looking for delivery people. Hidalgo traveled on to Shiprock and out to the reservation where he hoped he could get some insight into what was happening.

I immediately began to make friends; if for no other reason than my mysterious demeanor I had established. My athleticism drew attention from the coaches. I blended in well but was confronted by several simple problems. First of all, I could do the school work effortlessly. I found myself marking answers wrong just so I wouldn't appear too smart. My most common answer to any inquiry by the teachers or administration was "whatever."

Secondly, being very good looking, dare I say sexy? I found myself the center of attention from the local boys, which made the girls jealous. I solved that problem by connecting with Corey, making me unavailable to the boys yet allowing me to mix in. My romance with the so called new boy at the pizza place became the center of gossip for the school, but the hardest job I had was simply pretending to be bad. I knew that if I wanted to blend in with the rough kids who might have a few answers, I would need to play the part. Thinking of my experiences in Mexico I streaked my blond hair with black and pink streaks and then painted my fingernails black. I had become a rebel.

26

Corey thought I looked awful but understood what I was doing. It was the only way I could blend in, but he refused to join in on the charade. It was then that the so-called romance ended between Corey and me. Little did the students know that I had been married to Corey and hopelessly in love with him for some time!

Corey was the person who made a real break though. By just hanging around the pizza place he was privy to all the teenage gossip and it was only a short time until he discovered just how sneaky Dalton was. His suspicions were confirmed when he confronted Dalton with questions. Similar questions were showered upon Dalton by other students as well. The key questions that Corey needed to have answers to was; where did the gun come from, and who made the anonymous phone call to the police?

Further suspicions arose when suddenly Dalton became the main marijuana dealer in town. Jackson had accumulated a considerable amount of pot in his ammo box due to the money he had easy access to. Everyone knew about the pot but no one except for Dalton had any idea where it was hidden. Dalton felt like quite a big shot while he was a dealer, but within a couple of weeks his stash of marijuana was gone.

Dalton needed to do something else to feed his animosity to those around him. Reflecting upon what had happened at the baseball game his mind ventured into diabolical plots to get the thrill of watching the mayhem which he had created. Instead of driving to school he ventured into other communities, stopping near high schools and placing a phone call to the school with a bomb threat. It excited him when the entire school was emptied and the police were put into overdrive in a futile attempt to find the bombs. He repeated this on three more occasions until he realized that his treats were not being taken seriously. He concluded that in order to recreate the excitement, he would need to plant a real bomb.

Dalton's mind had been in overdrive ever since the murder of Jackson on that fateful spring day, now it actually began to bother him. He began to have vivid dreams at night. Dreams of murder and mayhem constantly floated in and out of his conscience especially during the early morning hours when everyone else was sound asleep. His dreams became diabolical plots.

Some mornings, after waking up early, he would leave the house, get into his truck, and just drive around thinking of the previous nights' dreams. Curiously there were always a raven or two perched on the tailgate of his truck or the porch railings when he got up but he never thought anything about them.

He was lost in thought, one morning, after a night of eventful dreams he decided to act on one of those dreams

Driving south into the desert county he encountered a pickup truck miles from any town. They were a common sight out there, used by the oil companies to transport every conceivable item used in the industry. He quietly come to a stop behind it and crept up to the cab. Inside was a man, fast asleep.

Dalton reached into his pocket where he had another twenty-two pistol he had traded some marijuana for, took it out, and shot the man in the head. Unfortunately, the man didn't die instantly as Jackson had, instead he jerked open the door and tried to tackle Dalton. Dalton pumped five more shots into him before the man stopped struggling and finally bled out.

Looking into the man's pockets he discovered a wallet with over five hundred dollars in cash in it, but even more importantly after looking in the bed of the truck he found tools, pipes and most importantly, a box of dynamite, caps and a huge roll of fuse, all used in the oil business. All would be incorporated into his business now.

The Navajo Police Force

Hidalgo met with the Navajo Tribal Council to discuss possible solutions to the problem of the four youths who had been transferred to the Farmington Correctional Facility. But by the time Hidalgo could arrange a meeting the boys had been released and they had returned home. It soon became apparent with the police that several people had actually seen the four boys coming in from Durango and it seemed pretty obvious to all that they were framed for the murder. Besides, by now the police were being overwhelmed with other, more pressing problems. Juveniles from all over the area were being incarcerated for crimes ranging from shoplifting to murder and the facility was bursting at the seams with inmates who all had to be walked through the legal system. The vast majority of the assault cases were a mystery to the under paid and over worked public defenders. Their clients knew what they had done but had no idea why they had done it. Most were in trouble for the first time in their lives. The only thing in common about them was that they were quiet, law abiding young people who normally would never consider getting into a fight or brawl. The troublemakers that the police usually dwelt with all were there in force which further complicated the situation.

The tribal meeting was of great importance, because the elders who made up the council were concerned about things that were occurring on the reservation. Just like everywhere else in the area, the quiet kids, the followers were getting into trouble. The Navajo shamans who normally were extremely secretive about what they did were now being rounded up and questioned by the tribal elders. They had no idea what was causing the problems, something was happening that even they couldn't control. Many people on the reservation were naturally superstitious but during the last month there were constant reports of supernatural occurrences.

Skin walkers had always been part of the natural mythology in the area but now reports were coming to the attention of the elders on a daily basis. Both the Tribal Council and the Navajo Police always took reports such as these very seriously if for no other reason than they often related to real trouble on the reservation.

Hidalgo had friends and relatives on the Navajo Police Force so he visited several of them to get their input and impressions. The reports were always the same; violence was on the increase. People were getting into fights over little things and then wondering later why they had been fighting at all. One young boy had been beaten to death after crossing a neighbor's property and getting too close to a flock of sheep. The man who beat the boy to death swore he was dealing with a shape shifter, not a boy at all. Not until he was later shown the body of the boy did he realize what he had done. When Hidalgo visited the man in jail all he would say was that a raven made him do it.

Ranchers refused to tend their stock, workers refused to show up to work. Even the Navajo Police began to report internal problems as many of them refused to leave their homes. Fear was obviously gripping the people who lived on the reservation. Fear in the form of apprehension. Nobody knew what was going to happen but everyone knew that something was happening.

Dalton

Dalton was called into the principal's office. Nothing new, he had been there followed by stays in detention many times before. This time was different. The principal explained to him something that every student in the school knew by heart. Each semester, a student is required to accumulate enough passing grades that would translate into credits in order to graduate. Not only would Dalton not graduate this year, it was doubtful that he would graduate the following year or even the year after that unless he took extra classes. He would be over twenty years old before he could conceivably graduate. The principal asked him point blank what he planned to do. Dalton stared at the floor, never lifting his eyes or making eye contact with the principal. "I don't know," was the only response the principal got.

"Have you considered taking some kind of technical classes, maybe auto or diesel mechanics, body work, or even culinary arts at the technical school?" asked the principal.

Again, "I don't know," was the only response the principal got.

Exasperated, the principal said, "Well you had better think of something fast. Perhaps you need to be in a restricted environment or something. Have you considered getting a job during the day and attending school at night?

Dalton didn't answer him. Academics were out of the question for Dalton, he was hopelessly behind. Instead he stood up, walked out the door and out of the school, never to return. In his mind two more years of school would be worthless, besides he would either be dead or in jail by then. Then, he began to justify his actions. It was the schools fault that he was failing. Certainly, he attended classes; he just never turned in a single assignment. It seemed to him in a sudden clarity of thought that the teachers had no right to expect him to actually work in school. After all, the school didn't pay him anything for what he did there. Besides, now that Jackson was no longer in the scene the teasing by the other students had gotten more intense. It was all, their fault!

It took only a couple of days to hatch a plan to get even with the school. Dalton knew that it would be impossible to get a bomb into the school but right behind the school building was a large facility where all the school busses pumped diesel into the bus tanks and several large propane tanks were located. Since it was an area off limits to the students with a chain link fence and locked gates there were no security cameras. They had just filled the tanks and Dalton knew it.

Early Monday morning Dalton snuck out of his house. Using bolt cutters, it was easy for him to get into the compound where he placed a dozen sticks of dynamite at the base of a tank and then unstrung a very long section of fuse. After lighting the fuse, he simply went back home and went to sleep.

The concussion of the blast shook his house awaking him, but he simply rolled back over and went back to sleep, despite the constant sirens. Dalton's father came into his room to inform him that there would be no school that day. Dalton rolled over looking at him and asked why.

His father responded, "One entire wing of the school has been leveled by some kind of explosion. The rest of the school is in shambles. You may not go to school for several days. Have you been here all night?"

A glassy eyed Dalton blinked and looked at him then mumbled, "Yeah." When the police went house to house looking for clues he provided an alibi for Dalton. If his father had looked into the old wooden box at the rear of the garage where Dalton had hidden several more sticks of dynamite and fuse along with a small twenty-two caliber handgun he might have said something different. Besides, who would suspect the laziest boy in town?

Increasing Tensions

When Corey and I awoke we casually got up and began to return to our normal routines. Corey, who didn't need to report for work for several hours went in and turned on the television set as he casually ate a bowl of steel cut oatmeal. He began to read the message that was being scrolled across the bottom of the screen. Realizing that something had happened in Bloomfield he immediately turned the television to the news channel. The explosion had been spectacular. The dynamite alone would have done the job but with the diesel and propane tanks exploding along with it, not only had most of the school been flattened, several close houses had received heavy damage. Fortunately, no one was hurt since it occurred so early in the morning but the community would be forever changed.

Follow up investigations brought detectives back to the Dalton home again after Dalton's name appeared on a list of problem students, but again his father provided him an alibi. All Robert Dalton would say was that he didn't know anything, which truly was in his character. Even I was questioned even though the police knew I was working undercover at the school. I had no idea who the perpetrator was.

A day later Hidalgo showed up at the door grim faced and looking very worried. "We need to have a serious talk about what is going on. There is much more to what is happening than meets the eye." I received curious looks from Hidalgo while he walked around me, studying my bizarre hair with the pink and black streaks. Looking up to the ceiling he then settled down at the kitchen table to talk.

Hidalgo got right to the heart of the matter as he saw it. "A thousand years ago the local natives fled from this area after waging war on each other. Once they left, war continued but with outsiders such as other tribes that they encountered such as the Navajo as well as many tribes that already lived in Mexico. As you know, archeologist who have studied this area are still mystified as to why the Anasazi culture waged war upon themselves but from the archeological studies they know that there were all kinds of strange things happening. Those people did not move into cliff houses out of convenience. They moved there because they were terrified of something. They were trying to escape and hide from something or someone."

"Sure, I get it," I responded. "When the Anasazi moved from the area, the creatures that were causing the problem moved south with them stopping in the canyon lands south of Serpiente where they produced another nest."

"That's right, Hidalgo replied. Our serpents that lived south of the ranch many centuries ago were living in peace with the native Indians because the Indians made sacrifices to them. They were shown respect."

Corey says, "Well if you think about it, all of history records people who made sacrifices to gods of some kind or another to gain favor."

"Well that's certainly true. Just pick up any Bible. Particularly in the old testaments there are stories of sacrifices going on," I countered.

"As we have talked before, you can bet that throughout history humans have had encounters with the serpents we have been dealing with." There was a pause in the conversation as everyone contemplated the gravity of the situation, then Hidalgo continued; "then along comes our antiquities thieves, Jose Garcia and Don Fernandez who ruined the whole arrangement that not only thousands of Anasazi cultivated but our efforts as well. Do you remember that last night at the cliff dwelling when I thought I saw two of them escaping?"

"Sure," responded Penny. "You could see them sparkling in the moonlight, but you weren't really sure what you saw."

"I am pretty sure of what I saw, there were two of them. They probably migrated back to their old home along the San Juan."

I looked deep into Hidalgos worried eyes and replied," So what you are saying is that they now have a new nest, somewhere around here."

"Yes." Hidalgo continued explaining how it must have taken some time but by now there were enough of them to wage war on humans again. "What is truly frightening about them is they draw energy from us. As you well know, they can control our thinking, causing us humans to fight among ourselves. Somehow when we fight among ourselves it creates even more power for them."

Corey interjected a thought, "So the harder we fight or wage war, the stronger we make them. That could lead to our own extinction."

I blurted out, "We need to tell the authorities!"

Everyone was quite for a moment then both Corey and Hidalgo began moving their heads to the left and then to the right. Finally, Corey said, "No one would believe us."

Hidalgo interjected, "There is only one group of people who understands what is going on. I'm sure the tribal elders suspected something like this was going on. A couple of them that I spoke to seemed to know as much as I did about the problem. How they did, I'll never know but they did. But when you try to explain to the civil government around here, how far do you think you will get? They will lock you up in a padded room with a strait jacket to wear."

I prepared dinner that evening for everyone. Afterwards we turned on the television set that was in the house. It was a rare treat for us to watch television as we didn't have television in Serpiente however what we watched on the local news was very familiar to us. People were complaining that dogs and cats were disappearing and occasionally found dead. Kittens were found dead but larger cats seemed to be spared. Then cows and even horses begin to mysteriously die. It was difficult to tell what had killed the larger animals. Since they had more body mass, the venom took a little longer to take effect. When found, they were discovered with huge bloated appendages. One had lived long enough for a leg to appear to rot off. The veterinarians easily diagnosed them as dying from snake bites but no one had seen any snakes. Watching television that evening was entertaining with the news of current events being interjected between programs.

It had become predictable for the historical detectives as they could foretell events that they knew would come about.

During the next few days patrols had been set up with groups searching the brush and even wandering through the surrounding foothills in search of rattlesnakes to kill. That seemed to only make the situation worse. When night came, the problems all started again. Finally, small children were found being mysteriously bitten; usually late in the evenings and several of them had died. They had all been outside playing with friends while their parents were pre-occupied with other things. The Center for Disease control was brought into the area with professionals attempting to isolate a contagion that was sweeping the area but as more and more puncture wounds were discovered on livestock as well as on children they focused on the snakes again. The problem was they could never find a trace of a snake other than the occasional rattlesnake that was discovered where one would naturally expect to find them, usually well away from civilization under a pile of rocks where they naturally hide.

But something else was happening in the communities that clustered along the banks of the ancient San Juan waterway. That evening they watched news reports of holdups, drive by shootings and assaults that were mysteriously occurring in the entire Four Corners area. Crime had shot up in only a few days but other things were occurring as well. As they watched, the perky but worried looking young news announcer began to talk about all manner of mysterious occurrences all over the area. Schools in the area began to experience constant fighting among the students as well as with some of the teachers. Teachers, as well as other workers, were refusing to show up to work which made control of everything even harder.

After a couple of commercials, the announcer came back on with a special announcement. The Indian burial grounds on the Navajo reservation had been desecrated as well as several state monuments where tourist explored Indian ruins over a thousand years old. The walls had been spray painted by a mob of young people who left as soon as the ruins were vandalized. When fear grips mankind, minorities become a target and the cherished items of civilization are destroyed.

Waging War on Humans

Robert Dalton was discovered at a truck stop taping a stick of dynamite to a gas tank on a diesel truck early one morning. Even though he proclaimed complete ignorance, a ploy that had always worked before, this time, he was caught in the act yet he seemed to have no memory of the events leading up to his capture. When the police searched his parent's home they discovered the last of a box of dynamite, fuses and of course the small pistol that would connect Dalton to the oil worker. Despite the fact that the items were discovered in the wooden box behind the family garage he claimed complete ignorance of the evidence. What was infuriating to the investigating officers was that Dalton apparently really didn't seem to know why he had been doing what he had been doing or even that he had done anything. He remembered the incident at the river where his friend Jackson had double crossed him but he couldn't remember anything else. In fact, he seemed heartbroken when he discovered what had happened to Jackson. He demanded to know who had killed him.

When truckers stopped making deliveries, a run on the food stores began to occur in the Four Corners area. It occurred slowly at first then mobs began to strip the shelves faster than they could be replenished. A siege mentality was taking place with people boarding up their houses and refusing to come out. Against the wishes of the authorities who feared spreading some kind of contagion, those that had the resources or a place to go packed up their belongings and moved from the area. Still the community drew little attention from the outside world until the oil producing facilities began shutting down as men were found dead while doing the thousands of odd jobs oil wells and refining facilities require. It was only a matter of time until the workers refused to go into the field. When that occurred they simply had to shut the facilities down.

The National Guard was brought into the area as a request from the state police who were overwhelmed with responsibilities. No one was allowed on the streets after sundown which is when all the deaths appeared to be occurring.

In order to keep people off of the streets after sundown, soldiers with automatic weapons were assigned to patrol in jeeps with nothing to do but to watch empty streets. When the soldiers tired of driving around they would pull over and just sit until one of them stepped out of the jeep to relieve a bladder. Upon returning to their jeep nothing would happen for several minutes until finally he would notice a searing pain, somewhere on his body. After examination, a set of fang marks could be found just above the knee, yet mysteriously, the soldier was unaware that he had been bitten. But within an hour he would be in agony. Every neuron and drop of blood would be on fire. It was so painful that the heart would literally explode. Soldiers began to die and not a single shot was ever fired. Desertion suddenly became a problem as no one dared to go out on patrol or to man a post.

Rumors and speculation spread at the speed of a telephone call. A rumor spread that a poisonous spider had moved into the area, but spider bites were immediately ruled out because of the large size of the fang marks. Clearly there were no spiders known to science large enough to inflict such marks. Like all conspiracies, they appeared and immediately disappeared. As the hospitals began to fill with people who were bitten, it soon became obvious that whatever kind of creature was biting them was a new species. Rattlesnake anti venom helped those who had been bitten, but it only postponed the inevitable death. Doctors were stymied; they tried everything they could think of, such as putting the victims on kidney dialysis. All children died. Only the largest, most heavy set healthy people survived the attack for more than a day. Two extremely heavy set men were still alive. They had survived so far. Both had been bitten behind the knee and where they had been bitten, the flesh died. One man had lost a grapefruit size chuck of flesh and the other had already had his leg amputated. They couldn't sleep. It took heavy sedation, normally administered only during surgical procedures just to induce sleep. When they did sleep, they continuously awoke, screaming in a state of complete terror and pain. They complained of dreaming they were in a small pit, chest deep with vicious snakes attacking them. It was always the same dream, yet scarier and scarier. They were in pure agony despite the drugs that the doctors gave them. Pain drugs taken orally had no effect at all. As the blood circulated, it left the victim in writhing convulsions.

The mystery they all reported was that they had no idea they had been bitten. They simply didn't feel the large fangs. Certainly, they never reported hearing the all too familiar buzzing sound a rattlesnake makes. Natural creatures seemed unaffected, particularly ravens and other birds. In fact, the local farmers were complaining about how crows were taking over their fields of corn. When the farmers would step out and shoot at the birds, they would swoop down on them, reminiscent of a Hitchcock Thriller. A day or so later, the shooters would be found dead from multiple snake bites.

It had taken three years for Quetzalcoatl and Kukulkan, as well as a multitude of their subjects, other serpents who had been away in other places doing the bidding of the serpent royalty. In the minds of those serpents, they could see what had happened and knew instantly what to do. They produced enough siblings to war on the humans as their ancestors had done thousands of years ago. A single serpent that had morphed into a raven could control many real ravens. They had complete control over such simple minds and as far as they were concerned it was all out war against the human clan. Despite their secretive nature and invisibility, as well as the serpents amazing mental powers over other creatures, they felt that their very existence was in danger. Being left on a strange planet thousands of years ago, they certainly had learned to survive with a singular priority of protecting the nest and the royalty that inhabited it. Even the five humans from Serpiente had intrigued them. They had taken time to study them individually and had even developed a respect for them, but as for the other humans, their fate had been already decided, they would need to be eliminated. The serpents were not worried about all the new toys that humans had invented, the serpents knew that they could manipulate their minds and make the humans use their new devices on themselves. But the serpents did have one weakness.

The Men in the Black Car

Corey, Hidalgo and I spent several days at the house watching the local news and wondering what the authorities would do. All the authorities could do was lock down the entire area. No one could get in or out without a complete inspection. We were helpless to do anything ourselves. At night, we would watch television or sit out on the screened in porch looking out at the community where not a single house light could be seen. Only the automatic street lights on the main road were glowing in the darkness. Indeed, most people had deserted the tiny community of Flora Vista and the ones that remained were hidden in sealed up houses.

Finally, one evening, a large black van slowly drove up the driveway and two men wearing sharp business suits and one in camouflage fatigues exited the car and carefully walked up to the screened in porch of the house. Hidalgo watched them carefully as they walked up the driveway. The men held canes in their hands and as they walked they moved them back and forth as if they were searching for mines. Hidalgo noticed the two stars that adorned the shoulders of the man in military wear which for some reason caused Hidalgos mind to flash back to the years he spent as a policeman in Durango. His mind was seeing a mirror image of himself in the uniform he used to wear. Uniforms in general change the way people perceive you. The man or woman wearing a uniform becomes the Policeman, Doctor, Fireman or 'whatever' as I had become accustomed to saying. Individuality is subsumed by the uniform worn. Some uniforms make the individual stand out and some make you invisible. A sanitation worker is often invisible to the public. The uniforms these men wore were business suits, standing out as if they wore flashing neon lights.

After they knocked on the door, Hidalgo invited them in and after formal introductions we all settled into the chairs that surrounded the kitchen table. Mr. Jones, who sported a neatly trimmed white beard and mustache, was apparently the spokesman of the group. As he explained it, Ken and June had personally explained to the governor about the recent history in Serpiente. Most governors would have rejected the story right away as a flight of fancy but this particular governor had known and respected June throughout her academic work. He too was a member of the historical society and with half of his state in paralysis, he welcomed any input he could receive. June had explained the situation in great detail, including the destruction of the nest. All this intrigued him and of course after phone calls were made, we were being visited. They announced that they were there in an official capacity leaving us very intrigued.

During the pause in the conversation due to the words 'official capacity' I had to stop and stare at Dr. Wilkerson for a moment. Despite the suit he was wearing, his disheveled Albert Einstein hair gave him away as a free thinker. He was much younger than the other two, just a little older than Corey and me. He was a scientist by trade but in reality, he was kept around because of his problem-solving intelligence.

Maybe, because I still looked like a very bad girl with the streaks still in my hair and black fingernails, I leaned over to him and asked him if he wouldn't be more comfortable if he loosened his tie?

Bless you, he says and immediately took the tie off. "We are expected to look our best on assignments like this one."

"What do you mean, this one," I asked while turning on the playful charm?

Dr. Wilkerson simply lifted one finger off the table and said to me, "I am fully aware of your life history since you first appeared at the ranch in Serpiente.

"How is your undercover work at the High School? Trust me, I can easily find out what classes you had in high school. I could even find out who your boy friends were there, and with a third finger coming out, I certainly know that you and Corey have been married for some time."

Corey says, "Finally, she meets someone who is smarter than she is."

I immediately backed off. Under all the makeup, I am sure I was blushing. Somehow, I had meant to do a simple tease, a way to understand the man. Hidalgo even winked at me.

General Armstrong who, after taking off his beret revealed a classic military style haircut, cleared his throat making it clear that he was not happy with the way the conversation was going and took off his mirror sun glasses revealing brilliant blue eyes and said, "You all can all joke all you want but the office of the president requested that we enlist you in solving the problem this nation is facing." With that said, everyone was back to business.

Mr. Jones, a government man with top clearance, answered only to the government agency he worked for and he started his proposition with a statement that if we could help, solve or find the cause of the current problem in the area all resources including the Army and Air Force were at our disposal. However, he had a real problem believing what his eyes were telling us. He was used to dealing with terrorist and outlaw nations. Dealing with alien serpents was something that he could never have imagined he would be involved with.

After spending almost two hours giving the men another accounting of their history and relationship with the serpents, Hidalgo laughed. "You do realize that the serpents live underground and that by attacking them they would only turn the resources of the Army and Air Force back against the attacker? Curiously, Mr. Jones who we suspected was using a pseudonym, listened to us intently. Due to the gravity of the situation the visitors were willing to try anything including the services of the historical detectives.

I listened to the discussion for a moment then said "We explained that the only way they knew to kill the snakes was to use poison gas." "Yes," replied Mr. Jones, "Gas would be the perfect weapon to use because it is heavier than air. As the snakes slithered further and further underground to escape the gas it would sink in the air and find them."

Hidalgo couldn't help himself, "How are you going to round them up and get them to wait for you at the nest? After all, they can change form and morph into any of a number of animals making them quite mobile. We know how to see them at night by using ultraviolet light, but in other forms such as coyotes or ravens they would be impossible to spot. Besides, how would you know you are attacking a serpent and not just a regular crow?"

The only answer we got was, "We don't know, that is why we have come to you for help."

Perhaps if we did find the nest and killed the leaders, in time the remainder of the serpents could be killed. You know, cut off the head of the snake and the rest will die." I explained to him that they have a collective conscience. "Other serpents would simply assume the role of leadership."

"How are you going to find the nest?" I asked.

Mr. Jones thought about the question for a minute then answered, "We need a description of the nest that was at Serpiente, that is one of the reasons why we came to you. We really don't have any idea what to look for. Certainly, few would be willing to go into the field and search for it."

I answered him, "Why don't you put those military resources to work and find a new hill that looks like a miniature volcano. It is bound to be easier spotted and infinitely less dangerous if spotted from the air."

"Sounds like a game plan to me," Mr. Jones replied. "Consider it done. Stay here and we will be in contact with you."

As they got up to leave, Hidalgo said to them, "You had better get your facts straight about these creatures before you attack them. Humans have made mistakes before and you can plainly see the results." Mr. Jones bobbed his head up and down and within a few moments they were driving out of sight down the road.

Overhead Surveillance

Geology and survey maps of the entire region were rounded up and put up on the bulletin boards in the largest of the offices of the Farmington Regional Airport. The airport was picked as a base to work out of because of the proximity to the actual airfields and the security that was already provided. Only incoming flights were occurring, few planes left the area. Military jets and helicopters along with an occasional government transport plane used to carry personnel to the base were the only air traffic over the area. When the transport jets arrived they never turned off the engines. Passengers were quickly unloaded and the jets returned to the sky within moments.

During the next two days, we sat in limbo wondering what to do. We talked through several scenarios as to what could be done, but we could not think of a game plan to deal with the serpents. From our point of view humans had lost all credibility with the serpents. Besides, one could run into a lot of serpents until just by accident they ran into Quetzalcoatl or Kukulkan; names Aunt June had picked because of the historical relationship given to Mayan serpent gods. Even if they did make contact, there was certainly no guarantee that they would be treated any differently than any other humans.

What the team was not aware of was that far overhead secret jets from a place known as area fifty-one were being flown with cameras busily snapping photographs. The photographs were then compared to previous photographs taken of the area to see if there was any change. Sure enough, within only two days a tiny but new volcanic structure was discovered far up a side canyon that flows into Chinle Creek which flows after rains into the San Juan River.

Suddenly it was becoming clear to the historical detectives why they had experienced apparitions and hallucinations on the river trip they had previously taken. They were getting too close to the serpent's home and the serpents wanted them to know. Now they could understand why, if not how, the serpents had controlled their minds. In a strange way, Hidalgo as well as Corey and I were relieved to understand what had been happening to them. Yet, Hidalgo was not sure and he wondered, "Why had they singled him out with the strange coyote like apparition? What was the symbolism?"

The Character of Dragons

Returning to the tiny house in Flora Vista, the government agents showed the historical detectives some large photographs of the Chile Wash area. When unrolled they were exactly one meter wide showing in amazing detail what was on the ground. Small animals could be seen as well as a boating party that had snuck on the river. Hidalgo, Corey and I were amused at the audacity of the river runners. They had assumed that the BLM had closed the river until the problem with disappearances had been solved but that would never stop a determined die hard river runner. They couldn't help but laugh when they saw the three small canoes on the river at the mouth of Chinle Wash, until they were informed that they were soldiers working with the government. Then Mr. Jones managed to find the map with the new volcanic feature, the nest.

Hidalgo examined the map closely and realized that the nest was located just a short distance up the canyon from where he had seen his earlier apparition. He also noticed that the canyon above the apparition site formed a narrow slot for a short distance until it opened up in a circle of cliffs with the nest in the center of the opening. Certainly no one could get a bulldozer or any other heavy equipment to the nest. On the other hand, it would make a perfect place to drop gas cylinders. The historical detectives explained how the black exterior of the nest was rock hard and impermeable to water while they suspected the inside was soft pumice like rock with interconnecting bubbles in it. Indeed, it looked just like a miniature cone volcano not unlike the thousands of real volcanic features that dotted the New Mexico landscape.

Hidalgo also suspected that by now the serpents had learned a simple lesson from Serpiente; there would be more than one way into and out of the nest. Besides, they had already dispersed all over the San Juan waterway. Hidalgo knew that a few gas cylinders would do nothing more than to leave the serpents angry. Like taking a stick and swatting a hornets' nest was the exact analogy he made to the three men.

Mr. Jones was dumfounded by Hidalgo's hesitation in using poisons to get rid of the serpents. "We do know they are out there, he said, we illuminated the entire area with UV light and could see them" With that he produced another photograph taken with a special camera from a helicopter that had hovered directly above the nest at night. Sure enough, several thin images of serpentine creatures could be seen slithering along the rock faces and entering the nest through the cone at the top of the nest. "Tell us more about these creatures," requested Dr. Wilkerson who hadn't said anything up to this point.

I began by explaining the historical aspects of the serpents. "Throughout all of history isolated cultures that don't know of the existence of each other, separately know about serpents; in English, we called them dragons. They have become symbols of power throughout history. Starting in ancient Mesopotamia, where written history is given credit for beginning, dragons decorated their architecture along with lions and bulls and was part of their creation myth. Romans, who were never willing to admit that mere humans could defeat them, officially blamed dragons for many of their defeats such as when they were defeated by the Carthaginians. Of course, everyone knows of the Vikings with the bow of their ships decorated in powerful dragon symbols. They, of course had their own creation myths that included dragons."

Corey continued the conversation, "Everyone knows of the stories of the Knights of the Round Table. The Knights were required to rescue damsels in distress. Curiously, the dragons always had a hoard of treasure that they guarded. It was in the nature of the dragons to hoard treasure. You remember that indeed our serpents in Serpiente hoarded treasure. Then when Christianity became a dominant religion, dragons were associated with the devil. From Adam and Eve on they were demonized."

"In the New World, they were thought of differently," Hidalgo said as he entered the conversation. "They were revered by the ancient Olmec civilization in Mexico. Their entire cosmology was centered on them. Then the Mayans worshiped Quetzalcoatl and Kukulkan, the feathered serpents, serpents that could fly, serpents that apparently taught them many important things, but one thing is certain, the serpents, dragons, or aliens or whatever you want to call them demanded respect from humans. Humans made blood sacrifices to them."

"So, you think that is the solution to this problem," queried Mr. Jones? "Do you think we simply need to take an obsidian knife and cut the heart out of a few people and that would solve the problem, sacrifice a few people," Jones sarcastically asked?

"No, I answered all we are suggesting is that dragons and serpents have been associated and even revered by humans throughout history and by people from the U.S., such as the Anasazi to faraway places such as China. The logic was there but I could tell there was a certain amount of disbelief in them despite the proof that they themselves had provided.

"They have to be some kind of new species of snake," argued Wilkerson, "surely with all the knowledge at our disposal we can find a way to contain them."

General Armstrong simply said, "Given enough bullets and gas we can eliminate them and be done with it."

"Not a chance," Hidalgo countered in argument, they are what the Native Americans call skin walkers or shape shifters and they have survived here in this area for thousands of years."

"Well, being a Navajo, I guess you would know," countered Dr. Wilkerson.

"Being an Indian doesn't give me any special powers when it comes to serpents. However, our cultural history, and therefore our point of view, is very different from yours."

"How so?" asked Wilkerson.

"We don't depend upon our technology to defeat our enemies; we use our personal courage and knowledge. We are a cooperative people, when we face adversity we work together even if it means working with the serpents,"

Wilkerson didn't say anything to that.

Corey, who could plainly see the conversation was getting a little heated, added a simple tidbit to the conversation. "You need to understand that the serpents can control any living creatures' mind. Change your perception; make you angry when you have nothing to be angry about. They can kill you with a thought or make you kill with a thought. We are dealing with creatures that cannot be defeated in any traditional way."

"So, you are saying that with all the resources the United States Government has, we are defenseless against them," asked General Armstrong?

"That's true," Hidalgo interjected," but there is one person here who has defeated them, even made friends with them."

"And who could that possibly be?" asked Mr. Jones.

They all looked at me and I was still trying to get the pink and black stripes out of my blond hair. "I did."

"Well, we're sure you will understand if we try?" Mr. Jones huffed.

"We understand, "answered Hidalgo, but you need to understand that you could just make things a lot worse."

Everyone was quiet at the impasse in the conversation. Then Mr. Jones proposed an entirely new take on the situation. "What if we told you that we didn't really want to destroy them; what if I told you that we would like to weaponize them to work for us?"

Hidalgo reached over and gently grabbed the tie around Mr. Jones neck. Pulling him over to within a couple of inches, Hidalgo said in a low threatening voice, "You have to be out of your mind if you think you can control those creatures."

An Attack Against Quetzalcoatl and Kukulkan

The following day, several gas cylinders were dropped on the nest, followed by incendiary bombs, followed by several large concussion bombs that left a ten-foot crater where the cone had been. The bombs left a greenish haze in the surrounding canyons killing every living creature for miles around. The yellow sandstone bluffs that had surrounded the tiny canyon were now scorched from the resulting fire and brush had been burned away for about a hundred yards in every direction due to the intense heat. The helicopters that dropped the poisonous mixtures then returned to Farmington where they landed at the airport. The airmen were then given leave to go into town to celebrate a job well done.

Leaving the control room at the airfield they all jumped into three of the black vans that were at the disposal of the team, and drove to a night club that was opened just for their benefit. During the evening, several of the men began to argue among themselves over who had killed the most serpents. It was a ridiculous argument considering that no one knew how many serpents they had killed, but the argument festered especially after several drinks. Then after several fights broke out which were entirely unnatural for the airmen, they got back into their vans and headed back to the airport. One after another, the vans began to weave across the lanes of the road and then slammed into the guard rails, trees and buildings that bordered the road. None of them got back alive.

Quetzalcoatl and Kukulkan were not fools. They had suspected what would happen as soon as the first artificial birds had appeared in the sky above their nest. They evacuated the nesting area immediately. Then following the noisy machines back into Farmington where they waited until the men drove into town to party, the serpents followed them and then changed from ravens back into their natural state and crawled into the cars that the soldiers had arrived in, while the soldiers were in the bar. The distracted and arguing men never saw them. As they left the night club to return to the base, the men were still arguing among themselves. In each car, the driver decided it would be the right thing to do, to floorboard the accelerator and return to the airfield as fast as possible. When the military finally got to the cars they discovered, in the cars where fire had not consumed the occupants, that they had multiple bites from serpents. Only one car was still intact after the wreak, using a UV filter and a simple loop of cord tied inside a metal tube to avoid a snakebite, two serpents were captured and taken to the airport where they were enclosed in an empty aquarium with a heavy glass lid placed over it. Now the government agents and biologist had two specimens to study. Conversations again returned to the prospects of weaponizing the serpents; literally putting them to work for the army.

That evening, somehow jubilant news leaked out about the destruction of the nest, prompting one television announcer to announce that the problem with the serpents had been solved. People started to come out and enjoy the cool air that summer nights have to offer, but by the following morning it was estimated that over two hundred people had died for one reason or another but most of them had died from snakebites from an invisible adversary. The war had now begun in earnest.

By early morning a caravan of black cars drove down the gravel road and turned into the driveway that was in front of the house where we were staying. After gingerly stepping out of their cars with walking canes probing ahead of them as they walked, several of them came to the door, knocked on it and nervously waited with their hands on their shoulder holsters. I answered the door this time and asked them what we could do for them. Looking rather sheepish, Mr. Jones simply said, "Pack up your things. You and the two men with you are coming with us."

Intelligent Aliens

"Now I know what it's like to be drafted into the military," Corey said to Hidalgo. "What right do they have to order us to go with them?"

"They are scared," answered Hidalgo. "In the real world, you realize at one time or another that you really don't own anything. Land, cars, it doesn't matter. If the government needs it they will take it. It can be dressed up in fancy words like imminent domain, the military draft or treaties. Despite the reason, whether it involves making a profit, obtaining land, or simply power, sooner or later, despite those powerful words that are put on pieces of paper, the government will take exactly what it needs. Right now, they need us and they are not going to take no for an answer. If we refuse to go they will put us in handcuffs and haul us out of here anyway."

We were separated and escorted to the waiting parked cars, and driven to the airport in Farmington where a makeshift headquarters had been set up. We were allowed time to unpack our meager supply of clothes and camping gear in two of the small rooms where normally the airport personnel and pilots stayed between flights and then shuffled to the war room where those in charge were trying to develop a strategy to deal with the serpents.

There, on a large table at one end of the room was a huge aquarium with two coiled serpents in the corner of it. The serpents were aquamarine in color, like the glass, I watched in amazement as one of the serpents morphed into a black raven that tried to drive its beak into the lid and lift the glass off. As soon as the raven decided it was a wasted effort it immediately morphed back into a serpent and returned to the corner of the aquarium blending into the glass like a pool of water. The only parts that was visible; a black forked tongue that occasionally flicked out of its mouth and two eyes with a pale green color like thick glass. The pupils of the eyes were also visible, two angry black slits that never blinked.

Several men and women entered the room where the serpents were being imprisoned. Scientist, government agents, and military men in camouflage uniforms, who all had one thing in mind; how to deal with a new threat to the people of the United States. The first order of business was containment. Mr. Jones who was directing the meeting asked around for ideas on keeping the serpents contained.

"Contained to what?" asked Corey.

"The range of the serpents appears to be limited to the San Juan River and possibly the Animas as far north as Colorado. There have been no reports of any problems in Durango as of yet, nor has there been any reports as far west as Mexican Hat."

The three historical detectives looked at each other and grinned. Penny then explained to the team, "Let us explain to you what happened at Oljeto Wash."

The three of us took turns recreating the entire story from their previous river trip down the San Juan. The story left the scientist spellbound but the military people looking incredulous. "And as for containment, added Hidalgo, you may have blown your opportunity for containment when you bombed the nest. Now they have no central place to return to or to protect. They may disperse on their own now or simply build another nest somewhere. I would like to propose to you that containment is really not an option. They will go where they want to go. After all they can morph into a raven and fly anywhere."

I added, "They did come all the way up here from Serpiente and Aunt June is sure she was dealing with one as far southwest as Zuni, New Mexico. You boys need to face facts; they can go anywhere they want to, anytime they want to."

Hidalgo then asked, "Have any of you bothered to ask any of the people who have lived with them before; that is the Native Americans?"

"Well, we have you!" Mr. Jones exclaimed.

Hidalgo could only smile as he made his point. "The Native Americans who live around here have encountered serpents for thousands of years. If you would take the time to talk to the tribal elders you would discover that you are not dealing with indigenous biology. According to the elders and the shamans who know far more about these creatures than we do, they are creatures who were left here by star people. You are dealing with intelligent aliens."

The room became very quiet at this point. With all eyes focused upon him, including the serpents, Hidalgo explained the serpent creation myth that he had learned from the shamans. When he finished, he realized that everyone was still silently staring at him. Obviously, their preconceived ideas of what they were dealing with were inadequate.

I added, "These creatures communicate with each other by what you would call extra sensory perception. I guarantee that the other serpents out there are seeing exactly what those fellows over there are seeing." Everyone in the room turned and looked at the serpents. The serpents rose up out of their coiled position and blinked in unison at them. I could visibly see the hair on the back of everyone's neck rise. The serpents knew exactly what everyone was talking about.

Serpent Undulations

A week had passed and the entire four corners area as well as the airport control room had taken on a siege mentality. General Armstrong simply was not convinced, no matter what he was told about the creatures. He held fast to his idea that they were dealing with simple biological creatures. At one time, he was entertaining everyone with the prospect of moving all the people out of the infected area, then applying liberal amounts of poisonous gas from helicopters to the entire area. The problem was he was dead serious. Dr. Wilkerson was totally exasperated and Mr. Jones, who was the psychologist of the group, was being psychological. A true diplomat, yet he was out of his league, after all, as General Armstrong would explain, the United States had been attacked by some terrorist group or country who was using biological weapons to conquer all of America; period. He was obviously at a loss to explain who that terrorist group was or what country or ideal they represented. No one had called the United States to take responsibility yet his scorched earth policy was the only viable solution that was on the table.

Mr. Jones who had, until the nest was bombed, appeared to be the leader of the government men had digressed into a blabbing encyclopedia of psychological theories. He was mostly concerned with communicating with an alien life that he didn't know how to communicate with. How does one communicate with a creature like they were dealing with?

Dr. Wilkerson was the only one who seemed to have his wits about him He would stand in front of the serpents staring at them with them starring back at him. He wanted to solve the problem without killing every creature with a nervous system for miles around. He stared at the serpents and they stared at him. He would close both eyes in an exaggerated blink and they would mimic him. So far that was the only communication he had managed.

Finally, after several days of this standoff, General Armstrong began to demand action. He was tired of being cooped up in a high security facility. He wanted action, and action now before the serpents could escape into the rest of America. I finally confronted him and demanded to know what he really understood about the serpents. He knew very little, and expressed the attitude that he really didn't care about them. They were the enemy, they had to be eliminated and that was that.

Dr. Wilkerson argued incessantly with him to no avail. But I broke the impasse with one simple question. "How are you doing to keep your test subjects alive? They require among other things, food to survive." So, while General Armstrong communicated with the powers that be and made plans to drop thermonuclear bombs or poison gas on the entire area, Dr. Wilkerson and I made arrangements to have some baby chickens delivered to the facility.

The baby chicks arrived only an hour later due to the entire effort of the combined forces of the United States government, a nervous scientist by the name of Wilkerson slid the lid over to expose entry into the glass container and I gingerly dropped two baby chicks into the cage.

Nothing happened for a few minutes, but then like all serpents they focused in on the very terrified baby chicks and within a micro second they struck.

Despite the fact that the venom took effect almost immediately, the serpents remained motionless for a full fifteen minutes. Then ever so slowly they slithered over to the dead chicks, who had plastered themselves as far as they could to the other end of the glass container. The serpents spent several minutes sniffing the chicks. Obviously, they were very suspicious after the ordeal they had been through. Then after swallowing the chicks starting with the head, they returned to the middle of the cage where they rose up and moved back and forth in an undulating motion.

The historical detectives immediately recognized the motions. They remembered seeing the same motions at the ranch house in Serpiente. In a flash of inspiration, I cupped my hand and moved it in front of the serpents in the same undulation motions. Everyone watched in amazement as the serpents again rose up and repeated the undulating motions. Dr. Wilkerson exclaimed in awe, "That is the first time I have ever seen communication between two species like that. What do you suppose it means?"

Nobody said a word for a moment as they watched the serpents assume their normal curled up position in the corner of the glass container.

Finally, Hidalgo replied hesitantly, "The motion indicates approval, I think. However, that is just a gut feeling I have. I could be wrong."

"No, I think you are right," I proclaimed. "We have all experienced the same thing in Serpiente. It means something to the serpents."

Corey thoughtfully replied, "It reminds me of dancing, maybe we need to experiment."

Dr. Wilkerson then added, "I suspect that the motions are just a ritual. Not true communication. However, I agree with you all that they can read our minds, even play with our minds. It is obvious that there is far more to them than what meets the eye."

Releasing Quetzalcoatl and Kukulkan

Despite the heat of the summer, the deaths due to serpent bites dramatically declined. This produced several outcomes. General Armstrong was furious at his missed opportunity to obliterate the entire area. In his communications with people even further up the military chain of command, he repeatedly voiced his personal point of view that a scorched earth solution was the only option. But then, there was a distinct geographical area; namely the San Juan and Animas Rivers where all action was occurring. There were no reports of bizarre behavior as far north as Durango nor as far west as Mexican Hat. Military people who had floated down the San Juan looking for anything unusual found nothing. Nor did they experience any unusual apparitions or hallucinations. It seemed too many of the humans that were being housed at the Farmington Airport, that the serpents realized that they were on the precipice of bringing an ecological disaster down upon themselves and backed off. Everyone came to the conclusion at the same time, which in itself caused a lot of discussion and disbelief. Everyone, except for General Armstrong, who believed everyone's mind, had been altered except for his. General Armstrong's mind had, of course, been altered more than anyone's.

Then there was a break in the situation. The three historical detectives as well as Wilkerson awoke after a troubled night of nightmares. Meeting over coffee at five in the morning, all four of us had dreamed of dealing with serpents all night long. Suddenly things seemed much clearer. We were suddenly aware that the serpents had allowed themselves to be captured. The serpents had introduced themselves to us as Quetzalcoatl and Kukulkan. Long before we awoke, we had all come to the same conclusion, almost a compulsion, an intense desire to release Quetzalcoatl and Kukulkan. To see what would happen.

Defying the United States Government

*I*t only took a few minutes of comparing dreams before the four of us decided on a plan to release the serpents. The problem was there were always two armed guards in the room who never left and were under strict orders to instantly notify everyone of any change in the situation. Certainly, the release of the two serpents would be a change in the situation. The four of us ventured into the large room where the aquarium was kept and certainly the guards watched every move we made.

I took the lead, walking up to the glass and moving my hand in an undulating motion as I had done before. Color returned to the serpents as I did this and they reciprocated by doing the same undulating motion. Then I did something that was unexpected, in my mind I asked the serpents for help with the guards.

Nothing happened for a moment, but both guards began to squirm. They both apparently needed to relieve themselves in the worst of ways yet they knew they couldn't leave the area. Dr. Wilkerson, who understood what was happening, walked up to them and said, "Don't worry about it boys, I will take responsibility for these people."

Thanking him, they both bolted out of the room and down the hall to find the nearest bathroom. Corey slid the lid off of the glass structure and then the four of us stood there not sure what to do next, but with a sudden inspiration, I reached into the tank and gingerly scooped up both serpents. They coiled around my arms but didn't bite me. Without saying a word, we walked to the nearest exit being careful not to encounter anyone. One of the guards passed them in the hall returning to his sentry post but said nothing as the lid had been replaced on the aquarium and the serpents were almost invisible anyway. The guards suspected nothing.

Upon reaching the last door we were confronted by another guard who asked us where we were going but without doing anything the guard suddenly turned on his heels and simply left. Obviously, the serpents had used mind control to make him uninterested. We stepped through the door where upon I dropped to my knees and allowed the serpents to crawl off of my arms. The serpents again went through the undulating motions which everyone now knew to mean 'thank you,' they morphed into ravens, and flew away.

Returning into the building all four of us felt a degree of satisfaction but knew we would be in deep trouble as soon as the authorities discovered the serpents were missing. The real question that was pressing us was what would happen next. Corey stopped in the hallway and turning to me asking how I had the courage to reach into the aquarium.

"Easy I responded while pulling out the owl amulet from under my blouse, I was protected by magic." While at the house in Flora Vista they had again tried to make contact with Mr. Owl but discovered again that there was absolutely no evidence that he or even his children ever existed. The motel that Corey had stayed in had no records or knowledge of Mr. Owl's daughter who had taken care of Corey while he was recouping from his injury, another mystery to solve.

It took several hours before Mr. Jones realized the aquarium was empty. Realizing what had happened he ran into the lunch room where we were all eating sweet rolls and drinking coffee. Demanding to know what had happened to the serpents Hidalgo casually answered him with the truth. "We let them go." All hell broke loose. The sentry guards were immediately summoned into the room and the four of us were handcuffed.

"How dare you defy the United States Government," bellowed Mr. Jones. General Armstrong, who was now disappointed that his new weapons had escaped demanded that we be put against a wall and shot for treason but clearer heads prevailed. Instead we were locked into holding rooms used by the airport personnel for unruly passengers and smugglers.

We were kept in those holding rooms which fortunately had adjoining bathrooms but nothing else except chairs and a table for three weeks. At the end of that time we were escorted into the large room where the serpents had been imprisoned and seated behind a table. Some thirty or so people watched every move we made without uttering a word until finally Mr. Jones said, "Something has happened and we don't understand what it is."

"What do you mean?" retorted Hidalgo, who was angry at the treatment we had been receiving.

"Nothing has happened," replied Mr. Jones.

"What do you mean, nothing has happened," demanded Corey.

"It is, as if the serpents have vanished," was the reply he got. "There has not been a single incidence, not a single bite, not a single death, nothing. They have vanished.

Hidalgo replied with a smirk, "They didn't vanish, they simply made peace. If we leave them alone they will leave us alone. All they wanted to do was teach us humans a lesson."

"Well, I should have all four of you put into prison for not following my orders," replied a still angry General Armstrong.

I laughed out loud at that remark, "We are private citizens. We don't take orders from you or anyone else. We simply offered the serpents a small degree of kindness. As a matter of fact, we solved your problem just like you asked us to."

There was silence in the room for a moment until finally Mr. Jones bobbed his head up and down and said "Yeah, consider yourselves and your friends, those serpents released."

Don't Wake up the Sleeping Dragons

It took several weeks before another nest was discovered far up Chinle Creek on the Navajo reservation. Within only a few days the military had constructed a chain link fence around it with signs posted, warning humans of radiological danger. The fence would certainly not keep serpents in the five-square mile enclosure the fence created but it would certainly keep humans out. Twice a month a helicopter flew over the serpent reservation and dropped a container that released hundreds of live mice and baby chickens. Then strangely the serpents disappeared from the nest and the fence enclosure. They vanished and no one had any idea what had happened to them. This caused considerable apprehension with the people who worked for the government but for all intent and purposes in the small communities that have grown along the banks of the San Juan River it was as if nothing had ever happened, except that the surrounding cemeteries had grown with many new occupants.

Corey, Hidalgo and I were content with returning to work at the ranch in Serpiente while solving new mysteries. As far as the mystery of the serpents was concerned, Hidalgo said it best; "Everything will be fine if they don't wake up the sleeping dragons."

Part 2

Hopi Prophecies

Don't be afraid to cry. It will free your mind of sorrowful thoughts.

—Hopi Proverb

A Visit by the Hopi

Ken, Corey and Hidalgo rolled out of bed two hours before sunrise so they could enjoy the cool morning air while doing the hard-physical work all working ranches required. But early on this day, it was already getting hot. Normally at this time of year they would come in for a small lunch and then do light work indoors waiting out the heat of the evening until almost sundown when they would return outdoors to tend the cattle and other farm animals. Ken, who was sitting on a farm tractor well up on the sandy mesa, a part of the Luna addition, noticed the car first. A brown car was working its way down the winding dirt road toward the ranch stirring up the dust in the dry roadbed. Shortly he noticed Hidalgo and Corey had noticed it also and were pointing to the car. Hidalgo and Corey had been stretching barbed wire over metal fence post they had driven into the ground the day before.

With the ranch house located so far out in the country it was a rare sight for them to see company coming and their curiosity was immediately piqued. Ken turned the tractor off leaving the key in place and walked down the hill until he was where Hidalgo and Corey were waiting for him and all three of the men began their long walk to the pickup truck which would take them back to the ranch house. They and the brown car arrived at the parking lot at the same time. Exiting the pickup truck, they noticed that the men who were getting out of the vehicle were Native Americans. Three of them were dressed very neatly in brown shirts with bolo ties. The fourth person appeared older and much more casual. He wore classic Indian apparel and even had a long black feather tied into hair that fell over his shoulder.

Looking at the emblem on the side of the car it was obvious where they had come from. The emblem on the front doors was a characterization of Kokopelli, a common Native American motif depicting a humpbacked man playing a flute and written under the symbol was Hopi Cultural Center.

As the men exited the vehicle they all said *"Loloma"* which Hidalgo immediately recognized as Hopi for 'Hello.' Herman Homanie, Ronald Hoyumptewa,
Todd Hoyacoma and Charles Youvella introduced themselves as representatives
from the Hopi Nation and requested an audience with Ken and June Anderson
along with the historical detectives. They were graciously invited into the kitchen
and seated around the family meeting place, the kitchen table. Cool drinks were
served to all by me and June. After further introductions, they settled down to
talk with Herman Honacoma taking the lead.

"We represent the Hopi people of northeastern Arizona, and were directed to seek you out by a representative of the government of New Mexico. You
see, several years ago many of our most precious ceremonial mask and *Kachinas*
were loaned to the Hopi Cultural Center which we now represent. The federal
government put up a tremendous amount of money to build a beautiful building
that was secure, where they could display some of our precious objects. There are
many things on display there that we are proud of, but we as a people objected
to the display of many of our most sacred objects. However, because of the vast
amounts of money that could be generated by the displays and the simple fact that
it eliminated many nosy people called anthropologist, not to mentions thousands
of tourists who wanted to know every detail of our faith, we gave in and allowed
them to be put on display. Only a few of the most important objects were we able
to hide away from the prying eyes of outsiders."

At that moment, interrupting Mr. Honacoma, Mr. Hoyumptewa, the man
with the feather tied into his hair asked a very pointed question of Hidalgo, "You
are Navajo are you not?"

Hidalgo, who was looking a little uncomfortable at the gruff manner of
the question, politely answered, "Yes I am of the people known as Navajo, but I
certainly value and respect the ways of the Hopi. In fact, I admire your culture
that has existed for thousands of years in this part of the world. Just because my
ancestors and yours have warred over the years does not mean that I am at war,
nor does it mean that I will not do everything in my power to help you."

June spoke up and said, "Hidalgo is certainly a proud Navajo, he is a proud
Navajo American. He has done much to encourage the advancement of his people
such as setting up a trust fund for the Indian Polytechnic School in Farmington.
That school welcomes all native students including Hopi students. Trust me,
there is no one that I would trust more than Hidalgo, he is a genius even among
geniuses and much more than just a member of our historical detectives; he is

a member of this family. We simply wouldn't attempt to help you without his assistance."

Mr. Hoyacoma says, "I'm sorry but I'm sure you understand our concerns as well as our families' histories. However, we have been assured that you people are certainly the most trustworthy people we would find to help us. If Mr. Hidalgo is a member of this team, I consider him a friend of ours and a friend of all Native Americans." Mr. Hoyumptewa held out his hand and exchanged handshakes with Hidalgo, Indian style, but he did not let Hidalgo's hand go, not until Mr. Honacoma reached over and lightly touched him in the arm.

"You are not going to embarrass us, are you Hoyumptewa?

Hoyumptewa pulled his hand back and replied "I am very sorry but you see; Mr. Hidalgo truly is much more than just a Navajo. He is very special. I can feel an energy emanating from him. Everyone starred at Hoyumptewa for a second until Mr. Honacoma says, "Our dear friend here is much more than just a representative to the Hopi people; he is a shaman. He has the ability to see into people, into the future and sometimes he makes prophecies."

I turned to Hidalgo and asked, "Would you mind explaining to me what that conversation was all about?" Then I turned to the four guests in a gesture of explanation, "I am not as educated to the ways of Native Americans as the rest of you are. I am originally from East Tennessee and would like to understand what the problem is."

Hidalgo explained to me, "Our tribes have been at war for many generations. The Hopi is a very peaceful tribe of people who have lived since the beginning of time in Hopituskua and have maintained a sacred covenant with Masaw, the ancient caretaker of the earth. Most Hopi live as peaceful and humble farmers who are respectful of the land and its resources. The only time they have been at war is when they were attacked or raided by outsiders such as my people. They now live on a reservation that is completely surrounded by the Navajo reservation which is why Mr. Hoyumptewa has his concerns. The Hopis have tried to coexist peacefully with all other tribes who have invaded the area. Tribes such as the Navajo and Apache have been raiding them ever since they wandered into this country. It was just the way things were. Today, there are still many small battles being fought between the Hopi and the Navajo, only now they are usually done in the white man's court. I simply have no bone in those dog fights, this is my home," waving his hand in a circular motion around the table, "and this is my family."

Mr. Hoyumptewa says; "Contrary to what everyone believes, we have not always been a peaceful people. There are some interesting events in our history if one takes the time to look back in time." He looked around and everyone was looking at him. "Hidalgo is obviously a very unique individual. Your soul seems to be centered, but there is something else about you. Something that is mysterious and interesting."

Hidalgo didn't quite know what to say so he just said, "Thank you."

I asked, "Why would you care if people viewed your religious objects? I would think that you would be proud to show others your religious items?"

Mr. Honanie explained, "The Hopi believe that the moral character and the thoughts of spectators influence the efficacy of our prayers. We have learned that it is best to keep many of our ceremonies secret. We do not allow outsiders, particularly pahanas or whites, to view even the public portions of the ceremonies. In the past when white people were allowed to view our ceremonies, they became spectacles with cameras taking pictures and very dangerous thoughts being generated. We felt like we were nothing but entertainers for the visitors. Since that time our people, the whole Hopi community has been called upon to be upright and conscientious in keeping our ceremonies private."

I answered his point with, "I have been to enough places where large crowds of people gather to understand what you are saying. Crowds of people seem to always get unruly."

Hidalgo simply says, "Thoughts are like arrows, once released, they strike their mark. Guard them well or one day you may be your own victim."

Mr. Hoyumptewa says, "I have heard that proverb before and it is true, there is much wisdom in your words."

Mr. Honacoma says, "It is obvious that you understand our feelings about our sacred objects, for this we respectfully thank you all. We contacted the State of Arizona which has offices that work with tribal issues and they suggested that we speak to Mr. Manny Aragon who worked with people in Washington concerning Indian affairs. Mr. Aragon immediately suggested we seek you out and was extremely positive about your abilities as detectives. We were particularly instructed to speak to June Anderson who was an expert in Indian affairs."

June blushed a little bit and said, "Well I am a licensed archeologist. That is why you can see many Native American artifacts setting on shelves around this house. They are mostly on loan for educational purposes, or were collected by the original inhabitants of this property long before we moved here. As I'm sure you know, immediately south of here is extensive Anasazi ruins in the canyons of Serpiente. With our work, as historical detectives we have crossed paths with some interesting people, both good and bad and some of them certainly were people who stole from the ancient sites."

Mr. Youvella asked, "So it is understood that you have had experience with antiquity thieves before?"

June answered him with, "Yes, we have all had experiences with antiquity thieves. Those thieves are now spending time in the New Mexico State Pen. None of us would ever consider making money from the objects found in native ruins."

"Good for you, Mrs. Anderson," says Mr. Youvella.

Mr. Hoyumptewa frowned after June's statement but didn't say anything.

"Please, just call me June, that is what my friends call me and I certainly consider you all friends. So exactly why did you come to see us?"

Mr. Honacoma continued, "It all has to do with a Jonas Jernigan who was assigned the job as Director of the Museum which is part of the Hopi Cultural Center. The State of Arizona assigned the position to him, to oversee the entire operation of the center and to see if it was possible to create a profit from it. The idea was to bring in more money than the center needed for its operation. The remaining money would be used to better the Hopi tribe. We as a tribe agreed that making money from the cultural center was acceptable as long as our own people had full access to the displays and it was understood that the objects were living entities of our religion and would need to be released to us when our ceremonies were performed. Mr. Jarnagan didn't like the idea but, after much pressure from the tribe, he finally agreed to allow us access to our own sacred objects."

Mr. Hoyumptewa interjected sarcastically, "Can you imagine that? We have to have permission to use our own ceremonial masks and we hardly saw any money from the operation of the Cultural Center! He kept his own books and the legers he showed us were suspicious."

Pausing, Mr. Honacoma continued, "But he did relinquish the objects but complained about the difficulties of having to redisplay them over and over. We didn't care. We had our own homes for our objects but again, we wanted to live in peace with the outsiders. We were also aware that if we didn't cooperate with them the objects could just as easily be forcefully taken from us and taken to the Smithsonian Institute where we would have no access to them at all."

"Frankly," June responded, "Most Native American ceremonial objects that wind up at the Smithsonian Institute are stored away and few get to examine them. There are whole warehouses there with Anasazi treasures that even I would not be able to examine without receiving written permission and taking a trip to the place. If you are unaware of those objects they disappear from history.

In fact, there are rumors that there are many objects hid away because if people were aware of them, there would be a dramatic impact on the legal status of the United States. This is why any evidence of European visitation to this country before Columbus is so vehemently denied. It is feared that other countries would claim ownership of all of America."

"I still don't understand but I certainly do understand that many Native Americans claim ownership of the entire continent since they were here long before Columbus arrived."

"Well," June replied, "You know that the discovery of the Estancia man caused quite a stir in anthropological, as well as, in some legal circles. But what if I told you that there is historical evidence that a race of giants occupied the entire east coast of America, creatures that were on the average eight feet tall and had a double row of teeth. In fact, there are historical documents by people such as Abraham Lincoln, George Washington and many others who understood the existence of giant people and some who had examined the remains of the giants who lived here at one time. The remains of those giants have supposedly been hidden away in the Smithsonian."

"What happened to those giant men," I asked?

"They were hunted down and killed by the ancestors of the natives who now live there," Hidalgo says. "Apparently the last of them became extinct about the time of the Woodland culture that incorporated what the giants had created, that is the actual mounds. It is thought that they were built over a long period of time by many different societies from mobile hunter-gatherers to sedentary farmers. Anyway, they are all extinct now. They were replaced by the cultures that live there now. Of course, after Columbus and the Spanish incursions into America, most of them died out."

June reentered the conversation, "While you were in Tennessee you visited a place near Manchester known as the Old Fort." Supposedly it was built by the Mound Builder Indians, but some say they conquered the giants and took the sites away from them, incorporating the sites into their own culture, which is why archeologist found much evidence of their presence at the sites. Like much that has to do with real history, truth as well as written history, depends upon the opinions of those who won the wars."

June looked at the four men. "I'm sorry, all of this has little to do with your problem but it is true that much is hid away from the public because those history books would all require rewriting, and the lawyers would have a field day."

I said, trying to get the conversation back on task. "I realize that maybe

I'm a little naïve, but what good are ceremonial objects if they are locked away in warehouses?"

June answered my question; "The problem arises when there is confusion over what is an older archeological object and one that is currently being used. Many of the ceremonial masks are hundreds of years old, yet they are still used in ceremonies. The archeologists tend to forget that they are dealing with living people, not a dead culture."

Mr. Honanie continued the explanation started by Mr. Honacoma. "Mr. Jernigan was very good at cataloging our material things but he had little insight into what we as a people were all about. He worked there for about ten years and when he discovered that he was going to be replaced by another official, an official who was Hopi, he disappeared along with a large truckload of our most ancient possessions; mostly ceremonial mask and *kachina* dolls. They were artifacts that were irreplaceable. No one had any idea what has happened to them despite the fact that the disappearance was reported to the State Police and the Federal Bureau of Investigation. Not a trace of them or Mr. Jernigan has ever been found."

"When did this all happen," asked Hidalgo?

"Over ten years ago," answered Honanie.

Corey, who hadn't said anything to this point asked, "If this stuff was stolen ten years ago how do you expect us to find it now?"

Mr. Honanie looked at Corey and slowly answered him. "We now know where it all is. It is in Paris, France. If I understand the facts correctly they intend to auction them off at the end of the month. They expect to make a lot of money and of course, once they are sold we will never be able to round them back up. They will be lost to us for all time, scattered all over Europe. That is why we came to you."

Hidalgo asked, "I don't understand all of this. Isn't there a repatriation act or something that by law means stolen goods must be returned to the rightful owners?"

Ken says, "Sure there is, that is how many of the art treasures that the Nazis stole during World War II have been returned."

"That is true," says Mr. Honanie, "but we have to prove that they were stolen from us. Can you imagine that? They were very carefully photographed and cataloged by Mr. Jernigan. They are even advertising the fact that they are selling authentic ceremonial objects taken from the Hopi people and yet we have no legal means to prove that they belong to us! Mr. Jernigan took the records with him. All we have now is our own word and photographs made by tourist which evidently carry no weight in a legal argument. Even if we went to the auction and tried to buy our own things back it would only raise the price of the objects. There will be very wealthy collectors there who will be bidding on those objects and we couldn't afford to buy even a few of them, much less all of them."

"Did you contact the government officials in France and explain what the situation was," asked Corey?

"Of course, we did but it only tipped them off to the fact that we wanted our mask and *kachinas* back. They immediately started putting up roadblocks and informed the auctioneers that we were contesting the sale; besides being a private auction they cannot really apply any legal pressure on them. They contend that under international law they cannot stop the auction. All we can do is buy the objects back, besides the government is expecting to make a handsome profit from the taxes collected on the sales and in Europe there is more of a demand for Native American artifacts than there is here in the United States. Anyway, they know who we are and will do anything to block our efforts to stop the auction. We feel helpless to act ourselves, which is why we came to you."

June says, "I just don't know what we can do. We have done little work outside of the United States, certainly not in Europe, and although Hidalgo speaks several languages, I doubt if French is one of them." Hidalgo was shaking his head back and forth in a 'no' gesture. "Besides it would be very expensive to fly all of us all the way to France and then we would need to stay there long enough to actually accomplish something. Frankly I don't know anything about international auctions other than people bid on very rare and expensive items. None of us have ever had any experience with that type of work."

Mr. Honanie answered June sadly. "If you think it all seems impossible to you, just imagine the position we are in. We have absolutely no experience in foreign matters such as international auctions. We would be laughed at for even considering being bidders. Those people all know each other and have been making money on art for many years now. They can afford to buy priceless works of art and store them for many years before even considering reselling them. It works a lot like the price of gold. For many years, it was only worth a few dollars an ounce and now it is worth many hundreds of dollars."

Mr. Youvella, with a sheepish look on his face, answered slowly. "We realize that we cannot ask you to work for nothing, however we are an extremely poor people. The majority of the Hopi are humble farmers. We have some resources but every dollar that we spend on retrieving our stolen artifacts is food out of our children's mouths. We are prepared however, to pay the price of your airline tickets there and back, but we cannot afford to really pay you a salary nor living expenses while you are there. Mr. Aragon said for us to tell you to contact him if you decide to take the case. He insinuated that he might be able to 'discover' some funds that would help but we simply cannot afford to pay a lot of money for your services. We are going to be lucky to have enough money for the gas it will take to return to our homes today."

"Oh dear," June says, "This sounds like a very complicated situation. It always amazes me how the least able to pay are the most victimized and the crooks always manage to make the most money off of them."

Mr. Honanie says, "Well, we felt we had to try anyway, and you were our last hope. We will leave now and if you can help us we would appreciate it and even if you cannot help us we want you to know that you are always welcome among us. Thank you." Everyone got up to leave except for the Hopi with the feather in his hair, Mr. Hoyumptewa. Everyone turned to look at him and he waved them all back to their seats. "I have more business to take care of. I want to talk a minute more to the Navajo."

Mr. Honyacoma says, "Mr. Hidalgo has a name, you should use it"

"Hidalgo is not his real name!"

Hidalgo, who was taking all this in stride simply answered, "He is correct, my real name is *Naalyehe Ya Sidahi,* however I have been called Hidalgo since I was a small boy. I do not know why, other than the fact that most people cannot pronounce my real name and it simplifies things. I just use my nickname. It is the name everyone calls me, it is even the name on my driver's license."

Mr. Hoyumptewa reached up and rubbed his hand over the raven feather that was in his hair and slowly spoke, "I felt energy from you the moment I touched you. You and your friends here are the ones who battled the serpents, are you not? You didn't mind making money from the gifts that the serpents provided for you."

Everyone starred at Hoyumptewa and sat back down at the table.

June says, "You know, there are very few people who have excess to that knowledge. It was Penny here who figured the serpents out and even made peace with them."

Mr. Hoyumptewa says, Yes, someday her children will become royalty but first many terrible things will happen. Most people will disappear and the ones who survive will enter another world, a world that is very different than this world. It will be more like it was thousands of years ago, before the Spanish and white men came to this land. Tribes will war against other tribes for the satisfaction of the serpents until you change it all. It all has to do with an evil human Shaman who wears stars on his shoulders. He is even more evil than the serpents are. He will cast spells. Flinging bundles of pure energy, cast like invisible fireballs that plunge into the hearts of all the unknowing victims. There will be many, many victims. Hidalgo and the rest of you will survive but only if you isolate yourselves from the remainder of humanity."

June replied "Well, I don't know if we can do that and find your ceremonial mask."

Hidalgo who could feel the gaze of the man's eyes upon him, finally says, "I will take your prophecy very seriously but I don't understand what it all has to do with me."

"You and this family are the key to the future for us all," says Hoyumptewa. "That is all I have to say about that for now, perhaps we can talk again when we have seen what happens."

I then asked the Shaman a simple question in a flirtatious way. "Do you have any predictions for us? Perhaps something not as serious as what you were talking about before?"

Mr. Hoyumptewa grinned and answered, "Sure, my friend Mr. Hidalgo here will soon have a beautiful girl attempt to conquer him, she will try to use him. Hidalgo will have problems with plumbing."

Hidalgo blushed and with a puzzled look said, "I can't imagine what you are talking about."

Mr. Hoyumptewa continued, "This young lady, Penny, will be very embarrassed and will manage to break the heart of a man who lives on a pool of oil. Her husband will be greatly relieved afterwards."

Finally, Mr. Hoyacoma says, "You all realize that he is kidding you now."

The Hopi delegation again got up to leave, leaving the historical detectives in a quandary as to how they could help them get their ceremonial mask back and in even more of a quandary as to what the Hopi prophecies meant or even if they should take them seriously. One thing they were mystified about was how the shaman could have known about their association with the serpents. Those that knew about what had happened in Farmington were sworn to secrecy and no one out of the immediate family was aware of the emeralds and bits of gold that the serpents had traded for baby chicks and mice. Mr. Hoyumtewa's insights would create a great deal of concern for them, but we were intrigued with the new mystery.

Hopi Ceremonial Life

Before the representatives left, June had collected phone numbers and a mailing address as well as a list of the people who the Hopi had contacted so that the Historical Detectives would have some people to talk to in France, but we could offer no assurances that we would or even could pursue the matter. Then, after saying goodbye to the Hopi officials, we all gathered around the kitchen table to discuss the possibilities.

We all wanted to help but had no idea where to begin. June made a call to Manny Aragon in Santa Fe who the Hopi had mentioned but he also had no idea how to legally acquire the artifacts; however, he was willing to say that if we would pursue the investigation, he would make certain government funds and services available to us. This sounded good, but he seemed rather secretive about it all.

Aragon had been aggressive about recruiting the historical detectives because he had personally been involved in the prosecution of artifact thieves. He knew that it was a multimillion dollar a year industry which involved the destruction of vast amounts of material goods from peoples who were the least able to defend themselves. It was their culture that was being looted, stolen and resold for vast amounts of money. Everyone profited except the people who created the beautiful artifacts. However, being a government official, his ability to help in retrieving the artifacts was limited except for the things that he could do under the table.

While preparing dinner, I asked Hidalgo to educate me more into the Hopi culture as I, being from East Tennessee, had never even heard of the tribe much less had a working knowledge of it. I began by asking why those masks are so important and why didn't the Hopi just make new ones.

"Well, first of all the Hopi are one of the most ancient of peoples who first appeared in the Southwest. They are living manifestations of the ancient Anasazi who appeared here thousands of years ago. The Hopi language is categorized as belonging to the large group of *Shoshonean* Indian languages of the Northwestern

United States. Specifically, it belongs to the Aztecan family of languages that includes Nahuatl, the language of Mexico's famed Aztecs.

"The Hopi people have retained many of their ancient connections with the spirit world because their whole way of life was a manifestation of their spiritual beliefs, and because they were isolated from most non-Indian influences until recent times. Their beliefs and rituals are especially rich in symbolism that explains and celebrates their spiritual link with each other, with other life forms, and with the cosmos at large. In true Hopi tradition, the mask does not merely represent spirits, but embodies them, making it a sacrilege to collect and display them. It must have been a real debate among the Hopi people to finally agree to let Jernigan display them. I'll bet many of the older people in the tribe complained bitterly when they were put on display."

I turned around from the sink where I was peeling potatoes and ask, "That sounds like all Indian tribes around here, what makes the Hopi so different?"

Hidalgo continued after offering to help prepare the food, but I shoved the knife between us and said, "You need to talk, I'll peel the potatoes."

"In all ancient cultures, they believed that all cosmic matter such as animals and plants as well as the earth itself was physically as well as spiritually connected. In ancient times, the Hopi as well as all ancient people recognized their cosmic link with other life forms, and created a variety of religious rituals and totems to reflect this relationship. All of those earliest religious beliefs from Buddhism, Christianity, Islam and other present day religions are derived or began as manifestations of reality as the people of those times knew it. This reality included the sacrifice of living creatures and in many cases humans as well, then eating flesh and drinking the blood of the sacrificed to represent the fact that life comes from death, and they merge the spirits of the living with the spirits of the dead. In time, in societies that became civilized, those rituals of perceived reality were gradually transformed into symbolic acts, some of which remain conspicuous today for their reflections of the ancient beliefs. In Catholicism, for example, adherents symbolically eat the flesh and drink the blood of Jesus Christ. In all religious ceremonials, whether symbolic or real, the sacrifice completes the cycle of death and life, and joins the spirits of the dead with the living."

"It all sounds a little like what we have learned from our serpent friends." Hidalgo ignored my point so I asked, "They are Native Americans who came from Mongolia during or before the last Ice Age, right?"

Hidalgo answered my question despite the fact that he was lost in thought. "All Hopi children are born with the so called 'Mongolian Spot' at the base of their spine. It is a spot that all Native Americans have that gradually disappears as they grow older."

I turned to him again and asked, "All this talk of *Kachinas* and ceremonial mask, I have seen a couple of *Kachina* dolls that Aunt June said she purchased in Arizona years ago, is that what they are talking about?"

"*Kachinas* are spirits from the other worlds. According to their origin stories they traveled to the New World aboard reed boats as instructed by *Sotunkang*. They island hopped until they reached the Americas. Then *Sotuknang* disappeared when another spirit arrived, named *Masaw*. He is now their caretaker. All religions are marked by spiritual beings who act as intermediaries between the people and their gods. Christians for example believe in angels and saints; in the case of the Hopis, they are the *Kachinas*. In Hopi cosmology, there are an infinite number of *kachinas* since the spirits of ancestors may become *Kachinas* as well as animals and plants. They also have spirits that may be referred to as *Kachinas*. In the past, there were some Hopi elders who could name around five hundred *Kachinas*, but in more recent times the names of most of them have been forgotten. Now, most Hopis are familiar with only a few dozen *Kachinas*. There are about thirty *Kachinas* that now play key roles in the five most important Hopi rituals. They are the Hopi guardian angels and messengers."

I interjected, "Oh I get it. The little dolls are representations of those *Kachinas*. They are what Corey was talking about when he told us the story of the Zuni Mudheads. What is the deal with the mask that they were talking about?"

"Well," Hidalgo thought for a moment then continued, "Let me give you an example that you may be able to relate to, particularly after you and Corey start having children." I turned around and grinned at him. "One *Kachina* is the Whipper. He plays a critical role in raising young Hopis. The Whipping Ceremony is an initiation into the adult world. When Hopi children reach the age of seven or eight they are required to submit to a public whipping by *Kachinas* as part of a ritual to drive out the bad they had accumulated over the years."

"The Whipper Kachina wears turtle shells on his legs that make a great clattering noise when it dances and cavorts around. The male *Kachinas* are accompanied by a mother *Kachina*. She carries an arm load of fresh yucca branches to be used as whips. At sunrise three days after the whipping ceremony, the same *Kachinas* go to the homes of each of the children that were whipped and are presented with a variety of gifts made by their parents, aunts, uncles and god-parents. The last event in this ceremony is an all-night dance by the *Kachina* whippers, only this time they do not wear mask, allowing the children to see that they were not really magical spirits but men and women from their own village."

"When children are naughty, their parents secretly make arrangements for a fearsome *Kachina* to come to their house and demand that the parents hand over the children for them to eat. The parents always act as the protectors, finally convincing the ogre that he should accept a bribe of some meat or food in place of the children, after which the *Kachina* ogre leaves, warning the children in loud voices that they will return if the youngsters were bad again. The mask worn by *Kachina* players, are called *Kwaatsi* which literally means 'friends.' The mask comes alive when they are donned by players, and while being worn, tell whether or not the wearer has a pure heart, and the masks punish wearers whose hearts are not pure."

I said, "I'll bet that they have very little trouble with their children at Hopi villages, maybe we should all do something like that when raising our children. It would certainly scare the devil out of me."

Hidalgo answered, "You are right, just like in all small communities, there is very little delinquency on the Hopi reservation. The families there are very tightly knit together. Nobody does anything without everyone knowing about it. All Hopi rituals reflected their belief that all life is one. They believe that there is a great life force, a force that exists throughout the cosmos. When a living thing dies, it releases that life energy. When Hopis kill animals for food and other uses they first make an offering to the spirit of the animal, asking it to sacrifice its physical life and energy. The one who does the killing has to express his gratitude for the life of the deceased."

I should have long ago finished peeling the potatoes but instead was listening intently to what Hidalgo was teaching me, I asked, "Do you think they had interactions with the serpents?"

Well actually, they were one of the earliest peoples who encountered the serpents. It is one of the reasons they live where they do, far isolated from other people which is where serpents seem to aggregate. You need to remember that it was the serpents that drove great numbers of people from the San Juan area to the south where they isolated themselves. The Hopi seem to have been spared the interactions of the serpents but one of the things that I find most fascinating about the Hopi is their ability to make predictions. For example, they predicted the arrival of white people who would invade their land and missed their arrival by only a decade or so. It is uncanny how many of their predictions have come true. But there is one prediction they made that scares me more than any other prediction."

"What is that," I asked.

"They predicted long ago that the white men would invent a gourd of ashes that when dropped from the sky would boil everything in a wide area and nothing would grow in that area for a long time!"

"And sure enough, atomic bombs were dropped during World War II in Japan and nothing would grow there for a long time," I replied.

"Precisely," replied Hidalgo, "let's hope they drop no more of them."

Contemplating Roles

The conversation regarding the Hopi continued right through the evening meal. Everyone was talking but no one was coming up with any real suggestions when Ken who hadn't said anything interjected a novel idea, "We need to set up a sting."

Everyone asked for clarification. "We need to figure out a way use their greed against the people who want to buy the Hopi masks for their own collections or for profit. It has been my experience that people, particularly rich people, will make all kinds of stupid mistakes if they think they are getting even richer for nothing. For them, it is not the money that is important; it is the power that money buys that is important. Sure, they can sell the mask and *Kachina* dolls, figuring they can make a few million dollars but if they think they can make that money and still keep the dolls anyway, for a later sell, they certainly will change the normal rules of the auction. Instead, we acquire the Hopi mask and *Kachinas* and keep the money anyway. Who are they going to call, the police? The stuff is stolen in the first place and they know it. They won't want to involve the police if they think that they are the smart ones. Instead we will be the smart ones. Of course, then they will make every attempt to take their goods back and probably kill us in the process. We are going to have to be very careful however we do this thing. Maybe we need to make them an offer they can't refuse. An offer that will shut down that part of the auction altogether and that way we deal with them directly."

June laughs and says, "We have a little money put away and certainly we could put that money toward possibly purchasing one of those masks but an entire truck load? I don't think they would even let us in the door."

"That's true," says Ken while looking at Penny, "But if they thought that they were dealing with some sweet little thing that didn't know much due to her tender age and experience they might think they could really take advantage of her, if she represented someone who had vast reserves of wealth, or perhaps a Navajo who was actually a wealthy oilman. What if they thought they were ripping us off and all the while we are ripping them off?"

Hidalgo says, "There are no rich Navajos out there who made their money in the oil business but then again, they don't know that. We would need some really good cheese, some really good bait to lure rats like that. Who do we know that might be willing to take a chance by letting us use his name as a way of getting in the door? After all, they send representatives to those auctions who purchase goods for them, why can't we?"

Corey questioned, "Yes, but that person should really appear to be quite beautiful yet sophisticated. Someone who is extremely smart yet appears to be someone who can be easily tricked by professional con men. It would help if she could speak some French but it wouldn't be necessary. Most Europeans speak several languages and so speaking English would not really be a problem. She would need to be a distraction to them so someone else can do the sting."

I looked around and realized that everyone was staring at me. "I never thought of myself as a *fem fatale*, I never even thought of myself as sexy."

June laughed, "You need to take another look at yourself in the mirror without your work clothes on, your hair in a mess, and that drop of gravy from the mashed potatoes on your chin. A little make up would also help."

I wiped off the gravy that was on my chin and considered the situation.

"I could be the negotiator," continued Ken, but we would need to figure out several more things, such as what we are going to use as bait and how are we going to ship the items back to the United States if we acquire them."

June got on the phone and called Manny Aragon to ask what he knew of the situation and how he intended to help. Aragon suggested that they contact Clarence Morgan, an inventor and computer specialist who had made millions creating guidance systems for military aircraft. He was the one who had learned to integrate computers into the systems of missiles that could be used to knock down other missiles, while in flight, and that is just one aspect of his expertise. He had worked with Aragon and was a philanthropist who gave away more money in a year than most corporations make in a year. The most qualifying thing about him though, was that he enjoyed correcting a wrong. He believed in social justice and wanted to leave the world a better place than he found it. After considerable talking he agreed to contact Clarence Morgan to see if he would allow the detectives to use his name as the buyer of the ceremonial object. Aragon suggested that maybe he would pretend to pay them twice the asking price in bars of gold which could be forfeited if things turned out badly and the objects had to actually be paid for.

It only took a day until Aragon was calling June with some information. "Clarence Morgan thought it would be a fun game to play on the auctioneers. He has some personal problems with them because they make enormous amounts of money off the work of others and contribute nothing to the world themselves. He is willing to put up a million in gold as collateral but would prefer to get that money back. He certainly has better uses of it than to donate to the greedy pursuits of the people who auctions off the treasures of others. He suggested that he will ship the gold to Europe and there you will need to acquire it. He also said something very interesting. He suggested that he will send one bar of pure gold that would be marked because surely, they will want to have it tested, the other bars will be of lead that is plated in gold. That way, not as much wealth is lost even if you have to pay them for the objects. The real challenge will be to get them to take the objects off the auction block and negotiate with you privately. You should say that you are a relative of his and he will provide you with some fake documentation to provide proof of that relationship. He also asked if we had a young girl there that is very good looking and could act as a distraction?"

"Yes, that should be Penny," answered June.

"Good, she will go as Morgan's daughter and you might want to have a bodyguard for her."

"Yes, that should be Corey, her husband."

"You also need to have someone who can do the actual negotiations, and of course you to inspect the ceremonial masks and *Kachinas* to make sure that they are not impostors. Someone like Hidalgo who obviously looks like an Indian and June can authenticate them."

"You will also need to rehearse what you are going to say enough so you can get everything down to a fine science. By the way, if you are able to pull the trade off, you will need to have all the objects taken to the airport where we will provide an American plane that will carry them as well as your detective team back to the United States."

Two days later a package of documents arrived at the ranch house in Serpiente by a very exasperated and tired Fed Ex man who had never in his life had to drive so far just to deliver a small package. Inside of the package was the documentation for Penny that identified her as Melissa Morgan, the wealthy and very spoiled daughter of Clarence Morgan. Ken was listed on the documents as her legal representative, and June as Mrs. Marylyn Rothschild, an ex-employee of the Smithsonian Institute and an expert on Native American Artifacts. Paperwork for Hidalgo and Corey was also provided along with a letter of introduction that would give them access to the auction along with one way tickets to Paris and instructions on where and when to meet the Americans who would fly them and the artifacts back to America. There were also instructions as to how to acquire the gold bars that was part of the transaction. Basically, the real gold bar and the fake ones would be flown in on a military aircraft which would also provide security for the shipment. Documents of introduction had already been mailed to Paris to the auctioneers to set up a meeting. They then had to wait until notified if they would agree to meet. There certainly was no guarantee that they would agree to meet at all but they were given incentive to meet. The opportunity to make more than twice the amount they would make in auctioning off the artifacts was a strong incentive for them, besides the auctioneers had no guarantee that they would make the projected amount of money even if they did auction the objects off. Sometimes they made a killing and sometimes they had a cold audience. Anyway, they looked at it, everything was a crapshoot and anything could go wrong.

After looking though, the materials, June and Ken were amazed at the speed and efficiency everything was going. "Well," sighed June, "you all realize that we are now committed to this sting and only a couple of days ago we had no idea it was going to happen. Furthermore, we only have a couple of days to get our act together. We need to buy fancy cloths and practice our lines. If this thing is going to work, it will have to proceed like clockwork."

Paris, France

From Albuquerque, we flew to New York where we spent a day doing nothing but buying clothes that were appropriate to wear in Paris. It was important to arrive in Paris with first class airline tickets that showed New York as their departing site.

The corporate headquarters of Morgan Industries was in New York and immediately our plans were changed. Clarence Morgan, who was truly caught up in the sting, had his private Lear Jet ready for us and we loaded ourselves into the private jet early in the morning and by evening we were in Paris.

At least we could return the money the Hopi had given us to pay for the airplane tickets. Besides, arriving in Paris aboard a private jet held far more prestige than arrival in a public transport. As we departed from the airplane, a representative from the auction, a Mr. Giroux was there to greet us. He escorted us into the private lobby of the airport. This lobby was separate from the main airport so there was little checking of identifications, customs or officials to deal with. Inconspicuously sitting in a chair as we entered the lobby of the building for private parties we saw an old friend. There sat Dr. Wilkerson with a big grin on his face and his hair in its usual disheveled mess. As soon as we saw him he gave us a nod then disappeared into the busy building.

After short introductions with Mr. Giroux we were escorted to a limousine and after a trip to the outskirts of Paris, we were taken to a very private hotel. As we entered though the front doors I gasped as I realized just how luxurious our surroundings were. The tip that Ken gave the baggage carriers was more than most people earn in a week, yet they seemed unimpressed. There was no check in procedure. We were escorted directly to the elevators which dropped us off on the top fourth floor. We walked down a short hallway and there was our suite. We spent the next few minutes just admiring the place. There was a well-lighted central room with a large ornate table with matching chairs around it. At the other end of the room was a small kitchen. The refrigerator was already packed full of alcoholic beverages, and soft drinks, American brands. From the kitchen, going outside through a double door, a small balcony allowed occupants to step outside to a small table with wrought iron chairs. It was a place where one could sit and see everything that was going on below. People could sunbath, smoke, read or do just about anything people wanted to do such as what we were doing; watching other people in a new world, the entire city of Paris lay before us.

I was a little more than intimidated but it didn't last. We were all actors upon a stage but our façade soon was revealed. Hidalgo was the first to start asking questions about how to operate the bathroom facilities with something called a bidet which was unlike anything he had experienced in America, particularly for an old boy that spent a lot of time outdoors living on a working ranch. We all needed a minute to adjust.

We were all getting comfortable, setting around the common area on overstuffed couches discussing the obvious question, what were we going to do next? Instead, a knock came to the door. Being the closest, I opened the door and there stood Dr. Jim Wilkerson, looking as if he was having fun, with a mischievous look on his face. He quickly stepped inside. As soon as we made eye contact again, he frowned, putting his finger to his lips and then took out of his shirt pocket, a small electronic device. He brought it to my forehead and then waved it all the way down to my toes at which point he signaled me to bend over which I did while he examined me with the device. After he had examined me he walked over to the table and quickly passed it over everyone who was seated there, but without asking them to bend over and touch the floor as he had me. He then proceeded to study our room poking his device anywhere an electronic listening device would likely be hidden. During the entire routine, everyone's eyes followed him everywhere he went without saying a word. A quick walk around the living room and he finally turned and faced all of us, apparently satisfied. He sat down and simply said, "One has to be careful." He then looked at me with a curious look, as if waiting for me to say something. Not giving him a response he got directly to the point.

"We may already have everything under control, except for one small detail; let me explain to you what is going to happen. These people are hoping they can auction off a small catalog of antiquities. Some of what they are auctioning is legitimate, authentic antiques that naturally come to market, but they really make their money on objects such as the Hopi stuff because it is so rare. Rarely, would an entire truck load of these kinds of artifacts be available. There are many Hopi items which they can sell for a small fortune. The auctioneers have never been suspected of anything, they represented a very old and conservative company and I suspect that they have someone on the inside of the Paris Police who redirects any complaints that are lodged against them. The Hopi items were just some of what was being auctioned; the auction would take some time to complete. We want them to think that the entire cache of Hopi items was being sought by you and you intend to make payment with a large shipment of gold.

Instead we know something about them that they think no one knows. As an import - export business they have been dealing in far more than just antiquities. We suspect that some of the members of their firm have been bringing hard drugs into France and several surrounding countries and then laundering the money they make under the guise of their auctions. They are about to all take a bad fall and everything they own, including the Hopi goods are going to be confiscated and they are going to jail."

Mystified, the group was dumbfounded if not amused.

"What do you want us to do," asked Ken?

Wilkerson cocked his head for a moment then says, "We still need you to go through the motions of going to the auction and pretend to make a bid on the antiquities. If you fail to show up they may get suspicious and think something is wrong. Mr. Giroux will pick you up in two days at exactly two in the afternoon. He will drive you to the auction where you will go through the motions of bidding on antiquities. Be prepared, auctions like these are social events for the very wealthy. We have no way of knowing exactly what you will do until the actual auction is over. More than likely you will be terribly outbid but that is fine because there is no gold coming into France and, hopefully they are going to be arrested by the local authorities and taken to jail. They probably are using the same facilities to store their baled kilos of heroin and cocaine as they use for stolen artifacts. We just don't know which one of their facilities they store the drugs in. The auctioneer owns thirty-two separate facilities here in France, everything from warehouses to expensive homes; anyone of them could be used to hide contraband such as drugs in it."

"Why don't you just raid all of them," Ken asked?

"We don't have the resources to do it all at once. Besides, if we didn't stumble upon the right place, right away, they would just move everything around, kind of like the shell game. Which shell is the pea under? Besides they have many wealthy friends who would help them and being wealthy they have little fear of prosecution."

June asked, "How did you learn all that?"

"Simple, Mr. Giroux the driver for the auction house actually works for us. It was he who let us know about the storage of drugs there. It was he who helped us set up the real sting that is about to take place. The governments of France, as well as the United States, have been trying for years to find out how the drugs were getting into the country. We still don't know how but if we can nail them with the goods it doesn't matter. In a few days, a C-130 will arrive at the airport and the Hopi antiquities will be loaded onto it and returned to the United States. You can leave on that plane which eventually will return you to Albuquerque. Or, you could hang around and continue being a tourist but I would wonder about the unknown element. You all might want to board the C-130 and return just for your own safety."

"What do we do in the meantime?" I asked.

"You have all of tomorrow and the next day to be tourist, the day after that you do your thing at the auction, offering them several million in gold, which they will never see, and then you need to return here and lay low."

"What do you mean by lay low," asked Ken?

"Well, you never know who all is involved. We know who our people are but we don't know all of their people. They will be doing their homework and investigate you just as we investigated them. I suspect that after the sting occurs they will attempt to exact vengeance by those not caught in the initial bust. If they connect you to the sting your lives may be in danger so I recommend that you are seen in public for a couple of days. You do have options however, you could stay in another tourist hotel and blend in with the other tourist, or you could just stay here in this hotel but it would be dangerous. Of course, the best option would be for you to leave on the C-130 with the antiquities but that might be a little strange considering you have an open check book with unlimited funding. You could enjoy the sights and sounds of Paris and eat and drink anything you want, but after the sting occurs, we cannot guarantee your safety."

Everybody understood the obvious solution of leaving on the C-130. But Dr. Wilkerson seemed to be displaying a wry sense of humor. Finally, he says, "Call me if you have serious questions but don't call me unless you have a real problem, any questions now?"

Hidalgo says while pointing to the bathroom, "How do you operate the plumbing in there?" Dr. Wilkerson grins and says, "I would suggest experimentation. But you might want to test it before you really need it. If it makes you feel any better, it bothered me too, at first. Anyway, I'll leave that problem to your friends to explore with you. Laughing, he stood up and took a couple of steps then turning he looked intently at me.

"I did think about the pass you made that first day I met you. It really put me on the spot. I guess when it comes to women, I am a little naive."

"Oh, I was just playing." I answered him. "I just wanted to see what you would do. I'm sorry."

"You were teasing just to see what kind of a reaction you could get. I understand. And you were right. I was as uncomfortable as I could be in that suit. Believe me, it wasn't my idea to wear it in the first place. Well, I suppose if I hadn't of already known your life history, you could have made me extremely nervous."

He took a couple of more steps closer to the door, turned again, and again focused his eyes on me and says, "By the way, do you remember the electronic detection device that I used to check all of you and your room out with?"

"Sure," I responded.

"I was just playing. It was just a toy, we are now even." With that said, he disappeared through the door.

The Rich Americans

In a couple of days, an auction would occur and for a while, all would be business. Until then, we had about sixty hours to do anything we wanted, with unlimited funds, in Paris, France. We were to pretend, to be wealthy. The problem was none of us had the foggiest idea how to portray ourselves as truly wealthy persons which was what were expected to do. Except for Mexico, none of us had traveled outside the United States, much less Europe and even though we were wealthy by New Mexico ranch standards, we never showed it beyond having to dress up for events at the university such as the historical society presentations.

Living within their means was a basic part of the way we lived. The only truly wealthy people we had encountered were some of the owners of oil facilities in Texas. Most of the oilmen that Corey, Ken and Hidalgo knew were just hard working people who were liked by everyone. But there were some they encountered that no one liked. Their arrogance and lack of concern for others made them a pariah. The only friends they had were those they purchased. The family had actually frowned on displays of personal wealth, as well as the personal habits of those that live that way. It was because of the way all of us had grown up. To us, people who live extravagant lifestyles were usually consumers of other people's hard work.

Certainly, not all wealthy people were that way. In fact, most had accumulated their wealth through persistent hard work and deserved every penny they earned. It was those who have no appreciation of the hard work of others, who acquired their wealth easily and bragged about their lifestyle or wasted the wealth that bothered us. Now we were being asked to pretend that we were like those very people. It certainly wasn't the hardest job we had tackled but we certainly felt strange doing it.

We decided to look into the resources provided in the Hotel and ask questions about the sights and sounds of Paris we could explore in the next couple of days. We were immediately but politely snubbed by most of the hotel workers who could not believe that a wealthy guest would need to ask about happenings in Paris. We finally found one friendly clerk who took the time to talk to us. June explained that we had never been to Paris before and the clerk wrote us out a list of what to him were some great sights and fine restaurants. He also explained that despite the fact that it was very rare for Paris, this particular hotel had a large enclosed swimming pool where most of the younger people hung out.

I immediately rounded up Corey and Hidalgo and suggested that we go swimming in the Hotel pool. Everyone agreed that it sounded like a great idea until I realized that I had not packed my one swimming suit that was used at the college pool. June suggested that we should see if we could buy one here in the hotel so down we went to the main foyer where many small shops, all catering to the needs of the guest could be found.

Ten minutes later we were in a small shop that sold cloths to the tourist who managed to show up without some article of clothing that would be worn around the pool. But I quickly discovered that I had another problem. "They don't cover anything up!" I said in exasperation.

June says in a tease, "This is the style that people wear around here. Here in France, they have nude beaches that people go to. If you cannot find a swim suit, perhaps we can all just go to one of those beaches."

This brought a blank look followed by a grimace and I said, "Not a chance." I finally settled for a lemon-yellow bikini that was far more string than cloth and it just barely fit me. It was designed for people to lounge around in, an advertisement for the care free and well to do. Not for an athletic young lady to do some serious swimming in but it was the only one that would even remotely work. After also purchasing a large towel robe I marched out to the pool area. As soon as the towel came off I noticed male eyes on me. The young men who were sunning themselves around the pool watched every move I made making several other young ladies envious of me. Pretending not to know Corey and Hidalgo, the three of us slowly swam laps across the pool and starting with Hidalgo we stepped out of the water and found lounge chairs where we sat and watched the other natives. Then an unexpected incident occurred.

A striking young lady, with sparkling green eyes and long raven hair pulled up a lounge chair and positioned it directly next to Hidalgo. She slowly took off her beach robe and spread it over the chair and lay down. Wearing a string bikini that I would never consider wearing in public, she quickly started up a conversation with Hidalgo. Unfortunately, the conversation was one sided as she was speaking in French. Hidalgo had no idea what she was saying knowing only a few words in French because of their similarity to Spanish. She was persistent and obvious in her flirtations which made Hidalgo very nervous which delighted the young lady.

Corey who changed his mind and returned to the water, was delighted watching the spectacle and would angle himself in the water so he didn't miss anything. Sitting down in the shallow water of the steps, a good-looking man who was obviously older than me moved his lounge chair over to where I had been setting. I was curious about the man who waited for my return. I let him wait on purpose.

Finally, overcome by curiosity, I returned to my lounge chair and the gentleman immediately introduced himself. Mr. Basheer Ahmed was the son of Damascus Ahmed who was the president of Ahmed Corporation, a mechanical company that serviced one of the largest oil companies in Saudi Arabia. Basheer Ahmed explained that he was one of the bidders at the auction. He seemed to be the classical playboy who spent his serious moments working with his father's money. I looked over at Hidalgo who was still squirming in his chair trying to understand what this astonishingly beautiful woman was so persistently trying to say to him. He tried conversing in English, then Spanish then finally in Navajo. All of this seemed to excite the girl as much as it did to frustrate Hidalgo.

Corey seemed to be busy talking to another couple while standing in the pool water. I excused myself from Mr. Ahmed and walked over to Hidalgo who was looking for an escape from the flirtatious girl. I had not seen him in such an uncomfortable situation since the time they had spent at Sand Island on a river trip down the San Juan River. The young girl glared at me as I approached so I backed away, much to the chagrin of Hidalgo and then dived back into the pool. Instantly I knew something was wrong but it took me a moment to figure it out. Suddenly all the men at poolside jerked their heads up or even stood up to get a better look at me. As I had dived into the water the top to my bikini had cupped water and slid down around my waist and for a few moments I was oblivious to the dilemma. Then I realized the dilemma I was in, being unable to bring the bikini top back to its original position without exposing myself even more. Corey and several other young men offered to help me bring the strap back to its original place while I floundered in the water attempting to cover my breast. Finally, Hidalgo appeared with a towel which he wrapped around me and the three of us left the pool together leaving the French speaking girl who was flirting with Hidalgo to find someone else to pursue and Mr. Ahmed alone. We had utterly failed at our first attempt to be sophisticated and suave.

That evening everyone settled into the hotel dining room to enjoy their first real meal since we had left New York. Having missed lunch, Ken and June were starving but nothing like the three of us who had been swimming. Hidalgo and Corey were finally able to kill their hunger pains by ordering two complete meals for each of them. The conversation was lively and full of giggles after Corey delicately explained how I had been embarrassed at the pool. It was June who brought up the subject of the Hopi prophecies.

"It sounds like Mr. Hoyumptewa was exactly right about what he said the other night."

"How is that?" asked Ken who already knew the answer to his own question.

"Well let's see," June says, "first of all he said that Hidalgo would be pursued by women who would embarrass the devil out of him."

"That's right," I chimed in. "She was putting major moves on him and he just laid there on the pool chair like a floundering whale out of water and by now he is just figuring out how to use the local plumbing. Two of Mr. Hoyumptewa's prophecies have already come true for Hidalgo. The third prophecy was wrong however."

"What do you mean, asked Hidalgo?"

"Well the shaman said that Hidalgo had very special powers that would appear. If it has to do with dealing with women like that 'hottie' that was pursuing him at the pool, I'm afraid Mr. Hoyumptewa was completely wrong. Otherwise Hidalgo wouldn't be eating dinner with us; he would be eating dinner with her and making plans for the evening."

"Well," Hidalgo counters, "he certainly was right about you. For a couple of minutes, I thought there was going to be a riot at the pool. You know there is a rule posted over the door of the pool that says, do not run in pool area. I thought several of those men were going to break a leg or something running to get a better look."

I was blushing again and said, "At least I had a Navajo knight who came to my rescue. Corey tried but just didn't think as fast as you did."

Hidalgo says, "I would do it all over again if I needed an excuse for an escape. I like rescuing damsels in distress but if you keep kidding me about my plumbing problems, next time I'll let you solve your problem all by yourself."

I said, "There is not going to be a next time. Before I ever get into a swimming suit again there had better be some kind of straps or something. But wasn't it very strange how Mr. Hoyumtewa could foresee those things, I really thought he was just kidding, even the other Hopi gentlemen said he was just kidding."

Hidalgo says, "A shaman doesn't kid around. I have never met one yet that would joke around. What concerns and worries me were his other prophecies."

The first thing we did the next day was to decide where to eat breakfast. We had seen what was being served in the hotel restaurant and decided that surely there was a better place to eat. June suggested a simple solution. She suggested that we get on the metro and travel to a place that was recommended in a guidebook that she had bought. It was called 'Breakfast in America'. The guide said that it was an American style diner that was started by an American who came to Paris for school and then just decided to stay.

After a short ride on the metro, we discovered that the restaurant served breakfast all day and we enjoyed the English that was being spoken around us. Although, most of the people we heard, had a strong British accent.

Everyone had a hearty breakfast of French toast, omelets and biscuits with gravy. We enjoyed ourselves despite the fact that some of the other guest spoke under their breaths about the gluttony of the Americans. Corey complained that they didn't have steak on the menu. We Americans were used to eating a hearty breakfast and then burning off the calories in a hard day's work. Few of the other people at the restaurant had ever done hard physical work in their entire lives. At this point we were concerned because we felt like we stood out so much. We were certainly not behaving like New York sophisticates. But to our faces, everyone in the restaurant was very polite. We decided to just be ourselves.

Digging up the Evidence

After breakfast we walked around the neighborhood which was near Sorbonne and visited the Pantheon, which confused me. I had no idea that Paris had a Pantheon as well as Greece and Nashville, Tennessee. We spent the entire remainder of the day seeing the usual sights that tourist see in Paris such as Notre Dame Cathedral, Champs-Elysees and the Arch of Triumph. We then went back to the Eiffel Tower where we shopped in a multitude of small shops finding nothing we could really use and explored the surrounding garden walks. We hung around until it became dark and was amazed when the tower was lit up and the tourist started to take photographs from it which made it seem to sparkle.

The following day after another breakfast at the Breakfast in America diner we took the metro to the Louvre. The Louvre is the most visited art museum in the world and Ken, June and I spent the entire day there attempting to explore the entire museum. Hidalgo and Corey snuck off to explore the Catacombs which seemed interesting to them. That evening everyone returned to the hotel with sore feet but a whole new understanding of the world they were visiting.

After two days of sightseeing we had exhausted all the normal tourist places. As Hidalgo said, "If I eat at another restaurant where a tiny plate of food is more expensive than what a cowboy earns in a week he was going to give up eating." They were already homesick for real food and the simple pleasures of life that Serpiente offered. We were also looking forward to getting on the job we had come to Paris for.

Finally the time came to go to the auction. Mr. Giroux informed them as soon as they opened the door that things were going to be interesting. The auctioneer was getting nervous about the gold transaction. Giroux overheard him talking to another man about getting the gold because he couldn't understand why anyone would pay so much for the artifacts and besides there was a buyer from Saudi Arabia who had his heart set on buying the artifacts and had done business with him before.

Arrival at the auction house was not at all what we expected. After we showed our identifications to what appeared to be an official we were escorted to a large dining room instead of going into a room where the artifacts and other treasures were presented. We were expected to socialize over finger foods and fine French wine. Ken and June graciously accepted a glass of Champaign. Corey and particularly Hidalgo refused to drink the wine which caused suspicious looks from many of the other participants. None of them could imagine Americans who refused to drink fine wines. They were ostracized but June and I had better luck. I particularly had good luck as the same middle aged man from Saudi Arabia, the same man who had flirted with me at the pool and spoke perfect English who had went through every motion available to separate me from the rest of the Americans. I played the part and remained friendly even when the man made several suggestions as to places he would like to take me. He certainly had plans for me before the auction and he seemed not used to having someone say no to him. The power that comes from being wealthy had intoxicated him along with the French wine. He was dead set on a conquest, and I was his target, he walked directly up to me.

Corey was amazed as he watched me play this fellow, I was having fun but Corey was also getting mad until I turned to him and winked at him as we walked the short distance to the auction hall. Corey had to remind himself that it was all part of the sting. Meanwhile the young girl who had flirted with Hidalgo at the pool also showed up, and spoke to him briefly in perfect English which perfectly flummoxed Hidalgo.

I sat with Mr. Basheer Ahmed, the man from Saudi Arabia while the other four Americans sat at a table near the rear of the room. Meanwhile the Arabian took out his notebook and wrapped his arm around my shoulder which brought a groan from Corey. I glanced over my shoulder and managed a grin as the auction began. The auction began with oil paintings that should have been hanging in museums. In fact, a couple of them were paintings I was sure I had seen in a book somewhere. The Peruvian pottery was put up for sale, one pot at a time. Hidalgo thought to himself that this is where those items wound up after they were pilfered out of burial grounds that are supposed to be protected by law. He thought back to Garcia and Fernandez who were now in the New Mexico State Penitentiary.

Finally, a portion of the collection of Hopi ceremonial objects was brought up to the gavel. Penny now realized who she was setting with. The man easily outbid everybody in the auction. Ken never won a single bid. We watched as he added up the items along with what his bids were and the total was several million dollars. We then were informed that there would more Hopi items at a later auction. They were being held back for future auctions, the value of them would only increase over time.

I whispered into Basheer's ear, asking if we could at least see the other Hopi artifacts before leaving Paris.

"Sure, you can, if you promise to ditch those boring Americans that I hung around with and consider returning to Saudi Arabia with him for a short visit. I agreed to consider the trip and pressed him about examining the other items. He stood up, took me by the arm and we walked out the room. He stopped at the door and spoke to two men who were manning the entrance. One of them immediately called for a car and the three of us loaded into it.

After we had traveled several miles we found ourselves in front of a private residence with a large wall around it and security cameras everywhere. The metal ornate gate to the compound opened after a code was punched into a keypad mounted next to the gate. Once inside, we were escorted into a house every bit as ornate as the hotel we had been staying in. Two new men met us at the door and escorted us into the living area which was stacked from floor to ceiling with antiquities stored in created boxes.

"You realize that I am the only person in the world that could have gotten you in here, you are going to owe me something very special," he said while patting me on the butt. I was glad that Corey was not there, he would have blown our cover for sure. He would have killed our Saudi businessman.

After examining several crates that contained artifacts that at first glance would not have received much attention, he asked me. "Do you feel better now that you have seen the Hopi pieces," he asked me.

"Yes, I do feel better. I still want to acquire them if there is a way."

"I'm afraid that would be impossible. I have already purchased them. In a few days, they will be shipped to my home. But at least, I let you see them, again you owe me something."

"Ok, I owe you something but for now I would like to return to the hotel unless you have something else here that could interest me."

"Well, we have bedrooms here."

"Do you have something that could make it all more interesting?" I asked, hoping to worm as much information out of him as possible.

"How about a couple of lines of coke" he asked.

I answered him with, "I'll bet if you have all this stuff here, you have more than just a couple of lines of coke?" I was hoping to get him to brag, and it worked. In a few moments, he was showing be a metal box that was stacked alongside several other metal boxes he opened. Sure enough, the inside was full of bales of powdered cocaine.

Grabbing my arm and directing me he says "Let's do a couple of lines and go to bed, I'm tired of waiting."

"Well, you are going to have to wait a little longer. I am not in the mood for that tonight, besides it is the wrong time of the month." I hoped my lies would be enough to delay the inevitable. "Will you be willing to accept a rain check? I will make it up to you, trust me, I will truly make it worth your time. You will appreciate it when you finally get it."

He was seriously disappointed but finally agreed to the fact that nothing was going to happen this particular evening. "You own all of this, don't you?" I casually asked.

Well, I don't own the auction firm but I certainly do own everything else around here."

I thought, you may own everything around here but you don't own me.

"Come on, I'll have the driver drop you off at the hotel." With that said, I immediately took him up on his offer and within a half hour was walking into the lobby of our hotel.

Meanwhile the girl who had flirted with Hidalgo made another appearance but only raised her shoulders in a sign of defeat and then says, "I could have made a really interesting evening for you."

Hidalgo pulled her up to him in a hug and says, "Yes, that is probably true but then, I would have to lie to someone else who is very important to me."

"She will never need to know," the mysterious girl says.

"Yes, that's true but I will know. Thank you anyway."

At that, the young girl walked away, clearly showing her disgust with the situation. They returned to the hotel to discover me there waiting for them. We never heard a word from Wilkerson but early the following day he appeared at the door to our suite.

Running from the Cartel

Wilkerson got right to the point. "We followed you after you left the auction last night and we raided the house you were taken to but the sting didn't come off as we expected. First of all, we caught them with half a ton of drugs so we were able to arrest many of them. We think they were in the process of removing the artifacts and indeed had already removed a couple of truckloads of goods but not the Hopi artifacts. We don't know if we were able to get them all out. We managed to find several containers that were labeled Hopi Ceremonial but we have no idea what is missing. But it is better than nothing. We also found several boxes of art work and pottery, several of them marked with the name Peru. Anyway, they are all leaving for America on the C-130. The problem is we don't know where they hid the rest of the auction items. Evidently, they have another warehouse somewhere around Paris but at the moment we don't have a lead as to where it is. The problem is, we don't know what they know and I'm sure they are going to seek some kind of revenge for messing up their operation. I don't know if they have connected all of you to the sting but if my guess is right, they will eventually try to grab anyone who they suspect was involved, mainly people they have not worked with before, such as the American delegation to the auction."

"This all sounds very serious," says June.

"Well, we do know that they were watching you carefully. Hidalgo, that sweet girl who was flirting with you was one of their agents. If you see her again I would watch myself very carefully if I was you. Trust me, she is no sweet little thing as you may imagine."

Hidalgo answers, "I had my suspicions from the first moment she showed up. Good looking girls simply don't come on to me like that. At least that has been my experience.

Penny asked, "What about the fellow that was coming on to me? He obviously is one of the ring leaders."

"True, but actually he is just a player for his father. He is an investment broker; that is he buys art and artifacts as cheaply as he can and then puts them into his father's private collection. A piece of art that may have sold for fifty thousand dollars twenty years ago could easily bring a half million dollars now and as for you Penny," he paused and looked at Corey whom he knew would be uncomfortable with this conversation, "He is a playboy who likes to use women and then disappears. If you had of developed a relationship with him, in time you would have been discarded like dozens of other women he has known."

Corey says, "I would like to get my hands on him."

Wilkerson laughs and says, "Well, for what it's worth, he just spent millions on goods that he will never see and I assure you that he will never see the money again. When he finally returns home to his father, it will be after he has spent another fortune getting him out of jail. I suspect he will be on the hot seat for a long time.

"Good," Corey says.

"I wouldn't be too mean about it all," I said, "after all, it wasn't like I wasn't playing along. He may feel that I trapped him. He may feel that I am responsible for his money disappearing and getting him into trouble."

"Perhaps," says Wilkerson, "but I wouldn't give him another thought. Right now, the problem is getting all of you out of Paris without running into any of them. I really doubt that it will be a problem; after all, they are hiding out from the law as we speak. But this whole operation is a lot bigger than we thought. I would like to suggest that you take a cab which we will provide for you, directly to the airport and I'll be along shortly."

We left the motel letting Wilkerson deal with paying the bills and headed to the airport. Within a few minutes after we arrived at the airport and before passing through any security, we attempted to go to the same building that we had arrived at. We could see the C-130, a monster of an airplane with large props, setting on the tarmac and trucks were taking turns delivering things from the warehouse. We knew that as soon as they loaded the artifacts on the plane we would need to be on that plane too. We remembered what Wilkerson had said, "I warn you, it will only take a few minutes for them to load that plane and it will immediately leave for London, gas up, fly to New York and then on to Albuquerque. Once there, we will go through the artifact creates and return as many of the antiquities as we can. Anything that cannot be accounted for will be sent to the Smithsonian."

Charged with Being Antiquity Thieves

The problem arose when airport officials noticed us. We were never asked for any identification when we arrived in Paris and now that we wanted out in a hurry the security officers, who we suspected could speak fluent English, choose to speak only in French. We were kept from venturing into the corridor that allows egress to the private jets. The building was off limits without an examination of our visas and an examination of our luggage. The team finally figured out that the problem arose as a result of the fact that no private jets were scheduled to leave that was not accounted for and of course none of us had any kind of documentation, not even a ticket for a departing flight. All we had was documentation that allowed us into the country in the first place. The real problem was as news of the police action that had occurred earlier they were looking for suspicious characters. The police lead us to an interrogation room where we were told to wait and locked in.

False identifications weighed heavily on our minds. With the massive props tuning, the pilot of the airplane had already done his pre-flight checks and was waiting for clearance from the tower. Suddenly, Wilkerson suddenly appeared at the door and waved us out. We were escorted directly to the tarmac and boarded the ungainly but powerful plane. The entire trip back was spent setting on tiny metal seats alongside an airplane filled with antiquities. We were beginning to wonder if leaving Paris was such a good idea. We could have changed our identities and truly went tourist, but then we could have been killed one at a time by people we had never met before. It wasn't worth the risk to stay in Paris, but our posteriors were now paying the price.

After taking two full days of flying an arduous and parabolic course from Paris then England, followed by Iceland, then setting down in Canada before landing in America proper, we were finally able to exit the airplane just as the sun was rising over the city of Albuquerque. Dog tired, we had to go through a security check with all our false documents which seemed to raise eyebrows. We were escorted into another private part of an airport and asked to wait. Several government officials came and went asking us to explain our circumstances over and over. They wanted a full description of what had occurred. We noticed that no representatives from the Hopi Indian Nation was present, nor was there any of the representatives we had been working with and wondered why.

The security agents in Albuquerque asked us why we were asked to participate in the stealing of artifacts if the government was going to steal them anyway.
Ken explained that they needed plausible deniability. First of all, Clarence Morgan
has never heard of the artifacts nor had any desire to own then. His daughter was
only eight years old. However, he had agreed to allow Wilkerson to use his name
in order to pull off the sting. He personally had plausible deniability, certainly his
lawyers would be challenged by the father of Basheer Ahmed, but they couldn't
get anywhere, besides Mr. Morgan certainly had his own security forces.

We seemed to be at an impasse with the officials gathered around us. We
had an entire airplane full of Hopi antiquities and by the time our interview
was over, we had the distinct feeling that something else was planned for the
antiquities other than returning them to their rightful owners. Politics were at
work and we were finally informed that the artifacts, as well as the airplane they
were loaded in needed to be redirected to the Smithsonian Institute. Then we
learned that not only were the antiquities on board the plane but several crates
full of drugs were also aboard. Evidentially they were in such a hurry to load the
artifacts out of the Parisian home owned by Ahmed, they didn't look at what was
actually inside the boxes. However, after an inspection by the airport security
officials, the drugs were quickly discovered. Now we were being charged with
smuggling drugs into the country. Everything was going to be confiscated and
we were all going to jail. When we asked, what was going to happen to the Hopi
antiquities we were told that at this point it was none of our business.

June went ballistic on them, she had heard of many instances of artifacts
being directed to the Smithsonian and disappearing. It wasn't that the officials at
the Smithsonian were dishonest, the artifacts were simply redirected somewhere
else. People with powerful connections and unlimited funds would pull strings
and the shipments would never arrive at the Smithsonian. Particularly items
which were controversial would disappear. June was able to cite several examples.

"What happened to the thousands of skeletons of giants that once lived
here in North America? Even Abraham Lincoln mentions them in his papers.
Skeletons of a people who lived here thousands of years ago have vanished. The
Smithsonian seems to have no record of eight-foot-tall skeletons with double rows
of teeth. They have all vanished, all because it would change our very notions of
human evolution. Yet we recently found proof of another race of people when we
discovered the cave in Estancia."

"What about the treasures that were taken out of Chaco Canyon.? Only a tiny portion of what was excavated is now available for study. Where did the rest of it go?"

"What happened to Geronimo's bones? Were they dug up by the participants of a club at Yale University, the skull and bones society?"

We still had the phone number that Dr. Jim Wilkerson had given us and asked for access to a phone but the guards denied us that call. "Even a convicted criminal gets at least one phone call," Hidalgo muttered.

The phone call was not to happen. We could only imagine that the auctioneer's lawyers had attempted to have their stolen loot returned to them. After two hours of arguing with the guards and politicians it became obvious that they thought we were using the facilities of the United States military to purloin the auctioneer's items as well as bring hard drugs into the country. We were handcuffed and not allowed to communicate with anyone. We were now the antiquity thieves.

We were obviously amateur players that were dealing with far more powerful people than we were. June could only state the obvious, that many of the greatest archeological treasures of America certainly have been stolen but we were not the thieves.

Returning the History of the Hopi

Several hours later, adding to further posterior fatigue, the door to the room that we were being held in opened and in walked Manny Aragon. "Boy, are we glad to see you!" June exclaimed.

"I can imagine why," Manny Aragon says. In all fairness, the people here in Albuquerque didn't know what was going on and certainly didn't know that the federal government was involved. We have explained to them that you were operating as agents of both the Hopi people as well as the federal government.

"So, what is going to happen to the antiquities," an exasperated June asked?

"Simple, we are going to make an inventory of what is on the airplane, remove the drugs, then we want you to fly with the airplane over to Arizona, you will land on the Hopi reservation, and there the contents will be presented to officials of the Hopi people by you."

"We have not had a bath or even a decent meal for three days now, can we at least change our clothes before we board that monster?" referring to the C-130.

"Sure, how about if we set you up in the airport motel, loan you a car which will allow you to do some shopping and of course you can eat in any restaurant you want."

We looked at each other, and June says, "We don't need to go shopping for clothes we just need to have the clothes we have with us to be laundered."

Aragon says, "That is not a problem at all, if you will come with me." Twenty minutes later we were checked into the airport motel with a plastic credit card that Manny Aragon handed us. Report back to the main airport tomorrow at ten and you will be flown to Arizona, with the antiquities. In the meantime, we will contact the officials you spoke to at the ranch and ask them to meet us there."

June says, "Just one thing, I would like it to be a surprise to them when we get there. We would like the opportunity to tell them what was accomplished."

"Fair enough," they said as they turned and left.

At ten the next day we were ready to go but the plane was still being serviced so we didn't leave Albuquerque International Airport until eleven, arriving in Arizona shortly afterwards. We landed on a gravel runway that seemed to be out in the middle of nowhere.

Walking out to great us was Herman Homanie, Ronald Hoyumptewa, Todd Hoyacoma and Charles Youvella, the representatives of the Hopi people that we had met at the ranch. Behind them was a long string of pickup trucks full of people who had followed them out to the airstrip.

The team stepped out of the plane and after shaking many hands Mr. Hoyacoma says, "I believe we know what you are doing here."

"How could you know what we are doing here," asked Hidalgo.

"You are going to give us an update on our problem we discussed out at your ranch."

June says, "No we are going to give you a solution to the problem we discussed out at the ranch, and before I forget it let me return this to you." It was a check for the amount of the airplane tickets. In the end, the entire venture had only cost the tribe the cost of a couple of tanks of gas to visit the ranch. The antiquities were unloaded from the plane and carried back to the cultural center where the people unpacked their history.

We were driven to a motel operated by the tribe and were told that we could certainly have anything we wanted to eat in the adjoining restaurant. The following day we were honored by the tribal council and given a formal letter of thanks by Mr. Hoyacoma. Then Mr. Hoyumptewa, who was still wearing the same black raven feather, stood up and walked to the center of the stage. He ignored the microphone that was being used by the speakers. The hall became very quiet so all could hear.

Mr. Hoyumptewa says, "Recently we traveled all the way to Serpiente, New Mexico in order to enlist the help of these fine people. I am afraid that one of those people, I may have offended. Mr. Hidalgo, we are truly grateful for your assistance in rescuing our religious objects. I am sure it is the beginning of a bond between your people and ours, besides now I understand your name."

"What do you mean," asked Hidalgo.

"Hidalgo, the name means nobility. The serpents spoke to me. Someday your descendants truly will be nobility."

Part 3

The Contagion

*Each of us is merely a small instrument; all of us, after
accomplishing our mission, will disappear.*

—Mother Teresa

Attending College Classes

One day a week, Corey and I would drive into Albuquerque to attend college classes at the University of New Mexico. It was a personal choice; it was like taking a day off of work. Unlike most young students who attend college in hopes of someday getting a good job, Corey and I were already doing several jobs; with jobs hidden within jobs; multitasking. Ranching and the family was the foundation of everything for us. If nothing else worked, we could at least rely on working the ranch for survival. We could live comfortably depending upon each other.

Everyone was a partner in a family as well as a business. Farming was being implemented on the Luna section of land. Now, because of the availability of this new land with an ample water supply flowing under it, we decided to clear large sections of the land which would be easy to irrigate and turn into agriculture.

Using a borrowed bulldozer, large fields were being created in order to grow such crops as alfalfa, hay, oats or anything else we could get to grow. We were not at all sure what we could grow there. We mostly researched what kinds of crops could be grown that could be easily raised without a lot of physical labor or requiring daily attention. Besides the obvious alfalfa and hay fields that would be used in raising and feeding cattle, we settled for onions and chili peppers as possibilities. Hidalgo had suggested a long peach orchid be built alongside the actual stream valley. Once the trees had well established roots, they would water themselves by taping the underground water.

Although we had Manuel and his family for help, because of the responsibilities of detective work, we never knew when we would be required to be away from Serpiente for days on end. With only one day a week available and expendable, I found myself taking an art class because it was the only class offered on the same day and time spot as Corey's geomorphology. Eventually we would want to take as many college classes as possible, but for now, taking one class at a time seemed like a logical move, besides art was one of those classes that I wanted to take whether or not I earned a degree in the field.

Corey was already well into a degree because he tested out of many of the prerequisite courses. Two hours later, Corey was sitting in his geomorphology class when the formal weekly lecture finally ended. Geomorphology was a science that Corey was already well versed in. His late father had been a geologist and living with Ken who was a petroleum geologist was an education in itself. Ken had even taken him into the field on occasions and Corey had been offered high paying jobs but he preferred the ranch work, particularly after a certain young blond, me, decided to live there.

It was the next portion of the class that intrigued Corey. It was question and answer time as the professor called it. Corey finally had a chance to ask questions. Raising his hand to get into the bidding, he knew that the professor would expound on student's questions after his formal lecture was over. The students loved it. Sometimes they learned far more from question and answer sessions than they learned from the formal lessons. As long as the subject of the question had a geological slant to it, any question was fair game. It was a game the professor took as a personal challenge and he enjoyed the game. Out of the same four hands that always went up, this time he called on Corey.

"Yes Sir, can you explain to me what happened in North America that resulted in the current tribes of natives that live here now?"

Geological History

The professor, who was known to have ideas of his own about the settlement of North America, took a long pause before he answered Corey's question. Then slowly he walked over to a chair and sat down.

"It will take a few minutes to answer that question but if you have the interest, I have the time. Well, let's see, after the Pandean Breakup, a sliver of landmass that stretched from the polar regions down to almost the south pole was to become North and South America; the Americas, forever separated from Europe and Africa. It is obvious that there were common dinosaurs everywhere during that time. After the geological break up, they were exposed to different environments and after vast periods of time, they became very different looking because they were adapting to different habitats. Yet they were similar in many ways biologically because of a common ancestry, but they evolved differently and were forever separated from their biological brethren."

"Then sixty-five million years ago, the earth was hit by a cosmologically speaking; small asteroid. But large enough that almost everything died out as a result of the impact and there followed a world-wide ecological collapse. Most animals that lived out in the open, or couldn't fly away from the resulting fires, died as a direct result of the impact and resulting compression waves that circled the planet with a series of sonic booms. It was a tsunami of heat and compression waves that knocked down forest and instantly started world-wide forest fires. System failures occurred in every environment except one, the mud dwelling world."

"Most animals died very shortly after the impact either by suffocation and burns or in a few weeks later by starvation. Herbivores would have survived only a few days as the food they usually ate was baked and dead, although pockets of food were undoubtedly available, it would only be a matter of time until it was all eaten or dead from the nuclear winter that was created. Predators may have survived a few brief extra weeks but as their prey rotted, it would only be a short time until they made war on each other, eventually tearing each other up until the last one, had no one left to fight. They could find nothing to eat. Each dinosaur, each one a monster and each one a survivalist who was the meanest left in each little corner of the world, died. Doomed from the start; most land species died."

"The animals that survived were the ones that could burrow under water and mud and just by luck avoid the obvious flash sunburn that would occur after an impact. Crocodiles, turtles, and most importantly, small mammals survived by burrowing into the soft mud along the banks of a river or riparian environment. Any animal that could survive avoided the concussive effects of the impact and the following rain of fire that burned everything. Most plants have long range mechanisms that insure their survival. Seeds, seedlings, do come back after a fire, even though it might take years for a forest to eventually reestablish itself, just like now after a forest fire."

"The vast oceans were another color then, much redder, with far less oxygen dissolved in them so only in pockets of the oceans could life survive. It may have taken some time, but without sunlight and the addition of toxic sediment from the landmasses the oceans soon putrefied, killing millions of ammonites and other common sea creatures. Yet, some animals like jellyfish may have thrived in the new ocean environment. The additional heat created by the impact along with vast amounts of volcanism that occurred took time to be absorbed by the oceans which moderated the climate of this planet. Being so big, the earth heals itself, but it takes a long time."

"During the vast time span that occurred until the Quaternary Period, mega animals of all kinds evolved. But as the dawn of the Quaternary Period appeared, the temperature became cooler over the entire earth. Polar ice advanced and retreated many times during this period. Scientists have cataloged over sixty cycles of glacial expansion and contraction during the Pleistocene Epoch."

"There is a reason the polar ice advances and retreats. It isn't random. The variations are because of changes in the Earth's orbit. These are called Milonkovitch cycles. The last major glacial advance was about eighteen thousand years ago. Some scientists say that we are still in an ice age and the current warming trend is just an interglacial period or temporary retreat of the polar ice. The ice will return again, certainly not in our lifetimes but someday."

"Actually, I could use some ice in a glass of tea," the professor casually interjected. The professor looked around the classroom. He really didn't think anyone would get the joke and sure enough, no one got up to find the professor a glass of tea with ice so he continued his talk.

"Humanoids evolved during this period and expanded out of Africa all over the old world. Anywhere people could find a way of making a living by obtaining food, they thrived and as their populations grew they explored to find new habitats. I suspect that there were many waves of humans who pushed into the Americas from both the Pacific and the Atlantic side. Contrary to what most modern people think, when the ice caps grow it was actually beneficial to human exploration. There was a lot more shoreline back then, as ice piled up on what is now Canada, and Europe the sea levels dropped exposing vast new areas of land. The ice would have pushed humanoids out of the interior and concentrated them along the ice-free shores. From Europe, they would naturally explore north adapting their ways of living and culture as they explored. Also, contrary to what many modern people think, those early people were just as smart as we are. They could easily stretch animal hides over frames made of bone and wood, water proof the hides and seams with animal oil and explore in kayaks just as Inuit's do now."

"They didn't use bull boats," referring to the upside-down umbrella shaped boat some early American explorers used. He paused for a moment as if collecting his thoughts. "A sixteen-foot covered canoe can easily carry over a thousand pounds of weight."

Polite frowns came to several of the students faces; of course, the professor could read those faces like a book. Since it was Corey's question, he felt a little brave and commented, "The professor is right, it is amazing how many things can be packed into a large canoe. It is easy to live out of one."

The professor nodded, then continued, "They lived out of their boats. Their covered canoes or kayaks were an efficient means for mobilization during the day and their tents during the night. Exploration was their way of life, exploring far more territory than has previously been thought possible. The oxygen rich, cold water would have supported an abundance of fish, seals, and even shelled creatures that can be found along shorelines. How many of you have eaten sea kelp?"

Looking around he did not see a single hand. He didn't expect to see a hand. "Sea salad, it is loaded with vitamin C and it tastes good. In cold water, it grows really well and is easily obtained from a boat. Living along a coastline had its dangerous sides of course, a fall through the ice would have resulted in probable death and you can bet the early explorers ran from their share of cave bears."

"It is my belief that there were at one time, many tribes of people who lived along what is now the western edge of North America. They most likely all used boats, much like those that modern day Inuit's or Eskimos use, to exploit the food rich coastline that goes all the way to South America. Then population pressure, curiosity or some need such as the desire to eat red meat caused them to abandon their boats and explore inland. Due to the geography of the area many would have been funneled back north. That is why, in my opinion, many modern Indians originally came into places like present day New Mexico from the south."

"Who knows how many pulses of peoples came into the Americas during the Ice Ages? But there is ample evidence that they were here, their Clovis style artifacts have been discovered all over the Americas. Many people are convinced that early human hunters killed off the mega fauna but I seriously doubt it. Even though there is evidence that some animal species were disappearing naturally, more than likely the population of humans never reached a critical point where animals started to disappear or even thin because of them. Something else killed all of them. What really happened was another extinction event."

Younger Dryas

*I*t was supposed to be the end of the class, but none of the students got up to leave. The professor continued, "The Younger Dryas Ice Age lasted for about one thousand two hundred years before the climate warmed to what it is now. Throughout most of North America, much colder summers were being experienced. Ice packs in the mountains simply never melted. In time, they formed ice sheets that were miles thick in places. Then an impact event occurred as air burst or impacts of a swarm of carbonaceous comet fragments set most of the North American continent on fire causing the extinction of most of the mega fauna in North America as well as the demise of the North American Clovis culture."

"This swarm is hypothesized to have exploded above or possibly on the Laurentide Ice Sheet in the region of the Great Lakes, though no impact crater has yet been identified. An airburst would have been similar but many, many magnitudes larger than the Tunguska event of 1908. Perhaps, hitting the ice sheets, the impact creators simply melted away in time. Animal and human life not directly killed by the blast or resulting coast to coast wildfires would have likely starved on the burned surface of the continent. The evidence claimed for an impact event includes a charred carbon-rich layer of soil that has been found at over fifty Clovis dated sites across the continent. On top of that layer is a two-foot-deep layer of dust. Windblown dust would have formed as a result of the deforestation that occurred. In effect, the entire continent suffered through a vast continent wide dust storm that would have made the Oklahoma dust bowl tame by comparison. Then the climate slowly warmed up, plants reclaimed the land, and the climate has continued to heat up until the present. The earth is experiencing an interglacial period. But some day the continent will cool, and the ice will return. But not before this class is over." The clock hanging over the podium said it was four o'clock. The class was supposed to be over, and again no one left so the professor continued.

"Although the Polynesian's were not the only ones who could cross the Pacific Ocean, they particularly found it easy to find islands; tiny dots out in an empty sea. They could navigate around them. How could they miss entire continents? That idea is just absurd. Boats must have been available to the peoples of Eurasia. As far as Australia, which was never connected by a land bridge, it was settled as far back as fifty thousand years ago. After the Younger Dryas period, many incursions into North America occurred but the majority of them, the ones that survived, were the Native Americans we are all familiar with now. Most Native Americans who live here now came from Asia, across the Bering Straits just like they had done before. They were isolated peoples who lived in small groups, but their populations grew as the world warmed and animal herds returned. A person needs to consider the vast amounts of time that occurred as people migrated into America. It has been some twelve thousand years since the last pulse of people that migrated into America. They lived here, for more than millennia, becoming over five hundred different nations and speaking as many languages."

"Then in 1492, Europeans discovered America. Europeans had not lived in biological isolation as those in America had. They brought with them diseases acquired from all over the rest of the known world, disease that they were now themselves becoming immune to. Diseases such as small pox and plague were deadly to anyone newly exposed, such as those living in isolated environments. It killed over ninety percent of the native peoples. Most of what we see here now is only ruins, a tiny vestige of what they were. The people who live here that were mistakenly called Indians by Columbus, survived by pure luck. Some of the local people carried a recessive gene or had just enough resistance in their immune systems to allow them to survive. It was fortunate for them that some had inherited at least a small amount of immunity, from somewhere. Normally you would have expected for them all to have become extinct."

Corey found himself thinking of Hidalgo, trying to imagine the circumstances in which his family survived that critical time in history. He had many more questions to ask but as he looked around the classroom, he realized that everyone was looking at him; he decided to wait for another time.

As he arose, he noticed me leaning on the door at the top of the *kiva*-like classroom. I had been listening to the professor's story and was intrigued.

Men Are All Cheaters

"We got out of art class early so I decided to come over and listen to your class for a while." I told Corey. We then left the university to find a restaurant for an evening meal, another earned treat for each other. We had made a game out of the dinners we were enjoying after the college class. Never eating in the same restaurant and never eating the same kind of food twice in a row. I loved it, it was like going out on a date, something neither of us had had the chance to do before. We were getting home later and later but for a newly married couple it was a joy.

But that night, the professor's story was on my mind. As we ate shrimp and fish, I kept asking what the story was about, from the beginning, but Corey wanted to be polite and ask me what I had done in class, and then, afterwards he could talk more about his story as we drove back to the ranch.

"Okay," I said, slowly. "I had to draw a charcoal caricature of a man with a very long nose."

"A long nose," Corey asked with a look of bewilderment?

"Yes, it was a caricature of a court jester with a long nose that came to a point. The original painting that was our study was placed on an easel upside down. We had to draw it correctly from the original that was upside down. It trains us to draw what is there, not what we think is there. Because it is a face, the optical illusion makes the brain turn it over in our minds. It was harder than you think. Mine didn't come out so well. But none who did the assignment correctly, did a very good job.

"What do you mean by us," Corey asked?

"Well," I answered, "the men all cheated. There are four men and seven women in that drawing class. Almost as soon as we started the teacher excused herself and left a few minutes from the drawing room. As soon as she left one of the guys left his table and went up to the print and turned it over so he could see it right side up, and of course all the other men joined him. They had good drawings that actually looked like the print but all of the ladies' drawings were not as good. The men all looked pretty smug and proud of themselves as they showed off their purloined drawings. They really did cheat. Well, I'm not so sure that they really cheated. I almost walked up to the print to turn it over myself. I felt impelled to do it."

"But you didn't," countered Corey. "Maybe the object of the lesson was more than how to paint a man with a long nose. Maybe the teacher wanted you to discover something about yourselves. Did the teacher ever figure out what happened?"

"She didn't say a thing until after we had all packed up to go. In private she walked over to a couple of us girls, winked, and said to us, "Those fellows think they really pulled one over. Did we girls learn something today?"

Though a big grin I said to her, "You bet we did." I jabbed Corey in the chest and said, "Men are all cheaters."

"I then got here just in time to hear the end of your lecture." I reflected upon that and said with a sly grin, "We have all been learning about ourselves."

Corey added, "And each other! I have never cheated on you."

"That's right and I'm not going to give you the chance to cheat on me."

"What are you going to do, lock me up at night?"

"No, I'm not going to give you a reason to want to cheat on me."

On the long drive, back to Serpiente, I finally got to hear the rest of the extinction story. For some reason, it seemed to haunt me; particularly the part about what happened to the Native Americans after Columbus arrived. I too began to think about Hidalgo and the circumstances of his relatives that allowed him to live. It was all facts I already knew by heart but hearing the professor say it made a difference to me.

Success is a Journey Not a Destination.'

Several months had passed since the incident that occurred along the San Juan waterway. Yet it took only a short time until everything had settled down in the small towns that dotted the flanks of the San Juan River that flowed through northern New Mexico. With the disappearance and placation of the serpents that had stymied the government agencies that had hoped to deal with the alien serpents, people began to forget what had really happened. Carefully constructed new conspiracies, misinformation, and theories were generated by the government as to the cause of deaths in the area and soon all mention of serpents was weaned out of the news media. It was hoped that in time, talk of serpents would be relegated to the same sort of scorn that UFO reports receive, despite the fact that the area was a focal point for such reports.

Most of the deaths that had occurred were explained by the presence of some virus that had evolved in the area and coupled with mass hysteria, outsiders began to doubt any relationship to serpents. Yet every two weeks a helicopter delivered a cage full of baby chickens and mice to a most desolate part of the Chinle Wash. There, miles from the San Juan River and protected by a chain link fence with razor wire on top of it and no gate, was a small volcanic appearing structure that was actually a nest. What really kept people out of there were the signs located every fifty feet or so along the fence that warned of extreme, radioactive, danger. A small amount of radioactive waste was dropped along the perimeter to stymie that curious few who just might show up with a Geiger counter. The nosy person who went there indeed found high readings of radioactive materials. The sleeping dragons, finally being left alone and receiving their due sacrifices which they fed on, appeared to blissfully sleep. Then, they vanished and no one knew about their disappearance until the helicopter crew noticed that the baby chicks and mice were not also disappearing but rather dying of thirst. No one knew where the serpents had gone.

Returning to *Serpiente* was a treat for the historical detectives. The mundane ranch work was a welcome relief from the intense pressure of dealing with all they had been dealing with. The historical detectives found themselves waiting for the New Mexico Historical Society to announce its next challenge and even though they had completed all the documentation for the Robert McKnight story and certainly would have won the contest, they failed to get the documents in on time; however, the university still accepted Junes work for publication. In time, it would all be worth the effort. We would need to wait for another time and a different challenge. June bought everyone coffee cups with pictures of a canoe. Each one said; 'Success is a Journey not a Destination.'

In the back of everyone's minds they had a mystery to solve without leaving the vicinity of their ranch. The pool, located well down into the canyons that undulated back and forth giving the ranch its namesake, still had a mystery to solve. After weeks of work in the area June had decided that it was a meeting place, not just for the local tribes but for tribes of Native Americans from all over. The rock carvings made that obvious. They were from places all over America including Mexico and in a couple of instances there was evidence of a carving that appeared to be Mayan. Then, of course, there was the problem of the enigmatic letters that seemed so out of place. Although the language appeared to be Phoenician it could also be Minoan. No one seemed to know for sure, it was truly another mystery for us to solve.

It took a lot of politics but with enough petitions signed and a need demonstrated, as well as a couple of favors that was owed them, a power line was strung out to a point ending at the edge of the ranch. Even though the power poles cost several thousand dollars, for the first time in the history of the ranch they had a television, although it was rarely turned on, a swamp air conditioner was installed in the house and most importantly, they had a phone. The trip into town just to communicate would no longer be necessary. It was on that phone that June received a long-distance call that would eventually send them on their next adventure.

Experimenting with Viral Agents

The call was about the deaths of livestock in Northwestern Colorado from Dr. Hartsell a biologist from New Mexico State University. The call left June a little confused as to what she could do about it. The tone of Dr. Hartsell's voice was alarming, obviously, she was very upset. However, June was an archeologist by trade, not a virologist. "I would be glad to help if I thought I could but what can I possibly do to help you?"

"I'm not sure, but let me share a couple of facts that I think you would be interested in."

"Okay," says June.

"First of all, there are many reports coming in from Utah, even as far away as Nevada. There is some kind of contagion that is killing livestock and I don't think it is natural. It appears that something has been affecting some of the cattle and sheep there. The poor animals that are infected wind up with brains that waste away. The gray matter becomes spongy over time. After a while the poor animals cannot even stand up or eat. They literally waste away."

"Has it spread?" asked June.

"Well, yes and no. The virus seems to infect cattle or sheep in a given area and then it stops. The epidemics do not seem natural."

What do you mean not natural?

Dr. Hartsell answered the question, "It is as if someone is experimenting with viral agents. Someone is developing something horrible."

"Oh my," exclaimed June.

Dr. Hartsell continued, "Well, first of all, this is all supposed to be top secret stuff. You certainly didn't hear about anything like that happening on the evening news. The point I would like to make is that based upon what I have learned, the animals are being attacked by a man-made pathogen."

"Who in their right minds would be exposing animals to pathogenic agents," asked June, trying to use the correct biological terms.

"Well, here is the clincher. I believe, well, we know, that there are secret government laboratories in Utah that are developing biological weapons."

June thought about it for a minute then replied, "Usually government facilities like that are very tightly run places. They are not sloppy."

"That's true," answered Dr. Hartsell, "but do you know who runs the entire agency that overlooks those laboratories?"

"I have no idea," answered June.

"There are several different laboratories out there, all overseen by one General Armstrong."

There was a long pause in the conversation as the reality of the situation came into focus. Because of what had happened to us kids, that is Corey, Hidalgo, and me with the serpents she knew what kind of person General Armstrong was. It certainly should have occurred to him that testing virulent agents on public herds in public spaces was wrong. But in his mind, perhaps the death of a few allows the living for everyone else. Cut off a foot to save a leg. The problem was the parts that were being cut off were actually good American ranchers, who themselves might be in danger of contracting a fatal disease.

"Any reports of humans being affected?" asked June.

"None that I am aware of, the problem is if they want to cover something up they can. They can make almost anything disappear. They have the entire Department of Defense behind them and they can simply buy the ranches if they need to.

June started to speculate and asked, "You want the team to find out if General Armstrong is doing unauthorized experiments? Then she added; I am not sure that I know how to go about doing that."

"Well you know far more people in high places than I do. One thing I do know is that there are some mighty angry ranchers up in that area and the problem is I have one account of it happening on a reservation here in New Mexico. I have received some interesting phone calls as you well can imagine. If word gets out about some kind of disease such as this, no one will buy beef again. The entire industry could be in shambles if we don't get some fast answers."

"Is there any way we can get together?" Dr. Hartsell says, "I really don't feel comfortable talking about this stuff over a phone. I'm calling you from a friend's home. I'm afraid the phones at the university may be taped."

After setting up a place to meet the following day so June and company could actually look at the documents and hear what Dr. Hartsell was afraid to say over the phone, June agreed that she would look into the problem and take it up with family.

As she hung up the phone she thought about something she had learned years ago while she herself was still just a student. It was about a tiny tribe of indigenous natives, the Wari, who lived in the rain forest of Brazil. It was thought that they could trace their ancestry back to the ancient Wari culture of Peru that emerged around 600 AD and lasted as a great empire until they dispersed in 1,100 AD. They had a peculiar funerary custom that almost lead to their extinction.

The stone-age tribe lived along the banks of a tributary of the Amazon River in grass huts. They were more than cannibals, they believed in eating their dead. They believed that the person, along with his life force or spirit, was being consumed and became part of the living. The descendant's children would not consume the body, it was offered to all other relatives and guests as a sign of respect. The soul or life force of the person was being kept in the living body of the relatives.

In a way, they were right, the bodies passed on nourishment but in another they were very sadly wrong, it also passed on a terrible neurological disease. The elders particularly relished eating the brains of their recently departed relatives but after a while they began to exhibit disagreeable symptoms. They began to shake uncontrollably. Then they had trouble walking. Soon they were unable to even feed themselves and they died. When their brains were to be eaten, it was noticed that the brains were spongy, as if something had eaten them from the inside out. But, following the local customs they were eaten anyway spreading the disease though out the village until a modern medical man found the few remaining villagers, and convinced them to stop eating their dead relatives, which they did under protest. As June helped prepare dinner for everyone that evening, she knew she would have an interesting story to share with everyone.

A History of Biological Weapons

Everyone decided to go with June except Ken, who simply had to travel the opposite direction on business. Leaving early, it was going to be a long drive for them, but even a much longer drive for Dr. Hartsell, but they had agreed to meet at a prearranged Mexican restaurant in Socorro. When we arrived there, Dr. Hartsell was already there, waiting for them at a large family room in the back of the restaurant. She had chosen the room because they would need plenty of room to spread out the documents she had brought and the room provided needed privacy.

Everyone said the niceties that must be said when meeting people that way, and before the waiter could take anyone's order, Dr. Hartsell pulled out a document and handed it to June. They would take turns reading it as they decided what food to order and while they waited for their food to arrive.

"It is some easy reading for you while we wait." It turned out to be a short inventory written by one of her students.

A History of Biological Weapons by Jonathan White of New Mexico State University

> *As far back as 1,500 BC, the Hittites of Asia Minor sent plague victims into its enemy's lands. Then in 400 BC Spartans and Greeks were devising methods to use poisons and even sulfur fumes on each other. They were using a type of napalm, called Greek Fire. The ingredients and how to make it were lost to history.*
>
> *In 55 AD Emperor Barbaossa poisoned water wells with human bodies in the city of Tortona, Italy.*
>
> *By 1346 Mongols were catapulting bodies of plague victims in to the city of Caffa, in the Crimean Peninsula. It was one of the reasons the plague spread so quickly throughout Europe, as it was used as a weapon.*
>
> *In 1492 Columbus inadvertently brought a plethora of disease to the New World. What they did know about was what they were doing with their enemies back in Europe. The Spanish mixed the blood of leprosy patients*

with wine which they sold for a profit to their French Foes, in Naples Italy.

In 1650, the Polish were firing saliva from rabid dogs toward their enemies.

In 1675, the German and French Forces made a deal not to use poisoned bullets in their guns. It was the changing paradigm of war that made the treaty viable. The object was becoming, not to kill your enemy, but rather to bankrupt his country. Governments spend far more resources to take care of the wounded than it took to bury them.

In 1763, British troops under General Jeffrey Amherst, gave the Delaware Indians blankets used by people with small pox.

Napoleon got into the biological weapons game. His soldiers flooded the plains around Mantua, Italy, to enhance the spread of Malaria.

During the 1860s the Confederates sold clothing from yellow and smallpox patients to union troops. A lot of that was going on, probably on both sides of the lines. Certainly there were gorilla bands that preyed on both sides and used biological weapons.

In modern times, it was the Japanese who contaminated food and released plague infested ticks during their conflict with mainland China during World War II. According to the evidence that has accumulated over the years they also poisoned over 1,000 water wells in Chinese villages just to study cholera and typhus outbreaks. Medical experimentation with live subjects was common at that time. Certainly, no anesthesia was used, vivisection was a common practice.

"I didn't want to spoil your appetite," says Dr. Hartsell who never dropped her worried look, "So I'll leave the heavier reading for after we eat."

The subject was interesting but hadn't affected anyone's appetite. Aunt June didn't know how to make some of the delicacies that were being served up. She continued reading the history article while the waiter cleared the table and Dr. Hartsell brought out more documents. They were official looking. Government documents with a Top-Secret clearance marking across the top of them.

June continued reading the highlighted portions of the history paper. The meeting, so far had started out mildly enough.

The United States' first interest in any form of biological warfare came at the close of World War I. The only agent the U.S. tested was the toxin ricin, a product of the caster plant. While the U.S. was spending very little time on biological weapons research, its future allies and enemies were researching the potential of biological weapons as early as 1933.

Germany used chemical weapons during World War I prompting everyone else to use them. When World War II erupted the United States Army still maintained the position that biological weapons were, for the most part, impractical. Other nations, notably France, Japan, and the United Kingdom, thought otherwise and had begun their own biological weapons programs. Finally, in November of 1942 President Franklin Roosevelt officially approved an American biological weapons program.

Under George Merck, several universities were contracted to participate in the U.S. biological weapons program. From them, outstanding personnel were drafted into work at several new and secure facilities; Namely, Detrick, and a biological agent production plant at Vigo County, Indiana. They built two facilities for testing biological agents at Horn Island on the Mississippi and another near Granite Peak in Utah. By 1950 the principle U.S. bio-weapons facility was located at Camp Detrick in Maryland under the auspices of the Research and Engineering Division of the U.S. Army Chemical Corps. The U.S. also maintained bio-warfare facilities at Fort Terry, and an animal research facility on Plum Island. From the end of World War II through the Korean War, the U.S. Army, the Chemical Corps and the U.S. Air Force all made great strides in their biological warfare programs, especially concerning delivery systems.

High grade chemical and biological weapons were created in those laboratories, but the programs were discontinued. The problems they were encountering were twofold. First, with the invention of the thermonuclear bomb, there was little incentive to continue the programs. Secondly, they could never develop a delivery system that would truly work. Then they discovered that experimentation was being conducted on unwitting military personnel and even civilians and the oversight committee that funds the programs went ballistic.

President Richard M. Nixon issued his "Statement on Chemical and Biological Defense Policies and Programs" on November 25, 1969 in a speech from Fort Detrick. The statement ended with, "The United States shall renounce the use of lethal biological agents and weapons, and all other methods of biological warfare. The United States will confine its biological research to defensive measures such as immunization and safety measures. U.S. stocks of biological weapons were destroyed over the next few years."

Cause for the Extermination

The paper was read by all as everyone had a large meal except for Dr. Hartsell who hardly touched her food. She then looked at every one and said, "It was all a lie you know. In 1968, the Pentagon was asking for the chance to use some of its arsenal against civil rights and anti-war protesters to demonstrate the efficacy of the chemicals. They said, 'by using gas in civil situations, we accomplish two purposes: controlling crowds and educating people on gas,'" said Major General J.B. Medaris. Now everyone just talks about it. "But nerve gas is the only way I know to sort out the guys in white hats from the ones in black hats without killing them."

"Then in 1969 Venezuelan Equines Encephalitis escaped from the government's Utah facility. Thousands of local sheep died as a result. Just like what is going on now but it was a different disease. Not all, but most exposed cattle, also died from something resembling mad cow disease. The disease attacks the central nervous system leaving their brains soft and spongy. Cows that become infected with it cannot even stand up after a few months. Then they simply starve to death and have to be disposed of. They dispose of a lot of animals like that by selling them to companies that produce dog and cat feed." With that said she pulled out another small pile of highly classified documents.

"Where did you get those documents?" I asked.

"Well Penny, as you all know, I'm pretty good at working with biological matters, and…"

"You certainly were helpful when we were dealing with the serpents," I said while trying to cheer her up.

"I'm sure that all of you have an understanding of how sensitive this subject is. I will tell you my source, but you will all have to swear to secrecy." With that said, everyone stopped smiling and assumed a serious look.

"I never told any of you but I have an older sister who works at Granite Peak in Utah. It is one of those government facilities that aren't supposed to exist. She was offered a great paying job there directly out of college. She loved the work. As a research scientist, she had great leverage with what went on but during the last administrative shakeup in Washington, her boss changed and the aim of the entire program changed. She received a request to develop agents that would kill all kinds of wildlife. The officer in charge wanted them to be species specific; virulent agents that only kill one species of animals; birds, or cows or sheep or rattlesnakes. Then she began to wonder, why would millions of dollars be spent on a weapon that would kill rattlesnakes? She thought that was preposterous. Certainly, she is no lover of rattlesnakes but they do have a very real purpose in nature; killing and consuming flea infested rats. She couldn't square it in her mind. Why would they spend that much money on a toxin just to kill snakes?"

"Keep in mind, the problem is not to create an agent that kills snakes but the problem is getting the poison to the snakes; a delivery system. She found herself working with a team of people who wanted to develop a benign pathogen that was very mobile, and a species-specific pathogen that could piggy back on it to get to the snakes."

"My sister risked her job and possibly her life to get these papers to me." With that, she pulled out several documents all signed by the same person, General Armstrong, who had worked hard to be put in charge of the facility. Right now, they are studying any organism that the army can weaponize."

"Hidalgo joined the conversation with, "You know, of course, that the general wanted to weaponize the serpents we were dealing with. Fortunately, the serpents outsmarted him."

"I knew he wanted to weaponize the serpents, but didn't he also build a reservation for them somewhere in extreme northwestern New Mexico?"

"That's true, but... Well, I suspect that they could read the general's mind and realized he was attempting to keep them rounded up so they could be controlled. They even rejected the food he was supplying."

Corey, who had said little up till now, interjected, "I don't understand. All natural creatures will hang around if they are receiving free food. But then, there is nothing natural about those serpents. Trust me, if these snakes want to and can find you, they can tell what you are thinking, they are alien."

Hidalgo joined the conversation again, "Let me ask you a question, do you know how to catch a wild boar?"

Dr. Hartsell could only imagine how to catch a wild boar but wanted to hear the story.

"I heard this from a fellow a few years ago who came here from somewhere in northern Europe. It's easy. First you take some corn out and dump it in a field. The wild boars discover it and soon they come back every day for the free corn.

Then you build a fence a few feet from the corn dump. The next day you build another section of the fence which will become a pen. Finally, you put a gate on the pen. It doesn't matter; as long as the corn is free, the boars will come to and stay in the pen. They have lost their freedom because of the free meal. The story is an analogy for the evils of socialism. But you understand, our serpents are not as stupid as the boars and they do value their freedom. Besides, I suspect that if they could not have been controlled or weaponized, the general would have made plans to destroy them all."

At that Dr. Hartsell lifted up a government document that was exactly as Hidalgo had described. The title of the paper was 'Cause for the Extermination of the Chinle Wash Reptiles' by General Armstrong. The main point of the paper was the cost of operating the facility. The cost of the facility was fifty-two million dollars a year. Money that was desperately needed and could be better spent on research for basic homeland security at Granite Peak. He proposed that the facility at Chinle Wash could easily be gassed, killing all living creatures. The cost of the gas operation was estimated to be sixty-five thousand dollars. It was a small price to pay for a yearly savings of fifty-two million dollars. Capital that would vitalize the homeland security facility that he represented.

Hidalgo asked, "How can a square mile of desert surrounded by chain link fence, even accounting for the helicopter deliveries of baby chickens and mice, cost fifty-two million dollars a year?" Everyone's palms came up briefly as they thought about it.

Hidalgo was enjoying himself, "Perhaps the serpents were reading the general's mind when he wrote it. Or, perhaps the serpents planted ideas in his mind. Maybe they have control over him now. Or more likely, absolute power corrupts absolutely. Maybe he is just protecting his investments. After all, he is in charge of vast amounts of money at that facility. He pulls everyone's purse strings. Who knows what kind of accountability they have at a facility like that, a facility that provides for homeland security? I wonder what kinds of products an agency called homeland security makes? My bet is, this guy is dirtier than oil sludge, and he is pocketing money so he can build his own empire somewhere, probably somewhere like the Cayman Islands where he doesn't have to pay American taxes. What is sad is that because all money that is designated for use on the base goes through him, everyone wants to protect him. He is the wolf who is protecting the hen house."

"And..." he let the word hang in the air for a moment or two then says, "I'll bet it didn't cost our antiquity thieves sixty-five thousand dollars to gas the nest at

Serpiente, I'll bet they only paid a couple hundred bucks for enough gas to kill an entire nest, almost ending a species. What is General Armstrong doing with the money?"

Dr. Hartsell replied thoughtfully, "Is he keeping the money for himself or is it being spent on a secret program? I suspect it is the latter."

A quick glance at the other documents that Dr, Hartsell's sister had smuggled out all pointed to one simple conclusion; General Armstrong held himself above the Washington bureaucrats that were actually his boss. In his own mind, he was defending the United States of America, even if he had to destroy it in the process.

Homeland Security

I asked the question that had been the eight-hundred-pound gorilla in the room. "What happens if humans are exposed to General Armstrong's weapon, the one he wants to use on the serpents?" Again, June thought back to the Wari village in South America that almost became extinct, before Dr. Hartsell began her answer.

"Well the active pathogen that they are developing sounds to me like some form of mad cow disease, but I cannot be sure of that."

"That's not very comforting," I countered.

"Believe me, I am not trying to be comforting. I'm scared to death. But let me explain mad cow disease. Mad cow disease, otherwise known as bovine spongiform encephalopathy is deadly to cows. But it is also transmittable to humans and then it is called *varant Creutz Jakob* disease. While, technically not mad cow, it is just as unpleasant and deadly. It is usually fatal to humans within 13 months after symptoms occur."

"First of all, people can't get it from eating regular cow meat. Generally, they will only become infected if they eat the nervous tissue, the brains or spinal cord of an infected animal. People cannot get the disease by simply eating ground beef or steak, or by drinking the milk of an infected cow. Humans cannot spread the disease through casual contact; in fact, they are discovering that some humans carry it naturally in their systems. They inherit the disease but never exhibit any of the symptoms."

For the third time that day June thought of the South American Indians, but she was confused, why was General Armstrong experimenting with this particular disease when there were many others that were available and acted much quicker.

Dr. Hartsell continued, "It has been documented that transmission can occur when a person is exposed to infected brain or nervous system tissue during medical procedures."

Hidalgo had to ask, "What about the butcher who cuts up an animal that is infected with mad cow disease? What if he eats some of the nervous tissue, would cooking it kill the virus?"

Dr. Hartsell though for a moment then says, "If all the butcher did was butcher the animal there would be no danger to him at all. If he took a sample of the brain home to fry with his scrambled eggs, he would certainly get the disease. It takes far more heat than a simple frying pan to kill the virus. It is an inactive virus until it regenerates inside a victim."

"What do you mean regenerates," asked Corey.

"Well, have you ever had a fever blister on your lips?"

I jumped in the conversation, "I hate fever blisters; I get them after I have been eating tomatoes."

Dr. Hartsell explained, "There is a multitude of inert herpes viruses that float in the air, naturally. When you eat that tomato, the acid in it dissolves the protective mucus off of your lips. Just by chance, if a microbe then runs into your lip, it enters one of your cells and then replicates using your genetic material. After it replicates, it forms a blister that releases new spores into the air."

I said, "I guess everyone knows that there are germs and virus all around us; but most people are not aware of the interactions that go on between humans and millions of other creatures. It is reassuring to know that few of them can get past the protective mucus on my lips." I was being a little silly now.

"I do, but then I'm her husband," Corey pipes up.

For the first time, Dr. Hartsell cracked a grin as she looked at us, then she continued her point. "I'm afraid that the general is trying to weaponize the disease. That is, he is trying to combine it with a virulent pathogen so it will spread quickly and naturally. I also suspect that because of the nature of the serpents, that is they are highly intelligent, he is focused on destroying the ability of the serpents to control a person's thoughts. Obviously, he has had some personal experiences with the serpents."

"I assume that they are developing vaccinations against their own creations?" June said cautiously.

"Sure, they are, but you realize that once released, the virus begins to change almost immediately. It mutates and adapts to the environment just like any organism will. How long the immunization will work is anybody's guess. Besides, I doubt that they are very worried. Usually they can create a species-specific agent. Snakes and serpents will die. Nothing else should be harmed unless the virus mutates, which is always possible. Maybe he thinks the risk is worth it, or maybe he is just being vindictive. He may have a personal grudge against the serpents if they have played with his mind. You know, there have been many people who appear to have gone insane after being contacted by serpents. Not everyone has the inner capacity to handle themselves when probed by the serpents. They may have terrorized him too many times, too many nightmares."

They laid out their options in front of them. There weren't many. Pressure could be put on General Armstrong but only from Washington and even then, it was doubtful. No one wants to engage in any form of politics that pushes against the Department of Defense; the military. Any investigation would take years to complete because of the top-secret nature of the labs and in addition to that was the nature of their work, Homeland Security. It all sounded too healthy and wholesome. Who would guess that they were developing weapons of mass destruction? Who in Congress would be able to be convinced that development of weapons of mass destruction was taking place right under their noses? There were few people who had the clearance to even discuss the facility much less look into what was occurring there. The accountants who doled out the taxpayer money to support the facility would be in the dark as to what the money was actually being spent for. As June well knew, there were many examples in the recent past where the military secretly spent vast amounts of money procured for everyday items. The government would supposedly spend eight hundred and thirty dollars for a hammer that cost twenty dollars at your local hardware store. Obviously, they weren't spending the money on real hammers but rather something else.

The security at facilities like Granite Peak or Dugway proving grounds is enormous. Located in central Utah on a dry lake bed, one would be required to cross through a multitude of security check points to get to Granite Peak. It was located inside the larger confines of Dugway Proving Grounds and there simply was no way anyone was going to sneak on to the base and get a look at what they were doing.

The other option was to make contact with Dr. Hartsell's sister who worked for the monster. But still, all that might accomplish would be to get the sister put in jail for espionage or it could accomplish getting the entire Anderson family put into jail for espionage or at least complacency.

June decided she would use her political connections in order to contact Mr. Wilkerson, the scientist who had worked with the team. She felt that he was the only person with integrity of which General Armstrong apparently had none, and sanity, which Mr. Jones seemed to have lost.

Jim Wilkerson had taken a personal risk to aid the team. He was the only person June knew who had the clearance and connections to find out anything; if anything could be found out. She thought to herself, if Mr. Jones lost his sanity, perhaps General Armstrong had also lost his sanity. Perhaps General Armstrong had fought the serpents in his dreams, who knows how it all affected him? At one time, he was a proud man with great integrity she thought to herself, the serpents have terrorized him. He is no longer the same man, June thought. She wondered if he had a family who wondered what had happened to him.

The Navajo Curse

The team loaded up the usual camping gear and ice chest into the family Cherokee van and headed to Utah. It was a long drive but before they left New Mexico, Hidalgo suggested that they stop on the Navajo reservation and visit the place where a virus supposedly escaped. There had not been a single entry in the newspapers about the incidence and they knew they would be lucky to find out anything.

Hidalgo had the respect of the older officers who made op the Navajo Nation Police Force. Although there were many new officers due to turnover, the older officers immediately recognized Hidalgo as he walked through the door. Coffee was ordered for him before he could introduce Corey and me, whom several of them knew anyway. It seemed that no one knew anything about an outbreak on the reservation. It was all news to them but after the meeting was over and they started to leave one of the new recruits, a tough looking young lady, followed them out to the jeep. Officer Yazee wanted to talk to them for just a moment.

In Navajo, she said to Hidalgo; "Aren't you the one that tried to get Alan Begay out of jail when he was accused of killing that man in Bloomington?"

Hidalgo simply says, "Uh Huh."

You need to talk to Ralph Tauglechee, he is a cousin of mine who raises sheep for a living. Recently he has come into a large amount of money. No one knows how he acquired the money and he won't admit to anything. He no longer tends a flock of sheep, didn't sell his sheep and yet he has money."

"Where can I find him?" asked Hidalgo. The young officer gave Hidalgo directions. Only a person who had been raised on the reservation would be able to find the man. Thanking her profoundly, the team loaded back into the Jeep and instead of turning to go to Shiprock, they headed down a dirt road, southwest, toward the Chuska Mountains. The Chuska Mountains are a sacred area to the Navajo nation and this section was hard to get to. It took most of the evening before Hidalgo found the right little road; none were marked. We found ourselves looking at a typical Navajo Hogan. The door was facing east, facing the morning sun and typical of every Hogan Hidalgo had ever seen. There in the front yard was a brand-new Dodge truck.

They started to step out of the jeep when several large dogs surrounded us, growling and barking. Hidalgo stepped out anyway and after he barked some commands in Navajo, the dogs returned to their crudely made dog houses. An elderly Navajo pulled aside the blanket that served as a door and stepped out of his home. In Navajo, he called out and Hidalgo answered him in Navajo. Hidalgo turned to Corey and me and instructed us to stay in the jeep. Then he walked over to the blanket door and went inside.

Returning some thirty minutes later, he got into the driver's seat and explained what had transpired inside the Hogan. "A helicopter had appeared about six months ago and flew all around the Navajo's pasture. A few weeks later, the sheep began to tremble and refused to eat. Then they started dying. That was predictable, but some *baligannas* showed up and offered the old man more money than he had ever seen before in his life if he would just keep his mouth shut. The first thing he did was use a rented back hoe to cover up all the dead sheep and then he went into Farmington and bought himself a new truck. He still has enough money so he won't have to work for several years."

Hidalgo tilted his head down a little bit and confessed; I had to get pretty rough with him to get him to admit it. I threatened him with a Navajo curse."

"A Navajo curse?" I asked.

"Yes, I told him I would expose him to the Navajo Tribal Council who would immediately take his truck away from him and..."

"And?" I prodded him.

"And that I would be back with shamans who would hurt him if he didn't tell me."

"You didn't actually hit him, did you?" asked Corey

"No, He was far more afraid of the unknown than anything I could ever do to him. The important thing is we know that testing is going on and the farmers and ranchers are being bought off. Those that cannot be bought off probably have their property confiscated by the government, some kind of imminent domain. Maybe that is where at least a little of that government money is going."

Dugway Proving Ground

Dugway Proving Ground is located some eighty miles southwest of Salt Lake City. It would be the following afternoon before we got there. Driving past the entrance to the facilities, we traveled on to the small town of Tooele where we hoped to find Dr. Hartsell's sister. The town of Tooele exists due to Dugway Proving Grounds and the money that it generated. Many of the scientists preferred to live there rather than on base. It possessed an entirely different atmosphere with restaurants and tourist going though. On base, everything was regimented. The barracks like houses that were provided for the workers and scientist were all alike, and the regulations on base made real living a dull experience.

The town of Tooele was just a point on the roadmap we were using but when we got there it turned out to be a fairly good sized town. It took us a while to find the cottage styled house that belonged to Dr. Angelina Hartsell. When we found the house, I got out of the jeep and walked up to the door. A timid looking Angelina Hartsell appeared at the door and I waved the rest of us in.

Angelina Hartsell looked just like her younger sister but appeared to be carrying the weight of the world on her shoulders. She explained, "There has been a huge turnover of personnel at the facility, over a third of the people who worked there left after they figured out what the real purpose of the facility was. I think some of them were arrested afterwards, but I don't know what for. Then rumors of sloppy research procedures were reported. Experiments were being done with no controls being used. It seemed as if the commander of the facility was in a terrible hurry to develop some kind of pathogenic agent." She looked at everyone and said, "You know, when you are working with biological agents like that, you cannot risk the chance of any of them escaping the lab." Everyone understood her added emphasis.

She started to reach into a brief case that was on the end table beside her. "It has become my job to develop precursors: harmless pathogens that are able to move through the environment with ease that a deadly pathogen could piggy back on. It is my research that allowed for the chromosomal reengineering. It really is difficult work."

"The director of the program is a General Armstrong, isn't it? What can you tell us about him?" I asked.

"I don't work with him directly, He seems like a driven man, He acts as if whatever he is doing is the most important thing in the world and it has to be done right now! It certainly has nothing to do with securing the safety of the American People."

Just then, there was a loud cracking sound and the front door to the house suddenly burst open. In walked several military policemen with combat gear on. The only difference between them and a regular police swat team was they were wearing silver helmets. Brandishing firearms they searched the house for a moment then the officer who was in charge looked around the room and said, "You are all under arrest for conspiracy to overthrow the government of the United States."

Hidalgo looked at Corey and me and said, "This is going to be a lot more complicated than I thought." We were put in military vans and driven out to Dugway Proving Grounds.

A Trip to Washington

All communication with us ceased and Dr. Hartsell soon discovered that her sister had apparently disappeared. Upon inquiry, all anyone could learn is that there had been no reports of foul play, although Angelina's neighbor was concerned that the front door appeared to be kicked in and would need to be fixed. No one had seen, or admitted to seeing the military police show up at the house. It was as if nothing had happened. June and Dr. Rebecca Hartsell were stymied, after calls to every police agency in the area produced nothing.

After packing clothes for any occasion, June packed her luggage into her personal car and headed to Santa Fe. The only person that she knew who might be able to help her was Manny Aragon, the up and coming senator who seemed to care about antiquities legislation which is how June became acquainted with him. She had no idea if he would even believe her story. She didn't know if he had any knowledge of the serpents. He might think she was crazy and have her removed from the capital building.

June entered though glass doors into a circular rotunda with large mahogany wood doors with nameplates on them. She entered the correct one and walked up to a very busy secretary. She introduced herself and said that she had an appointment to see the senator. She did, as it turned out Senator Manny Aragon was willing to see her, for ten minutes.

"I have a serious problem to discuss with him. It will take longer than ten minutes."

"Well, you take that up with the senator, go on in."

Senator Aragon was enjoying the time he had away from Washington. He actually got far more done for the people of New Mexico while in New Mexico. Looking up he offered his hand to June who shook it vigorously and then sat down.

"What can I do for you now?" asked the friendly senator.

June began her story with a summary of the recent occurrences that happened in the San Juan area of New Mexico. When she completed her story, she looked at him and asked if he knew anything about the military operations that had occurred there.

"Well, I've heard two stories, one was about a virus that went through the area and caused a lot of death. I have heard a different story though." He stopped talking and stared at June.

June was worried. But she knew she had to say it. She pointed at him and said, "We are talking about alien serpents here. Shape shifters who can change their shape whenever they want to. They are intelligent creatures who communicate with each other."

There was silence in the room. Then, slowly Senator Aragon gave in, "How do you know about the serpents, I thought the only people who knew about serpents was the military, a few Navajo sheepherders and shamans, and a ranch family that lives down in Serpiente, New Mexico."

June answered him. "Yes, that's true, the Anderson family. I'm June Anderson from Serpiente."

"Do you know about a fellow by the name of Hidalgo?" the senator asked.

"Hidalgo lives with us at the ranch house in Serpiente. We consider him part of our family," answered June.

"Let me apologize, I am trying to keep track of so many things that I lose track of who I am dealing with. First let me say, congratulations on your work on behalf of the Hopi people."

A bridge of trust had to be crossed before they could really talk. June couldn't help but wonder how the senator knew about Hidalgo but decided not to pursue the subject. She had too many important matters to talk about. They talked for over two hours as people piled up outside in the waiting room, and then gave up as the evening got late. June talked mostly, but the senator seemed fascinated. It was obvious that he knew more than he would be willing to admit. As she got up to leave, the senator did say one strange thing, stopping her exit. "If anyone asks you what we were talking about in here, let's agree to say we were talking about Hydrology problems associated with the excavation of the San Ysidro Indian ruins. Let's keep anything about shape shifters or serpents between the two of us."

The next morning, a young man dressed in a business suit, knocked on June's motel door and handed her a brown envelop. Inside it, she found a plane ticket to Albuquerque International Airport and another to Dulles International Airport in Washington. There was also hand written directions to an office in Washington. For some reason, the state of New Mexico had issued her a check for five thousand dollars. For services rendered was typed on the back. That day June found herself rushing to make her connections. She repacked her luggage so she only had one suitcase and a carry on. She locked everything else away in her car, bribed the motel clerk to watch the car for the next few days, and spent her evening flying through the air in an aluminum tube shaped like a bird. She thought it was foolish to have to go to the Santa Fe Airport when she could just as easy drive down to Albuquerque and board an airplane there.

It was late when she landed in Washington. Too late to get anything accomplished. She rented another room and made a call to Ken to find out if he had learned about Corey, Hidalgo and me. Ken had not heard a word. It was as if we had disappeared off the face of the earth. Even our Jeep Cherokee had not been found. No one knew anything.

The Office of Jim Wilkerson

It had been a while and June was undergoing culture shock. She was not used to the hustle and bustle of life in a large city. While eating a breakfast of waffles and cantaloupe, she took out the paper with the handwritten address. It simply said, 'The office of Jim Wilkerson." Strangely the address was that of a house in the suburbs of Washington. June could not imagine why Wilkerson's office was not in one of the capital buildings.

As she opened the door to a taxi cab there was a Jamaican looking man who was driving. "Where do you wish to go?" She handed him the piece of paper which caused him to dive into some notebooks he had in the seat next to him as he looked up the address. June said, "It is the office of Jim Wilkerson; it should be located somewhere near the capital. He has a government job."

"No, the Jamaican replied, this address is to a house address outside of the actual city. It is what you call, a suburb, close to Washington. It will take me a while to get there, could be expensive. What do you want me to do?"

"Well, let's go." June loaded her suitcase and travel bag into the cab and away they drove into the traffic that always surrounds an airport.

Indeed, it was well out of the way. June was thankful that she had cashed the check at the airport and had cash money to operate on. They drove up to the door and the register on the dash of the car was hitting eighty dollars. June gave him a one-hundred-dollar bill and asked if he would wait for a moment. "If I don't need you I will tell you," she added. With that said, she walked up to the porch and knocked on the door.

The door opened just a little and an extremely frail looking lady stood before June, she was working to steady herself on a cane she used. "May I help you?" she asked.

June had no idea what to say. This was certainly no government office of any kind. She asked the elderly lady, "Do you know how I might find Dr. Jim Wilkerson?"

The old lady sucked in her breath and held it for a second, then she said, "Who?"

"Dr. Jim Wilkerson," June repeated a little louder and with clear enunciation.

"Why don't you come in and we can have some tea."

"Well, actually I have a taxi waiting for me and if you don't know Wilkerson, I need to leave."

The fragile lady suddenly became animated, pushing past June and signaled the cab to leave, which it did. June was left standing on some lady's porch in the middle of residential area close to Washington. She really had no idea where she was or what she was going to do.

"Come inside and have some tea with me, I'm sure I can help you, somehow."

June thought to herself, that it was strange how easily the old lady became animated. She really didn't depend on the cane at all. "I would delight in a cup of tea with you." June smiled.

From the outside, this house looked exactly like all the other houses on the block but inside it was entirely different. The inner walls of the small house were covered in tiny crystal and cut glass dishes. They, and the selves they rested on, covered everything except utilitarian surfaces. She had covered every wall with crystal dishes making each room a kaleidoscope lacework of crystal color.

Sitting down on the sofa, June sat and admired the result of many generations of people, who had saved such objects. The lady already had a pot of tea on and it only took a few moments until they were sitting down to enjoy it. The elderly lady, looked at June, and then ask, "Why do you want to meet Jim Wilkerson?"

June was not sure what to say. She still wasn't at all sure if she was at the right address and whether or not this lady knew Jim Wilkerson or if she was fishing for information. Maybe she just wanted someone to talk to.

But this time she asked it in a demanding tone. "Why do you want to meet Jim Wilkerson?"

June asked, "Who are you?" They were at an impasse.

Again, June asked "Who are you?

The lady finally whispered, "Maybe I am Dr. Jim Wilkerson's mother, but then maybe I am just wanting some company, now would you be so kind as to describe Dr. Jim Wilkerson to me?"

June answered, "From the side, he looks like a young Albert Einstein; his hair is usually disheveled, a little like he just walked in from a sandstorm." June continued, "Can you help me get into contact with him? I assure you, it is a life or death situation."

"Well, I suppose I could try to get a hold of him if it was for a good reason, but you have to understand, Jim Wilkerson is a very important person with an important job. He is a government man you know?

June wasn't sure what to say,

The elderly lady then says, "Well there is only one thing that Jim has worked on during the last few years, the one that has really kept him busy, it had something to do with… serpents."

The word just hung there in the air. Instantly, June knew that the lady knew far more than she had admitted to. They had plenty of time to get acquainted. In the end, June would have to spend the night there as well as the following day until Dr. Jim Wilkerson, following the same routine he had used for years in order to stay in contact with his mother, called her. The phone rang at precisely six o'clock.

June listened to a short exchange of words, one side of a conversation where it was easily guessed what the other person was saying. Words, such as no, everything's fine, no I don't need money, finally Mrs. Wilkerson cut into the one-sided conversation with, "I have someone here who needs to talk to you," and she handed the phone to June.

Mildred

June was not sure what to say. Finally, she gathered herself up to do the job and answered, "Mr. Wilkerson, do you remember working with Penny, Cory, and a Navajo fellow by the name of Hidalgo in the San Juan area of New Mexico?

"I certainly do remember them. I consider them great friends as well as I consider you a great friend, June, I recognized your voice. I am mystified, how did you know that I would be talking to my mother? I didn't think anyone had figured out our system.

I seem to have stumbled into it and I'll explain it to you when I see you in person. Is that possible? The phone went dead. June called into the kitchen but Mrs. Wilkerson was occupied with cooking something. She would just have to wait to see what was going to happen.

Later that evening, an elderly lady was gently let off at the curb outside. Carrying a large bag in one hand and a cane that she leaned heavily on, she slowly walked up to the door and using her cane, knocked on the door. "Oh, it's just Mildred," says Mrs. Wilkerson, "You'll like her. She is a good friend of mine."

Leaning heavily on the cane the old lady entered the room, and turned to close the small curtains that hung on the window. Turning, she reached up and pulled off the wig. Underneath was Dr. Jim Wilkerson, disheveled hair and all.

"I think we have a lot to talk about," he said as he pulled the skirt and blouse off, stuffing them into the large bag. "It's just a precaution we take. In my work, there are all kinds of people out there that want to hurt me because of the kind of work I do. Actually, the agency I work for has hurt them.

"What exactly is your kind of work?" asked June.

Wilkerson poked a finger at June and laughed, "If I told you, I would have to kill you."

"Okay, you can kill me, but I still want to know exactly what kind of work you do?"

"I was appointed by the president to investigate any mysterious occurrences that could not be easily explained, involved scientific materials or national security. Basically, it is my job to protect you from the bogie man. For one thing, I am a CIA operative. Believe me, there are strange people out there."

"What do you mean strange people out there?"

"Think about it, there are corporations out there that have only one goal, to make a profit. The men that represent them make multi-million dollar bonuses usually while the workers that actually make the money for them are paid minimum wages or in some countries just a penance of a wage. Sometimes they cheat, usually in highly creative ways that nobody is even aware of or pay a million dollar fine on a billion in profits. It is my job to catch them without them even knowing it. And of course, there are the weird happenings, mysterious occurrences that happen that no one can explain. It is my job to actually access occurrences and report and resolve those problems before they really become problems. Who knows, maybe there are little green men out there, but right now I have something far more important to discuss."

June asked, "What about alien serpents?"

"Precisely," answered Wilkerson.

Jim and June along with Jim's mother, who had her own opinions about just about everything, discussed the disappearances of Corey, Hidalgo and me. This demonstrably concerned Wilkerson but his real concern was the Granite Peak facility.

"They are supposed to be designing technology to make America a safer place to live. Most of that has to do with making stealth technology work on small unmanned reconnaissance aircraft and making them capable of carrying armaments, in this case, biological agents. It is for use in a do or die situation and only if we are attacked. Just think, someday we should be able to fly an unmanned aircraft to anywhere in the world and drop a bomb with pin point accuracy," Wilkerson seemed proud when he said it.

June countered him with, "It has been my experience that if one country can invent something, any country can invent it. Do you really want to live in a world where nations are equipped with weapons that can destroy all life on earth?"

"We already live in that world," answered Wilkerson rather matter of fact.

"What about General Armstrong," June asked, "He is the person in charge of the Granite Peak facility and based upon what I learned from a biologist who works there, he has dropped all work except for finding a way to destroy all the serpents."

Wilkerson says, "I doubt that most of the people there have ever heard of serpents other than in storybooks. It is a lot like when they were developing the atomic bomb. Everyone worked on a tiny part of a project that only a few top scientists understood."

June countered his point with, "General Armstrong seems to be in charge of this whole project. Could it be him that is responsible for also making Penny, Corey and Hidalgo disappear?"

"You bet it is possible, and highly probable. When I was working directly with him I really admired the man. I thought that he was the most patriotic man alive, but I think the serpents got to him. I will tell you a secret, I personally had some strange dreams when I was working out there, but I kind of liked having them. They made me think about things in a different way. But when it comes to General Armstrong, I think he fought with the serpents even in his dreams. He may have thought he was going crazy at first but as he became more and more aware of the serpent's abilities, he freaked out. I think he decided that the world would never be safe as long as they lived, and the war was on."

Finally, around midnight Wilkerson made a phone call and an unmarked car drove up in front of his mother's house. A frail little lady walked out to the car and was helped in by the driver. June called the same cab company and requested the same driver that she had had before. He was available and within the hour the cab appeared in front of the house. June got in the cab and went back to her room at the motel where she had left her suitcase and carryon bag. Entering her room, she was grabbed by someone who put her in an arm lock while another man searched her rather crudely then handcuffed her. The two FBI agents as it turned out showed June a pile of documents on the bed that she had carried out from New Mexico with her. The leader of the agents looked at her and said, "You are under arrest for conspiracy to overthrow the government of the United States and espionage. You are also under arrest for the embezzling and miss representing state funds from the State of New Mexico." June was escorted out of the building and taken downtown to a large office building where she was put in a holding cell by herself. There she sat until the arresting officer came in to see her.

She was escorted to an interrogation room and asked about everything from atomic secrets to common American trivia, such as; what is the capital of Colorado and who won the football game this year between Michigan State and Notre Dame. June certainly knew what the capital of Colorado was but answered Santa Fe instead, on purpose. She had no idea who won the football game nor did she care. She refused to give them any straight answers and usually didn't say a thing. She knew that everything she said was going to be used against her in a kangaroo court probably set up by General Armstrong.

She was then escorted to a drab office building on the outskirts of Washington where she was dumped in a holding room with an armed guard.

Then, just when the FBI agents were strapping her down to take a lie detector test, in walks Jim Wilkerson. He flashed his credentials, and put out his palm, "Would you like to leave this dreadful place?"

"Absolutely," June exclaimed, "but how did you know I had been arrested?"

Wilkerson looked at her and asked, "Are you still having hydrology problems associated with the excavation site of the San Ysidro Indian ruins?"

June thought that only she and Manny Aragon knew about that code line. She was just getting an idea of the complexity of the situation. June was escorted by Wilkerson out of the building and into a waiting black car.

"I don't understand," June asked, "How did you know I had been arrested?"

"Easy," Wilkerson answered. "I was arrested too, well, Armstrong tried to have me arrested but I have a higher clearance than him. If anything comes of all this it will be me who will arrest him. You need to understand that there are hundreds of agents involved; some who work for him and some who work for me. They have no idea why they are doing what they are doing other than that they have been ordered to do so. From their point of view, they want to protect the security of the United States. They were just following orders."

June says, "So everyone is just following orders? It seems to me that I have read that line in a number of history books said by a dubious group of people." June's suitcases were delivered to her from the same two FBI agents who had arrested her and she and Mr. Wilkerson were escorted to the airport where they boarded a private jet. Within a short time, they were landing at Dugway Proving Grounds in Utah.

The Granite Peak Facility

Upon arriving at the Dugway Proving Grounds, they immediately met with the head of the military police, a commander Peirce. He had been the one who had ordered the arrest of Corey, Hidalgo and me after orders were issued by General Armstrong. Highly embarrassed, he immediately apologized to June.

"We were told that we had a mole among us, Dr. Angelina Hartsell was supposedly a traitor to the United States and feeding information to our enemies. It was our understanding that she was meeting with some agents of foreign powers who were attempting to gain knowledge of our technology. I have to admit, Penny and Corey certainly seemed like agents of something, but Hidalgo seemed completely out of place. He would only talk to us in Navajo and it took us a while before we could find another soldier who could ask him questions in Navajo. The soldier laughed all the way through the interview. Evidently, they had grown up together on the reservation and knew each other well. The soldier turned in a report on what Hidalgo had said, written in Navajo, knowing that it would get him in trouble."

"What about Penny, Corey and Hidalgo?

"Commander Pierce says, "I assure you, that if we can ascertain that they were not agents working for a foreign power, which is quite likely, they will be released in your care.

Mr. Wilkerson says, "You can take my word for it, you might as well have George Washington, Thomas Jefferson and Betsy Ross locked up. Those three-young people and I go a long way back and we have experienced things together that would scare the medals off of your shirt. If you need me to, I can arrange for their release though Washington. Would you like to speak to the President of the United States?"

With that said, the commander picked up a phone and in just a few minutes in we walked, wearing striped prison fatigues and nothing else. June and the team immediately hugged each other and shook hands with Wilkerson.

That afternoon, almost every soldier that could be released from active duty was rounded up and we all drove out to the entry gate at the Granite Peak facility. The guards there approached the base commander with a look of surprise on their faces and after a fast discussion; they quickly stepped aside to allow entry into the facility. There was only one person that was arrested that day, General Armstrong, for conducting his own research, manipulating and embezzling government funds and taking his own actions against the wishes of the government.

Conspiracy to Overthrow the Government of the United States

The black helicopters, along with all the noise they make, parked further down the road. This time they did not terrify all the living creatures; the chickens, cows, horses, goats, sheep and other small animals along with the humans. They landed well down the road and they walked to the assembly of structures that makes up the ranch. Jim Wilkerson was in the lead with two soldier escorts and General Armstrong with two soldier escorts. They walked up the well rutted road into the parking lot, and finally up to the front door of the ranch house. Everyone watched them land and waited for them sitting on the chairs of the front porch.

After formal handshakes, Jim Wilkerson immediately directed everyone to the kitchen table. The two guards that were escorting General Armstrong gently reached to his arms and directed him to the table. When they got to the kitchen table and chairs, they helped him sit down then stood behind him. Corey and I poured everyone an icy glass of lemonade including one for the soldiers that they didn't know. They drank them down and politely asked if they could have some more. Then, June insisted that the soldiers sit down and everyone just sat there for a moment waiting to see what was going to happen.

Mr. Wilkerson took out a letter, made a peculiar sound, something like a giggle, and read from the letter. "As representative of the Government of the United States we would like to take this opportunity to apologize for the egregious actions of a rogue entity of the United States."

Everyone looked at each other, and grinned. Mr. Wilkerson had a grin on his face and was enjoying the comedic position his job had put him in. But then, he was a genius at what he did, he could handle it, especially this time. He says, "I think we should clear up a few points here," then he continued reading.

"All charges of Conspiracy to overthrow the government of the United States and espionage as well as for embezzling and misrepresenting state funds from the State of New Mexico against one June Anderson, will be dismissed. No fault can be established for the circumstances, leading up to her arrest and imprisonment."

"Furthermore, all charges of, Conspiracy to overthrow the government of the United States and espionage against one, he paused as he looked at the Navajo name then just said Hidalgo, will be dismissed. No fault can be established for the circumstances, leading to his arrest warrant. Execution to prosecute will cease immediately."

"Furthermore, all charges of, Conspiracy to overthrow the government of the United States and espionage, against one Corey Anderson, will be dismissed. No fault can be established for the circumstances, leading to his arrest warrant.

Lastly, all charges of, Conspiracy to overthrow the government of the United States and espionage against one Penny Anderson, will be dismissed. No fault can be established for the circumstances, leading up to her arrest warrant. He reached over and cupped my hands when he said that.

"All judicial inquiries will cease immediately. Here is a check which should cover all your legal problems."

Everyone seemed happy. Then Wilkerson continued, "I believe General Armstrong has something to say to you."

General Armstrong, who had seemed quite jovial along with everyone else hadn't actually said anything. It would take a minute before the general would make a speech.

"It was the serpents; I fought them with every fiber of my soul but could not keep them from entering my dreams. They were incessant, they came every night. They attacked me. They hurt me." He stopped for a moment to collect his thoughts and then Mr. Wilkerson encouraged him to explain.

"Every night I dreamed of doing something crazy. Then one day I found myself doing something crazy just like I dreamed of. I found myself doing things and wondering in retrospect why I had done them. I didn't know if what I was doing was real or in a dream. All I know is, I fought the meddling of the serpents as best I could do. I felt violated."

"When awake, all I could think about is a way to destroy them. I was driven, that is why I did everything I could. All of the money I could acquire I shifted to the Granite Peak facility where biological weapons were being developed. I was in charge so it was easy to put all the resources of the facility to finding a way to destroy the serpents. One of my associates even managed to test some of the agents using isolated farms and ranches. We saved thousands of dollars by doing limited and harmless experiments. I sure hope the farmers and ranchers didn't mind. Do you think they did?"

Incredulously, everyone looked at each other but said nothing.

"Tell them about that other thing." prompted Wilkerson.

"Well, don't worry, I am not contagious but somehow a few months ago I was exposed to one of the pathogens. An agent derived from a strain of mad cow disease with no anti-viral agent. There is no cure. I already catch myself forgetting things all the time." Again, June's mind wondered back to the story of the tribe of Indians, the Wari, who had almost become extinct due to a spongiform virus.

Mr. Wilkerson rather sternly says, "General Armstrong has only a few weeks now before the symptoms will really begin to show. He won't be able to walk and then after a month he will probably have a heart attack. He wanted to come to you and apologize. Please understand that we humans are not designed to withstand the serpents mind manipulations."

At that, everyone just looked at General Armstrong, this frail man who knew he was losing his mind. But then, he had lost it long ago.

Wilkerson directed the two soldiers that were escorting the general to return to the helicopter but as the general arose, he turned to us and made a simple statement. "We found the agent you know, they are all going to die." He then produced a vindictive smile that crossed his face and he arose to return to the helicopter.

Part 4

The History and Demise of the Serpent Clan

Who controls the past controls the future: who controls the present controls the past.

—George Orwell

Understanding Molecular Transformations

Ultimately, the only true value contained in the universe is knowledge. Knowledge is prized more than any material object or substance. Gold and diamonds are easily obtained in the vastness of space. Diamonds are useless crystals which although they are hard, they are not as hard as the crystalline material commonly used in the construction of the crystalline city the star people live in. Gold however, is a particularly plentiful and valuable substance, because it is chemically inert; it was used in the construction of the crystalline city. A thin sheet of gold covers the entire exterior of the spherical structure to provide for radiation protection. Anyone traveling through space, looking at the crystalline city, would see a vast perfect sphere, the size of a small planet, appearing to be made out of pure gold. The star people who lived in the crystalline city were actually librarians who kept an inventory of the knowledge of the universe. They also ran a genetic zoo where interesting but endangered species were stored until practical homes could be found for them. Billions of creatures were kept there, in tiny glass tubes, kept for their genetic material.

The star people were benign creatures who long ago discovered that the greater the genetic diversity of creatures in the universe, the greater the continuity of all life. Life draws energy from other life. When the diversity of life on a planet drops below a critical level, such as when a critical link in a food chain breaks, everything dies. With a greater diversity of life on any given planet, the greater the odds were that life would survive.

Space is a violent place. Occasionally, stars did supernova, destroying the life on planets for light years around them. As new stars ignited and planets became hospitable, the star people sowed the planets around them with genetic material to encourage life.

The only creatures that the star people had experienced a problem with was the creatures from the serpent clan. The serpent clan, originally from a small planet in the Orion star system, survived by stealth, by being invisible to other creatures yet they could create a strong influence upon other creatures around them. They communicated much like the star people did, nonverbally by a telepathic thought process involving images that evolved many thousands of millennia before. If they had a reason to, the serpents could trace their lineage back, at least as far as the star people themselves. Being creatures that were virtually invisible, a few had managed to escape their home planet by sneaking aboard a visiting vessel that returned to the star ship. There, the serpents disappeared into the mechanisms of the ship, finding places to hide.

They found the energy source of the ship, a plasma ball, like a small star that was suspended in a magnetic field. There was little food available to them so they hibernated as close to the energy source as they could get and not be detected. They would hibernate there while absorbing energy directly from the energy source. But at least two of them always watched and learned from the star people. They managed to stay hidden and unnoticed until the star people finally realized that someone or something was pilfering through their data banks.

During that brief time, the serpents learned much from the star people. They learned the secrets of atomic transformations. With the stealth, they naturally had acquired though millions of years of evolution, acquiring the new information changed the very nature of the serpents. They could transform themselves into the likeness of any small creature. As they watched and learned from the star people they acquired a consciousness of such feelings as pride, lust, and above all, suddenly they felt powerful. At one point of time, they even plotted against the star people.

The leader of the star people was Viracocha. The leaders of the serpents, Quetzalcoatl and Kukulcan, appeared before Viracocha, introducing themselves through their undulating dance. Then they demanded that Viracocha and the star people release the knowledge from their library to them. They were also ravenous; they wanted live creatures to consume.

There of course, would be no transfer of knowledge or living creatures for the serpents. The serpents were dangerous enough already. For a short while, a war occurred within the crystalline city. The star people discovered serpents hiding in the mechanism of the starship, requiring a general house cleaning. They rounded up the serpents and put them into cages made from force fields. When a serpent brushed up against the field, it received a simple electric shock.

The star people then searched until they found an appropriate planet to leave their unwanted guests. A Goldilocks planet had to be found, one that was just livable yet miserable to the serpents, one where the serpents could not cause harm to the indigenous species, nor escape from it. It was only a short time until they located themselves above Earth. It was a perfect planet to the star people. From the point of view of a serpent, this was a God forsaken planet that would become a perfect prison.

But the serpents had already learned much from the star people. They understood molecular transformation and they could transform themselves into almost any creature they could see for short periods of time. Most importantly they could communicate. Serpent communication is symbolic. They could look into each other's minds or even most other species minds and see the images that were there.

Long before living with the star people, they had learned to share these images with each other. They were now dangerous creatures who knew how to plant images into another creature's mind and use that ability as a weapon. The star people immediately recognized what the serpents were up to and this necessitated the use of their own special tools. The star people developed amulets that sent out a force field, to negate the effects of the serpent probes. They wore these amulets at all times. It was the only way the star people could insure the clarity of their minds and therefore their own safety.

Housecleaning of an Undesirable Pest

Arriving in a triangular shaped exploration craft used to set down on planets, the Star people along with Viracocha himself; arrived here on the continent that would someday become known as North America; there were no humans. A continent away in a long volcanic valley there were creatures that might, if they were lucky enough to survive the vagaries of life in an ever-changing jungle, become sentient beings someday but here, isolated in North America there was nothing. The likelihood was slim, reasoned the star people, that any terrestrial animal would survive long enough to acquire any real intelligence on this planet. Everywhere on this continent, lived animals that would consider humans something easy to catch and eat.

Just by coincidence, there were also many life forms there that were similar to the serpents but they were just cold blooded animals, namely snakes of every kind imaginable. In the area, the serpents were unceremoniously dumped, there were rattlesnakes that the serpents could play with, or so the star people humorously thought. The place was picked because it would be the most unappealing place imaginable from the point of view of a serpent. Because the elevation was high, it was a cold place to live most of the year. Any creature that lived on a planet such as this would have to deal with seasons and changing climates. Surely the serpents couldn't get into too much trouble with the Pleistocene fauna.

Except for an occasional meal, the roaming animals would be useless to the serpents. Just to the north of where they were marooned existed huge sheets of ice. The serpent would suffer trying to stay warm. Again, the star people had little remorse about the sentence being served against the serpents. Besides, it was warm enough in the summer so the serpents could procreate. It wasn't considered a death sentence; it was considered a housecleaning of an undesirable pest, much like cleaning out an infestation of lice from your head. Perhaps if the serpents had been a little more polite and honest about their intentions rather than demanding, the star people would have been a little more understanding. But it was in the nature of the serpents to use other creatures.

Archaic Humans

An Ice Age was occurring on Earth when the star people encountered the planet. There, in a place that would someday be known as Utah, beside a vast inland sea, formed from the melt water of ice sheets, a small collection of serpents was dumped out of their electric cages to make do on their own. These serpents had no idea, whatsoever, where the remainder of their species had been unceremoniously dumped, or even if it was on this planet.

The serpents quickly discovered that they were in an alien environment; most of their newly acquired skills would be of little use to them. Slow to action, they existed there, deeply hidden in caves and borrows that surrounded the eastern side of the sea.

It was a cold and miserable time for the serpents. The sun was their only source of heat. Therefore, they slowly but naturally began to migrate south, as the sun could always be found somewhere in the southern sky. Finally, Quetzalcoatl and Kukulcan sent out spies to find a better home for them. As a tiny swarm of serpents, they slowly migrated south, realizing that as they traveled in a southerly direction, the seasons were becoming warmer, making life easier. By the time, they had reached what would someday be New Mexico, they built their first nest; a protective pyramid shaped hill that was filled with borrows and pockets where they could safely raise future serpents.

Because they had a collective conscience, leadership in the clan was forever changing. Whatever pair was the oldest and most experienced serpents in the clan, were the clan leaders who carried the consciousness of the clan. They were royalty, always referred to as Quetzalcoatl and Kukulcan. The problem was there were no other creatures out there that merited mind probing until finally one day, a group of archaic humans appeared. They were hunters who appeared from the south. The serpents enjoyed watching them as they singled out one of the huge elephants that had fallen behind the rest of his herd. They watched spellbound as the humans charged the animal leaving behind spears with obsidian points embedded in the lower extremities of the beast. The beast lasted only a few hours until it died. The serpents collectively relished the death of the huge beast. Then they watched as the humans began cutting away large chunks of meat from it. The humans, as well as the serpents knew that most of the animal would spoil under the warm summer sun, but many other animals would come to feed there. Eventually scavengers would strip nearly all the meat off the carcass but in time small rodents and mice would feed on the last bits of meat and bone marrow that the carcass would provide and the serpents would feed on them. The humans appeared to be helping the serpents, whether they knew it or not. The important thing was, now the serpents finally had an interesting creature they could play with.

The serpents continued their migration south, looking for where the humans were coming from. They stopped many times in many environments but there were few humans, only the occasional hunting band that was exploring north, where the serpents had come from. They finally found their way into what would become South America. There they found humans who were living like the small six legged creatures called ants that live in nest. They found humans there, mostly living in a nest along the sea coast where the humans had lived since leaving their sea kayaks.

The Norte Chico People

Although many other humans had come before them, most of the Siberian people that the serpents would encounter had crossed over the Bering Strait land bridge during the last maximum of the Pleistocene Era, when sea levels were far lower than it is today. However, the presence or absence of a land bridge from Siberia to Alaska was not relevant for the very first Americans took maritime routes.

The first people who settled on the coast were a sea faring people who had followed the coast all the way down from the Bering Straits. Where the rivers emptied into the sea all kinds of possibilities existed for farming which they immediately took up where they camped. Rivers drained the volcanic Andes Mountains bringing mineral laden water through a desert and finally out to sea. The wide meandering river left a flat flood plain bordered by small hills formed by the eroded canyon walls cut by the river. The archaic people learned to cut into the rivers, far upstream, and then build ditches that would carry water to the flat fields. Irrigation systems were built there that are still in use today.

They would become known by many names, but modern archeologist would call them the *Norte Chico* civilization, going all the way back to the twenty seventh century B.C. They began life under their boats which were used as tents until the obvious building material was put into use, adobe. They immediately figured out how to make adobes by taking a wooden slip and packing it with mud and straw. Leaving it in the sun, it became a sun-dried brick. Make a million bricks and you can construct a civilization, which they did. A basic hard wired drive of all humans; to build, they built huge buildings and pyramids. When later day archeologist first studied the pyramids, they were thought to be natural mountains. They were simply too big to be man-made. But, upon closer inspection they discovered millions of bricks had been carefully stacked to make those mountains.

The *Norte Chico* people were a peaceful agrarian people, there has never been found any evidence of warfare among them of any kind. They left no pottery as it hadn't been invented; and only primitive artwork. What they lacked in artistic abilities they made up for in megalithic constructions. Most of the massive works they built have still to be excavated by modern day archeologists. Then the *Norte Chico* people mysteriously deserting the place, leaving empty buildings and questions as to what caused their demise.

Living with Humans

Many of the descendants of the archaic humans escaped from the death of the human ant hill and explored into the interior of the continent, looking for a place that was more hospitable and had more available resources. It is where it all started, Quetzalcoatl and Kukulcan found them there. Their serpent spies had found a civilization that was flourishing to the north and on the other side of the continent, along the coast of the Gulf of Mexico. There, humans found good conditions to organize a civilization. The people created an urban society possessing a complex social organization of labor, politics, and religion as well as the ability to write. The Olmecs were the first truly civilized people in Mexico communicating by using a form of hieroglyphs, which was an early pictorial or symbolic form of writing. The Olmec civilization became famous for two art forms; one was figurines made of jade. These artifacts were usually made with jaguar faces combined with human bodies to create "were-jaguars." The jaguar represented a complex array of religious beliefs associated with the gods of rain and fertility. The other art form they are famous for are large stone heads measuring nine feet in height and weighing nearly forty tons each.

The problems associated with the vulgarities of El Nino had as great a grip on that part of the continent as Peru, but the serpents settled into and assimilated among the humans. During the rise of the humans all the serpents worried about were the occasional floods that accompanied hurricanes that occasionally visited the area. Quetzalcoatl and Kukulcan immediately left the poverty of the seacoast for the lush jungles of Mesoamerica. The serpents had experienced some bad reactions with some humans. Having their minds probed by the serpents was a terrifying experience for uninitiated humans, many of the humans went insane after an attempt was made to probe their minds. A few died shortly thereafter. As a result, the serpents grew fearful of being detected by their actions. They had to be very careful who they communicated with. Therefore, they would seek out only the shamans, those humans that were the most cooperative and least resistant to mind probes. Many shamans actually lusted for the delirium and visions the mind probes produced.

Attaining insight into many wonderful images and ideas, the shamans shared their visions and what they learned with their fellow humans who learned to apply the knowledge. The humans absorbed much of the style of the serpents' images in their own art work and writing. The panels on which these people drew were elaborated and stylized because they were much more than a simple scene. They were a written language adopted and developed from the stylized images of the serpents, a pictorial writing system that would astound and mystify latter archeologist to this day.

It was a slow process teaching the humans to do the serpent's bidding, but the humans did learn how to build and make things with the basic building materials around them. They built stone megalithic buildings where complex rituals were observed including humans sacrifice. For a long time the serpents relished living among the humans. They relished and absorbed the release of energy from the sudden death of human sacrifice, it was in their nature.

Serpent Physiology

A serpent's life is actually a very slow moving world; most of them would prefer to remain motionless for hours, and sometimes days at a time. But when active, they can be far faster than a typical earth racer snake and with far greater endurance. When the nest is stirred up, they all become active. They are all sensing the same fear, they all see it. But when it comes to seeking food, they all hunt on their own, usually just patiently waiting until a mouse or lizard walks by.

Serpents swallow their prey whole, just for nourishment. They have only rudimentary taste glands. Usually their prey is whatever appears in the serpent's highly developed sense of smell, or a serpent's eyesight; which is perfect. Once a serpent zeros in on a meal, the eyes never blink. After the serpent strikes their prey, they swallow it head first and the prey digests slowly inside their alimentary canals releasing the prey's life force to the serpent. There are many forms of life energy. The serpent relishes the energy released at the time of death more than the biological energy from the nourishment of the prey.

Humans place offerings of food and flowers on graves knowing that shortly the food will rot and the flowers will wilt. As any ancient Egyptian would tell you, it is the life force of the food and flowers that is being given to the dead, not the actual flowers and food. The energy is offered to the dead relative. Ancient people were fully aware that all living things have forces locked up in their cells.

It was in the nature of the serpents to enjoy seeing others die. They preferred being up close to the death where they could gain the most life energy from the death. Although the force wasn't much, a weak force like gravity, the serpents could absorb it. The amount of energy was minuscule but once the serpents tasted it, the more they relished it. Unfortunately, the energy was only temporary; it constantly had to be replenished. It was a stimulant to the serpents, much like a drug. It would require another death to maintain the high. The Olmecs learned from the shamans what was expected of them for all manner of terrible things could happen if they didn't cooperate. The very sun might not rise. In order to continue learning new and wonderful things the Olmecs would have to learn to make blood sacrifices. A certain number of humans would need to regularly die an agonizing death in order to fulfill the lusty demands of the serpents. Another death, another battle, another war would always need to occur. Otherwise, the humans would all die, or so the shamans thought.

It was in the nature of the serpents to not notice the hardship that the humans dealt with, they didn't care. The only thing that mattered to the serpents was their own comforts. The serpents had become addicted to the life energy they could absorb when a death occurred. Soon, due to their ways, there were few humans left. The human culture again dispersed to find a new home. In time, new peoples would wonder who had built all the amazing buildings that were now in ruins.

The Moche

A mysterious and little known civilization arose in the northern coast of Peru called the Moche. For the most part, like those before them, the earliest Moche were a peaceful people, it was in their nature and best interest. Their society was based upon cooperation. Everyone knew his place and contributed to the workload their society required. They were quite benign, like their ancestors they did not practice war and had learned to settle disputes before a court. The early Moche civilization blossomed. It was also in their nature, as all humans to build, it was a national identity. They built as a way to express themselves, huge and bizarre pyramids that still to this day dominate the surrounding country.

Because of the high degree of cooperation among the people, many of them had time to experiment and learn. The Moche culture blossomed. They acquired an appreciation for art. Many of the pyramids, known as '*huacas*', meaning sacred site in the modern local Indian dialect, contain rich collections of murals depicting both secular and sacred scenes from the Moche world. The Moche was pioneers of metal working techniques like gilding and early forms of soldering. These skills enabled them to create extraordinarily intricate artifacts. The ruling elite wore intricate ear studs and necklaces, nose rings and helmets, many heavily inlaid with gold and precious stones. The farmers that supported the ruling elite were irrigating an area larger than what is being irrigated in Peru today.

But something changed dramatically for them. The very nature of the people changed. They began to covet the treasures, whether material or ceremonial, that other humans have. Then, two thousand years ago, during a Renaissance period for the humans that lived in Mochica, the Moche was amazed when Quetzalcoatl and Kukulcan appeared before them. They were even more amazed when, in their dreams, many of them started to see images beyond their wildest imagination; images that would terrify yet intrigue them.

The Moche shamans were the first to know the serpents well. They had learned to see the occasional sparkle that firelight makes on a serpent's scale. Like the tiniest of mirrors. They were also the ones who had experienced many of the most bizarre dreams. Many of them went insane trying to talk to the serpents for hours on end, even if there were no serpents there to hear them. The snake couldn't hear them anyway, but they could feel the vibrations the shamans were making. The sound a serpent understands best is the way a rattlesnake shakes its tail causing vibrations. The same kind of sound that is made with a gourd filled with small stones. The Shamans would make that sound for hours trying to communicate with the serpents. The serpents finally made the humans understand that if they were to share more knowledge, the humans would need to arrange a death. The serpents understood the rattling sound and were drawn to it. It usually meant that a death was about to occur, an event they relished.

In the end, the serpents tricked the humans, teaching the Moche little in the way of technology; the humans were perfectly capable of creating and building their own empire, but the humans knew there were many other worlds out there and they sought knowledge of the forbidden fruit. The serpents certainly made an impression on them, changing the very character of the nature of the humans.

The serpents lived among them for many years, always remaining invisible and stealthy. They watched in awe as the humans built huge pyramids, made of blocks of mud hardened into bricks. They resembled the shape of the serpent's home nest but were much larger, the pyramids impressed the serpents. The humans were building their own nest but for reasons that the serpents could only guess.

The serpents thought in symbols and images, not words. As a result of probing the minds of the humans along with the impressions they made, it would only be a matter of time, until the images that the humans were creating would reflect the images they received and be turned into their own symbolic communication. The humans drew images provided by the serpents and those images would someday be turned into a symbolic writing system. Hieroglyphs would soon decorate the human's homes and palaces.

It was the pottery that first gave archeologists a real insight into Moche life. The Moche left little formal written record only hieroglyphic scenes that were a mystery to archeologist. But they did leave a fabulous account of their life and times in paintings on pots and vessels. Some images show every day events such as people with fish, birds, and snakes. Others show scenes from what, at first sight, look like a series of battles. But as archeologist studied them more closely they realized these weren't ordinary battles; all the soldiers were dressed alike, the same images were repeated time and again. When the battle was won, the vanquished were ritually sacrificed; their throats cut, the blood drained into a cup and the blood drunk by a God-like deity. It was, the archeologist slowly realized, a story not of war but ritual combat followed by human sacrifice.

But what did it all mean? Was it real or a mythological scene? The multitude of vessels found with the ritual wars on them meant that the practice had become a central part of Moche life.

When the human population grew too massive, there were simply too many mouths to feed. Daily life took a massive effort just to survive. It took a long time for a worker to carry enough firewood to support the family hearth. Sometimes the rain didn't come and starvation occurred. Hardship always occurred from over taxing the environment, and when it occurred the serpents took advantage and began to cull the humans. War would inevitably occur and the humans would produce more sacrifices. This cyclic pattern continued for hundreds of years before the humans realized what was happening to them.

Then suddenly, the climate changed. Years of severe rain would be followed by years of severe drought. The ocean that was their birthplace experienced what would come to be known as El Nino years. The drastically changing temperature of the ocean's water determined the climate of the entire continent. For thirty years or so, torrential rains would cut away entire sections of the pyramids they had built. Then thirty or so years of drought would occur, leaving everything including their gardens buried in fine sand. The unusual but continual vacillations in weather could not have been survived by even a modern community. To the humans, the only solution, by now ingrained into their nature by the serpents, was to practice war.

War and Human Sacrifice

Ancient Peru is, as it is in the present, is a land of four distinctly different worlds. An ancient human explorer would climb out of his ocean kayak onto a seacoast environment followed by a short walk up gradual hills into a vast desert. In places, it is the driest desert in the world. But where rivers emptied their water into the sea, the valley floors were very lush and green; full of wildlife. They were places that invited human habitation. If the explorer crossed the desert by following the rivers upstream, he found the source of the rivers high in the Andean Mountains.

The ancient explorer found himself in a world of snow covered volcanic mountains full of mineral deposits. Some of the largest deposits of gold, silver, copper, turquoise, lead and a wealth of other minerals can be found there. Then, looking over the crest of the snow-covered mountains, the ancient explorer eventually saw, to his astonishment; a vast green world, the Amazon rain forest, as far as the eye could see.

The archaic humans invaded the Amazon rainforest. It was shaped by those ancient people. The first European to travel the length of the Amazon River was Francisco de Orellana in 1542. He documented an advanced civilization that lived there, a friendly and cooperative people. There was no stone to work with and adobes melt in such humid places so they built their huts out of trees. Modern archeologist measure cultures usually upon their building accomplishments but because of the lack of concrete building materials such as stone they often assume that these people were a backward race, but that assumption is very wrong. They built roads, bridges and large plazas all made from local material. Some five million people may have lived there. They farmed the jungle, developing a soil known as the *terra preta* which is found over large areas in the Amazon forest. The development of the soil allowed agriculture in the previously hostile environment. With huge areas of the Amazon Rain Forest under human control, the jungles became very productive. Then European disease appeared and the people virtually all disappeared, and so has the knowledge of how to survive in such an inhospitable place.

In time, as the earth turned and the climate maker El Nino found equilibrium; humans could flourish again. Weather was manageable and they could farm again. This time, Quetzalcoatl and Kukulcan encouraged the growth of the human clans. They knew that a greater human civilization would ensure greater human sacrifices.

Kukulcan enjoyed passing images containing knowledge to the humans. For a select few of the humans, they experienced the greatest insights and ideas in their lives. They quickly shared these insights with what was to become the Wari humans, about the mathematics of constructing massive buildings, terracing the land to provide more level fields, metallurgy, a symbolic language and many other skills. The Wari humans were particularly interesting in learning about astronomy, the serpents themselves wanted answers to some of the strange memories they carried, and they wanted revenge upon the star people, the librarians. It was in their nature. They hoped that eventually the humans would help them find their own origins, if not provide them a means of escaping their prison, earth. Anything was possible given enough time.

With the telepathic communication they used, Quetzalcoatl and Kukulcan, welcomed new hatchings that occurred and as the new serpents arrived, they were immediately educated into the collective consciousness of the older serpents. Humans on the other hand were slow; they had to be patiently and laboriously taught and cultured to fit the mold that the serpents wanted them to fit in.

Some of the people fought it, but they were usually run out of the cities or disposed of. What was left was a culture that flourished but became more war like. For the first time, they would venture into the countryside, seeking other humans who were farming the available land. They would capture those humans, bring them back to their home and after enjoying the delights of toying with their captives they would eventually and ceremoniously sacrifice the captives. It would be another tribe of humans who would satisfy the serpent's evil desires.

Following the cycles of El Nino, many different tribes of humans arose and fell. Each time the serpents would be in the background, sometimes watching and sometimes directing. Only a few of these tribes are known by modern archeologist. The tribes that would later collectively become the Mayas, Incas and finally the Aztec, as well as the many tribes that lived in North America had all learned to make war as a natural way of life. Anywhere humans lived the serpents would soon follow and the serpents eventually manipulated them to make war. War was always followed by human sacrifice.

A Journey to Tiahuanaco

June answered the newly installed phone. "They want me to go to Bolivia," offering an explanation to a phone call that lasted for more than two hours. "There is a site there that is stymieing archeologists and they want me to investigate some of the things that they are discovering there."

"Oh really," I answered while spending the day working around the house while Ken, Hidalgo and Corey worked on the Luna fields. The fields had to be fenced in to keep cattle out of the fields where food crops were being grown. The cattle would then be allowed in the fields at the end of the growing season to fatten on the waste silage.

After some quick thrashing around the kitchen, June continued her explanation. "Some forty-five miles west of the capital of Bolivia is a ruin called *Tiahuanaco*. It was built by a very ancient race of people well before the Incas ever arrived there. No one really knows when it was built but they do know it was completely deserted around 11,000 A.D., about the same time settlements were being vacated here in New Mexico. What they have discovered is that the entire area was destroyed and deserted, including a mysterious place called *Puma Punka*. The ruins there defy logic. They are actually too well made. They were building things out of stone, thousands of years ago, that we have just obtained the technology to accomplish. In fact, modern day stonecutters who use all manner of power tools say that it would be possible but incredibly expensive and difficult to build them even now."

I was perplexed, trying to imagine what June was talking about. I had seen, in books, photographs of Mayan walls constructed of blocks of stone that were perfectly fitted together. No one had any idea how they constructed them. Just then, the 'boys,' as June called them, walked in the front door and immediately walked over to the kitchen looking for something to eat.

"Sit down boys, we have to talk," laughed June. "Dinner isn't ready yet anyway. You got in early tonight."

"Do you want us to go find some more work to do?" Hidalgo answered with a wry grin.

"No, this is important," June said as she poured them all an iced drink. She told them about the phone call and then retold what she had already discussed with me.

"The place has been pretty much picked clean by treasure hunters. Even the Spanish plundered the ruins when they arrived. But what is left is amazing in its' own right. When they first discovered the place, it was somehow covered by about six feet of hardened mud, thousands of years ago. Currently it is being excavated by the Bolivian government and they have discovered some strange things there."

"What do you mean by strange things," asked Hidalgo who was intrigued.

June continued, "Well, for one thing they have discovered a courtyard that has stone faces carved in the walls that look like faces from every race of people on the planet and that is not all." She paused for a dramatic effect, letting the thought sink in. "There appears to be two faces there that look like aliens. Even the rock that they were carved from is different from all the rest of the faces.

They are carved from a white rock that had to be brought in just for the two faces."

"You mean they look like grays, like the aliens who supposedly were discovered in Roswell along with a spaceship that was taken away and hidden by the government," I asked?

June answered, "I don't know what they found in Roswell. For a couple of days and newspaper runs the Air Force claimed to have found a UFO with occupants but only a day or two later supposedly it was only a weather balloon that they found. No little gray men just a lot of aluminum foil and wooden struts. There certainly were a lot of balloons being launched at the time. They were trying to keep track of the nuclear testing that was occurring in the Soviet Union. There are two considerations; there is a dramatic difference between a balloon and a flying saucer, surely the investigators knew the difference, a three-year-old would, and secondly, they may have let the cat out of the bag about the ship before they realized it needed to be covered up. You see, the government may have wanted to retro-engineer the equipment on board. I just don't know. After our experiences with the serpents I certainly have an open mind, but the Roswell incident seems like a different thing altogether. Let's finish dinner, and I'll tell everyone the rest of the story then."

An Archeological Mystery

Corey and I spent the next hour preparing dinner for everyone while June poured over books and articles that would give her a fast education on *Tiahuanaco*. Fried chicken, mashed potatoes with gravy, and wilted greens from the garden that Manuel and his family tended were eaten and relished by the whole family. It was a real treat that summer evening, eaten under the welcome cool air provided by an air conditioner. A great meal but it was tempered by the seriousness of the conversation. We finally got to the peach cobbler with generous scoops of ice cream washed down with ice tea and we settled down to hear June's story.

As June explained it, "some forty-five miles outside of La Paz, the Bolivian government archeologists had been excavating ruins. Near Lake Titicaca, they were already recognized as some of the oldest ruins ever excavated. They had no way of really dating the stonework that was all that was left. Everyone assumed that it was old, perhaps two thousand years old, but now there was growing evidence that it could be at least seventeen thousand years old. Two new theories had surfaced which seemed to indicate an extreme antiquity. One has to do with star alignments. As you may know all ancient pyramids and buildings were built on the compass points. All of them, exactly," June added for dramatic effect. "The alignment is now off by seventeen thousand years, or in another word, seventeen thousand years ago it would line up correctly."

"So, the building material was on site to build the structure," Ken interjected into the conversation."

"No, apparently, they have found quarry sites miles away," answered June. "The problem is, they have no idea how the people of that time moved the stones to the site. They could have used log rollers but just getting the logs up the mountain to the *altoplano* would have taken a herculean effort. The ruins were located well above tree line between twelve and thirteen thousand feet high, where there are no trees or anything else that grows that high."

Corey interjected a question, "What was the other method used for dating the ruins?"

"Well, Lake Titicaca is some twelve miles away and as you may, or may not know, the lake is subsiding. There are twenty-seven small rivers flowing into the lake and only one river flowing out of the lake. Because most of the water evaporates, it is getting saltier and saltier. Currently as the water evaporates the shoreline is getting further and further away from the ruins. If one takes into account the rate of evaporation, some seventeen thousand years ago the water would have been washing up on the shores of Tiahuanaco. But that still wouldn't explain how they moved the stone. The natives there use reed boats. It is highly unlikely that they could have built reed boats that could float stones that have been estimated to weigh some four hundred and sixty tons! I'm telling you, it is a complete mystery as to how they moved them." June looked at everyone defiantly.

"Not really," interjected Ken, "With enough ropes and men some amazingly large chunks of rocks can be dragged around and put into place. Anyway, that is how they supposedly built the pyramids not to mention such places as Stonehenge in England."

"That's true" answered June, "but these were enormous blocks of rock that were moved. It is impossible for enough men to get around one, putting their hands under it to life them. Besides, those rocks are made of andesite, one of the hardest rocks on the planet, rocks that are impossible to cut without power tools. Besides, the real question, like Stonehenge, is not how they moved these blocks of stone but rather why they moved them at all?"

Hidalgo decided to play devil's advocate at this point, "Well again, if enough people are turned loose with enough copper chisels any rock can eventually be cut."

"That's true, countered June, but there has not been a single tool unearthed at the site. They did use copper there, there is evidence that that joined the rocks together in places in order to secure them with copper ties, but apparently, they didn't need copper chisels or any chisels. At twelve thousand feet in elevation where it hurts to even breathe they built an entire complex without evidence of a single tool being used. It all goes against everything we know about archeology. It is the precision of the work that confounds everyone. The blocks of stone are perfectly cut; it would have taken many generations of locals just to dress a single rock. Just think about it, perhaps a single family would have been required to spend years to smooth a single rock surface."

"Something else was happening in Tiahuanaco. There, rock cutting was occurring that still could not be done by modern people. Well, it could be done, but it would be incredibly laborious and expensive to do. Cutting just one of the intricate blocks found in Tiahuanaco would take months in a modern plant. There are hundreds of them scattered around like a giant jigsaw puzzle. Sure, there are other ruins in Peru and Bolivia that have highly polished blocks of rock that fit together perfectly without mortar, but nothing quite as intricate as this work."

Everyone looked at each other, refilled iced drinks, and June continued, "The people of Tiahuanaco who built all the ruins apparently vanished while the construction was still going on. Most of the monumental archeology found there is ancient, with many newer and progressively less sophisticated settlements have grown over the older settlements. Anything and everything, including portable rocks were used by later peoples. Any artifacts left by the original builders were absorbed into later tribes who lived there."

"Who lives there now," asked Hidalgo?

"The region is currently populated by the Aymara Indians." answered June. "They are a desperately poor people who live by growing their own food on the same terraced landscapes that the original people built. They mostly live by eating corn, potatoes and consume a fermented alcoholic beverage made of cornmeal. The ruins are apparently a mystery to them just as they were to the Incas who came much later and even to the Spanish who investigated the ruins. One of the basic mysteries about the place is that the culture that created it appears to be full blown from day one. There are no antecedent cultures that preceded the culture that created Tiahuanaco. It is as if one day Stone Age people woke up and were able to construct a city that would be incredibly difficult or even impossible for modern engineers with modern equipment."

Discovering a book June thought she had misplaced or even lost, she read out loud,

"In 1540 the Spanish chronicler, Pedro Cieza de Leon visited the area and his descriptions of the statures and monoliths are the same as what we see today. The only difference is, the six feet of dirt that covered much that has been excavated and removed. The dirt, which covers everything, is itself a mystery. There are no high mountains around the ruins which could have accounted for sedimentation as a result of erosion and run off. No one knows how the hardened mud was deposited."

"Wait a minute, Corey interjected, let me get this straight, "When the Spanish arrived there, there was a six feet layer of hardened dry mud on everything and nobody knows where it came from. There are no artifacts under that mud?"

"No, apparently, the place was picked clean by other peoples in antiquity, before the deposition of the mud. There appears to be little left there but the foundations of several megalithic structures and cut building stones. Then there are the stone statues, one structure known as the gateway to the sun is ten feet high and thirteen feet wide, with some fifty winged creatures are carved on the front of it. The stone steps leading up to the platform where the idols are located are made of rectangular blocks of stone about thirty feet wide. There are many idols there, most of them about twenty-three feet tall and all of them representing unusual looking beings with typical Tiahuanaco headgear."

"One of the statues depicts Viracocha, the creator god, carved with a full beard and mustache. He appears to be Sumerian and that's not all, they have found ceramics with cuneiform writing on them. The same writing that is found in Mesopotamia and is considered to be the oldest writing in the world."

Hidalgo asked, "Well, I never heard of Native Americans who sported beards and mustaches. So, what were people from Mesopotamia doing in a desert at twelve thousand feet above sea level before the last ice age?"

Hidalgo was laughing at this point, then suddenly got quiet after he thought about it for a minute. "Let me guess, there are indications of winged serpents there."

"Of course, there are, but it appears to be much more involved than that."

I asked a simple question, "It seems from what I have read in my history books that Viracocha was a figure though out the Americas that supposedly came from another land and after teaching the people their great things, in effect giving them great gifts, he left promising to return someday. In Christian writings such as the Bible it is taught that Jesus would teach many wonderful things and then after he left, in this case after his crucifixion, he would someday return to earth. In fact, it seems to be a common concept of many religions that were springing up all over the world."

June says, "That is absolutely correct. Jesus changed the world but on this continent Viracocha seemingly changed the world. There are many examples of this throughout the world's religions, perhaps there is something to the idea that someone or something did visit different areas of the world in those days who improved the lives of humans but there is no way of knowing who he was or even what it was. There are many, of course, that claim that it was ancient astronauts that visited the earth and all these remarkable things that we see now days are a result of their visit. Some people even argue that they genetically improved the human race by culling out undesirable creatures among us such as Neanderthals and the like and mated with humans to produce a more intelligent human. There is some speculation that something occurred back then because civilizations arose all over the world at that time and suddenly humans did seem to become more intelligent. Again though, it is all speculation, I just don't know."

Ken reentered the conversation, "People have funny ideas about ruins; for example, pyramids. Everyone thinks that it is a mystery as to why pyramids are found on both sides of the Atlantic Ocean. But think about it; a pyramid is the only shape that is feasible to use if you are working with stone and want to build a structure that is high. Without steel girders, a pyramid is the only structure that won't collapse on its 'self and as for moving those stones, I have to admit that in some parts of the world it is a complete mystery as to how they moved those blocks of stone around. But then, with enough ropes and people I suppose anything is possible.

June smiled at him and simply said, "Sixty miles?"

"Sixty miles?" repeated Ken as a question.

"Although a small quarry has been discovered only ten miles from the site, it appears that the quarry where much of the rock came from is sixty miles from

Tiahuanaco. There is not a clue as to how they moved the megalithic stones. However, according to the legends of the people who live there, they say the rocks were floated into place. Perhaps there is more to the story of Viracocha than we know." June smiled as she answered his inquiry. "Besides, Tiahuanaco is not the real mystery here. The real mystery is located about a quarter of a mile away and goes by the name of Puma Punka."

Puma Punka

*J*une continued her explanation while everyone listened intently. "Puma Punka is a collection of stones that have been discovered a short distance away from Tiahuanaco. There, perfectly cut stone has been discovered that defies all logic. The place as described to me by Dr. Emory at the university looks like a bomb or something blew the structure apart. In places, the andesitic rock has been shattered but the large pieces that are left leave no doubt that something strange happened there."

Corey says, "Maybe there was a war among the star people who visited the earth and they destroyed each other's creations. According to beliefs of the Hindu and others, the star people warred against each other in the skies over medieval Europe and Asia. It was witnessed by humans who could do nothing as two factions fought it out in the skies above them. Maybe the war between those creatures was carried over to Tiahuanaco.

I added, "There certainly are many medieval paintings that showed scenes with strange flying craft in the skies above them. What else can you tell us about this place called Puma Punka?

June continued her story. "The stone structures that have been excavated there appear to have been machine cut with perfect right angles and inside cuts that could only be accomplished now days with a laser guided diamond saw. For example, they have found hundreds of interlocking H blocks. They have dove cuts in them, you know, like the interlocking cuts used to hold furniture together, without nails. They are all perfectly uniform yet massive. It is the inside corners that really makes them different. It is estimated that it would take many workers years just to construct one H block using ordinary tools. Considering that there are only two rocks that are harder than andesite and one of those is diamonds, it might take a thousand years to construct the original site if done by an army of humans."

Everyone stopped to consider this not so simple dilemma. They all suspected the existence of outsiders. Why would star people who could travel through space have needed to visit earth thousands of years ago and constructed or have constructed such an archeological site? Perhaps different star people visited the earth? After all, there may be literally thousands of different species of star people out there.

Building Puma Punka was a serious problem. Perhaps they were trying to impress the locals, who knows? Certainly, June did not have a clue as to why an alien life form would construct or have constructed such a place. But then, we all knew just how strange star people could be just by their dealings with their pets, the serpents that they discarded here on earth many millennia ago. But why would they have returned seventeen thousand years ago to build a structure like Puma Punka? Lastly, why was it destroyed? Was it natural destruction such as from an impact from an asteroid, earthquake, crustal shifting or something else such as another alien race who didn't want evidence of star people to exist there? June knew that there were many things that could have happened and it all could be easily explained if one believed that ancient aliens had been there but she was very conservative in her assumptions. Usually there was a very human answer to the megalithic constructions and achievements of ancient people. Humans, she thought, are perfectly capable of creating them but after her experiences with serpents she was questioning her own assumptions. Tiahuanaco and Puma Punka provided direct evidence of serpents in their culture.

Her conclusions were intriguing with many unanswered questions such as exactly who was promising to return to earth and when? She was also forming new opinions concerning the serpents and a history of humans who seemed to always involve cycles of peace and prosperity followed by warfare, human sacrifice and subjugation of lesser civilizations. Now June was beginning to realize just how serpents had influenced humans throughout history. She was herself beginning to suspect the serpents were parasites existing for some stimulation, perhaps the life force they received and relished when another creature dies.

Plate Tectonics

$\mathcal{J}$une, Corey and I traveled by airplane to Peru where we immediately found ourselves in an entirely different world than we were used to. After spending several days on the site, it was Corey who figured out a theory as to what had happened at Tiahuanaco. Thousands of years ago Puma Punka and Tiahuanaco were ports, located at the same elevation as Lake Titicaca. Then a dramatic uplift occurred, carrying the once beautiful temple thousands of feet higher in elevation. It was the only way to explain the ancient terraced garden plots that rise to elevations where nothing can now grow. Although the entire area is being slowly uplifted thousands of feet due to a subduction zone along the Pacific Ocean, what had occurred here happened suddenly, perhaps occurring in only a day or even in a few hours. It was as if the entire continent slipped over the mantle and the uplift was instantaneous. He found much to support his theory; first of all, he climbed all the way up into the glacial ice in the highest mountains. There, he found what appeared to be plants that only grew at lower elevations, frozen under the ice. As the ice melted the exposed plants were still green just as if they were just pulled out of a garden and put in an icebox. Thawing out, they were still relatively fresh.

He next attacked the problem of the layer of mud that still existed all over the ruins except where it had been removed by archeologist. It was easy to surmise that if the ruins were at one time at the level of Lake Titicaca, the convulsive movement of the earth would have caused vast waves to be propagated that would have deposited the mud. The same thing occurs now after earthquakes occur and tsunamis race across the land depositing vast amounts of mud and debris.

Even the transportation of the blocks of rocks would have been possible at a much lower elevation where huge trees grow and the air is more breathable but what he, nor anybody else, could figure out was how the ancient people who lived there managed to carve the rocks into the intricate patterns that are found there today. June and Corey concluded that the serpents must have shared some form of technology with them that has been lost to the ages.

A mystery that was uncovered was how did the continent rise, so quickly? Corey understood plate tectonics but what had occurred there was something far more dramatic and sudden. Scientist can actually measure the uplift in major mountain ranges today, usually at most only a few centimeters a year, but it is not understood how an entire continent could uplift thousands of feet in only a few hours, yet the evidence was there in plain sight. Perhaps, he thought, the crust of the earth slipped over the mantle, like the skin over an orange.

The Introduction of Disease

*O*ne of the serpent spies communicated a story to Quetzalcoatl and Kukulcan, through images of places far to the north. The serpent spies passed on images of a large Pueblo within a small canyon, Chaco Canyon, where a new human nest was found. There natives lived in peace and traded with other tribes from all over the continent. The serpents decided to send a delegation back the way they had come, this time following the trail of the humans as they returned to their old home in the north. Over many ages, many new Quetzalcoatls and Kukulcans came into being as the serpent clan followed the humans. Following their usual method of manipulating the shamans to do their bidding, in time the serpents caused the culture to collapse.

They would start by using witchcraft, setting humans against humans who would sooner or later begin to kill each other. In time, many of the people would become insane, gathering in groups and rampaging throughout the area. Those not affected by the serpent's spell would attempt to escape by secreting away in the most remote and deserted places they could find. They built their homes in cliffs where they could be easily defended. But in time even the most secret cliff dwelling would be found out and roving bands of blood thirsty youth would find them. Following the cycles of El Nino the entire area became deserted due to persistent drought and warfare with the affected young warriors.

For almost two hundred years the natives roamed throughout what is present day Mexico looking for a place to settle. They became the Aztec people of *Tenochitilan* which is the site of modern Mexico City. By the year 1,500 AD the Aztecs ruled all of what is now known as Mexico extending down into regions of Central America.

The Aztecs conquered and subjugated all other tribes of peoples that they encountered but they themselves were mystified when they stumbled upon a hidden city in what is now known as the country of Bolivia. There, they found a megalithic city of pyramids. The amazed Aztecs believed it was the home of the Gods. Tiahuanaco is a full eight square miles of stone buildings. To the ancient Aztecs the secret purpose of the pyramid builders that built Tiahuanaco was a complete mystery to them. It would never have occurred to them that they were seeing, firsthand, the work of the same serpents that had ruined their homeland of *Aztlán* and a new cycle of creation and destruction would occur, all under the manipulative eyes of the serpents.

Then in 1492 Christopher Columbus discovered America. It has long been suspected that he was not the first, however he was the one who unknowingly led many other Europeans into America and this influx of people introduced a plethora of diseases that decimated the humans as well as virtually all the serpents that lived there. Serpents as well as humans had no resistance to the microscopic plague that was released upon them.

At first the serpents thought that the Spaniards were just another group of humans who would provide entertainment and life energy upon their deaths. They relished the death of many natives when Hernando Cortez laid siege to and conquered the Aztec capital of *Tenochitilan*. Then again, they reveled in the exploits of Pizarro who ended the Inca Empire. The serpents were in love with the destruction that occurred as millions of natives perished but suddenly the serpents realized that most of the deaths were not occurring due to war or human sacrifice but due to some other insidious force that the new comers brought with them. That insidious force began to affect the serpents themselves. Not only were the native humans dying but the serpents were also dying. The survivors secreted away until they could become strong again.

Prehistoric Civilization in Western South America

The history of the west coast of South America, a region extending from northern Chile and western Columbia on the north and encompassing western Bolivia, Peru, and Ecuador, was catastrophe, conquest and plunder. Little of this region's true prehistoric past is known, largely due to nature and the rest as a result of European insensitivity and greed. To comprehend this void of prehistoric data, one must understand the events of the fairly recent past.

As a rule, the culture of western South America is credited to the Inca whose vast empire spanned almost its entire length and who were in power when the Spanish conquistadors arrived. However historically, there were and still are many diverse cultures in the region with different languages, customs, modes of life and dress. During recorded history, these never were unified even when subjugated by the Inca and, much earlier in history, appear more like remnants of past civilizations than unique cultures of more modern times. At the onset, the Inca leadership of Manco Capac was little more than a well-organized group of illiterate barbarians on a par with the European Huns. They were squatters at a prehistoric site who numbered less than forty thousand at their peak but who managed to usurp power through force of arms. Initially under the command of Pachacuti Yupanqui, the ninth Inca emperor, a small army began conquering neighboring civilized societies, subjugating them and absorbing their cultures to a limited degree. Topa Yupanqui, son of Pachacuti, continued to expand the Inca realm after his father retired from war. Most of the so-called Inca culture was plagiarized by Pachacuti, primarily from the Chimu whom the Inca conquered about the 14th century A.D. and assimilated into their empire. The Chimu was a high culture based near modern day Trujillo, Peru. They were experts at building elaborate structures, road construction, irrigation, textiles and metalworking; and were the largest and most important political system before falling under the yoke of the Inca. As a stand-apart society that never integrated with its subject cultures, the Incas relocated the Chimu educated elite, primarily artisans and craftsman, to its capitol near Cuzco as they did with all potentially rebellious groups. The Chimu civilization was plundered and it severely retrogressed.

Later in history, Huayna Capac, a cruder version of Alexander the Great, continued the Inca rampage of conquest with an elite corps bolstered by conscripts from groups under his control. Capac subjugated over a hundred diverse ethnic groups, drawing them into the Inca domain. He died a few years before the arrival of the Spanish, leaving his empire divided between Huascar his son by a lawful wife, and Atahulpa, a son by a concubine. Following his death, a civil war erupted between the two half-brothers which Atahulpa won and first imprisoned then murdered Huascar. The empire Atahulpa gained had been twice decimated, first by the bloody civil war and secondly by the pandemic of European diseases that had reached Peru and overall killed about two-thirds of the native population of the region.

Pizarro, an unscrupulous mercenary, had gained permission from Emperor Charles V of Spain to conquer Peru and was promised a major part of the spoils. When Atahulpa and his men sought to negotiate with the invaders, the Inca ruler was taken prisoner and held for ransom for a room full of gold. After the ransom was paid, Pizarro murdered Atahulpa anyway and marched on the Inca capitol at Cuzco. Subsequently, the Inca Empire fell and became a slave colony of Spain. The orgy of plunder was so rampant that the Spanish government issued "mining claims."

Millions of archeologically priceless artifacts of gold and silver, were melted down in crude smelters, were turned into bullion bricks, and shipped back to Spain. The Spanish Inquisition was also alive and flourishing in Spain and South America at that time. In less than twenty years, almost all vestiges of western South American civilization were rendered extinct. Illiterate squatters moved into the sites.

Prehistoric civilization in western South America appeared to be the ultimate anomaly. The earliest inhabitants of the region accomplished phenomenal feats in moving, shaping and using massive blocks of stone by means yet unknown. At the prehistoric city of Tiahuanaco, the ruins of which generally bears the same name and is located about thirteen miles from Lake Titicaca at the border between Bolivia and Peru, massive blocks of stone ranging upwards to one hundred and fifty tons were transported from a quarry ten miles away from the site and mounted upon each other. One giant block is estimated to weigh about four hundred and forty tons and one of the blocks has a six-millimeter-wide, precision cut groove several feet in length and, as modern machinists say, "perfectly true." Equidistant drilled holes run the length of the groove, holes that could not have been made by stone, copper, or bronze tools.

The apparent disarray of the area leads one to the conclusion that some great catastrophic event interrupted its construction. This view is supported by the ruins of Puma Punka and Tiahuanaco where massive shaped and polished slabs of stones are scattered about, one atop the other, as if tossed in the air and landing where they fell. Most believe that no mere earthquake could have created such a disorganized array.

An Evil Human Shaman

Although they were not the main band of the serpents who ventured into the continent following the humans, they rediscovered their original trails they had left. They also discovered that the spy had been correct. A new civilization of humans lived at the center of the human world called Chaco Canyon. At first the serpents were confused. Only a small population of people actually lived at Chaco Canyon. But delegations of humans were constantly coming in and then leaving. It took them a while before they realized that the humans were trading items. Corn, feathers, birds, minerals and jewelry, all manner of useful material was being traded. The serpents decided to acquire the community of humans. They would need to create fear in the humans, which is all it took to start another cycle of destruction with the humans. Soon the Anasazi world imploded, with people moving away from Chaco. They were hiding in cliffs in an attempt to escape the manipulations of the deadly serpents. They also were trying to escape their deranged brethren who the serpents had driven insane. When the society finally broke down, the humans found themselves living on the very edge of existence searching for an escape. The humans left the cliff dwellings, thousands of them, to escape to the south, in what seemed to them, the only possible escape route.

For many, it was all too late, a pattern played out in regular cycles ever since Quetzalcoatl and Kukulcan had first arrived in Moche, centuries before. For some, insanity had a firm grip on their souls. They were easily bewitched by the images and cravings of the serpents which caused them to take to murder. They traveled in roving gangs, living at the apex of their arrogant youth. Roaming the countryside, looking for someone to whom they could inflict pain; someone they could torment. The longer the victim stayed alive the more they enjoyed it. They were imitating a feature of the serpent's culture, the longer the death took, the longer they could absorb the energy they relished. Wherever the humans went, the serpents who followed them relished the unfortunate deaths that occurred.

The serpents lived for pure barbarism created by the humans who roamed as small bands of warriors; while the serpents harvested the life energy, created by their wars. If one of their fellow humans was killed, nobody cared, he like the victims, was eaten. Mindlessly exploring for the next available energy source, the warriors as well as the serpents lived off of the victims that they encountered.

Suddenly, everything changed.

An evil human Shaman arrived, far eviler than a serpent could be, and it was casting spells. Flinging bundles of pure energy, cast like invisible fireballs that plunged into the hearts of the unknowing victims.

After the humans dispersed from the Chaco Canyon complex, they returned south over the desert, hoping to find new ways and religions. In New Mexico, many of them became the Native American Peoples that are seen there now. The Hopi, Zuni, and later the Apache and Navajo and many others throughout present day Mexico, are the descendants of those early Anasazi.

The serpents experienced a sickness, nearly all of them died, just as the native humans had. As new people arrived from the east, they brought with them all manner of disease from another continent. The native people who lived in North America had no immunity to the disease nor did the serpents. After the dying, the survivors finally settled into Serpiente building their usual bond with the native humans, and hoping to escape further contact with nonnative humans. Later, they even found a useful relationship with one family, the Andersons, who treated them well. The family had offered them small sacrifices of mice and baby chickens. That was all they wanted at the time. Long gone, were the days when they could coerce whole societies into offering up human sacrifices for them. The survivors remained hidden, only the contact with the Anderson family would be allowed. All other outsiders were avoided but in time the nest was found. Then the serpents were gassed by treasure hunters.

Two of them, Quetzalcoatl and Kukulcan escaped and returned to the San Juan River expecting to find it deserted of human life. Instead, they were amazed at the rise of the foreign humans. They had built many small towns and roads that went everywhere including the backcountry where they had lived before. Angry over what had happened to them, and after they reproduced enough, producing enough warriors, they declared a very limited war on the local humans who had made them ill. They watched and learned from the humans who were oblivious to them. But now, they were even more secretive, they didn't trust humans, they had been exposed to too many humans. There had been too many of their own deaths.

Quetzalcoatl and Kukulcan Issue a War Decree

*I*n time, the serpent clan grew strong again. This time, instead of building a central nest, they would stay secreted away in the deepest and smallest rock crevasses available. As Hidalgo had said, they just dispersed into the back country. Becoming invisible was the strongest attribute that they processed and it didn't matter where they hid away, their spies would share visions and images of the biological organisms they might encounter. Life was, in serpent thought, all classified to clan systems with an individual hieroglyphic image that both identified it and reflected its interactions with the serpents. They were completely at piece and harmless to virtually all other clans, excepting a few small creatures they used for regular biological activities which they absorbed by chemically digested energy. In their interactions with other clans there were few that bothered then with the exception of the coyote, cats, and of course the human clan.

The serpent clan was unknowingly the victim of a spell. A small trio of serpent spies journeyed to the place where they were originally sentenced to live on this planet. The inland sea was now nothing but a vast salt bed with mountains in the far distance. Humans had built a huge city close by, the serpents admired the way the humans had learned to fly in large metal tubes that looked like birds. The serpents also had images of flying through the air. At one time, their ancestors had hitched rides to other stars. Although they had images of the vast worlds in space they once knew, they had for all practical purposes forgotten the world in which they had come from. Their home planet and the librarian's world was now nothing but a series of obscure, dream-like, hieroglyphics.

The serpents that lived on earth did have something of a belief system. They believed that Viracocha, the head of the star people as well as the head librarian, would return someday. He would rescue them, releasing them from their earthly prison. By returning to the stars perhaps they could return to their home planet or be placed on a planet with more comfortable features than earth. What the serpents really wanted more than anything else is to find places where living beings would, through the process of death, release their life energy to them. To the serpents it was simple farming, no different than a human farmer who cuts up potatoes with sprouts on them and plants them, with the intention of sometime later digging them up and eating them.

The trio of serpents traveled to the place it had all started, where their ancestors had commenced their migrations after being sentenced to earth. But as soon as the trio reached the area they began to realize that that something was terribly wrong. They found themselves wondering though a countryside where all the natural wildlife had died. All reptilian life, as well as most birds had vanished. Rattlesnakes, usually immune to the shaman's spells and biological agents that cause death were also being found dead. The dead rattlesnakes appeared to have decomposed from the inside out. They died in an agonizing stupor, in pain and unable to move.

The serpents had no idea what had killed the rattlesnakes. Rattlesnake clan was important to the serpents. Physiologically, they were the closest terrestrial creature to the serpents. The only real difference in them was that a rattlesnake's brain acts on instinct, whereas a serpents' brain, when active was a super computer. A collective brain, they experienced the world individually but when something occurred they could communicate visually and share images with any other serpent, usually with Quetzalcoatl and Kukulcan.

Then, before they completed their return journey to the San Juan River area, the serpents began to notice that they were becoming sick. First it was just an involuntary shaking of the tail, like a rattlesnake they added a button to their tail every time they molted out of their skin. Their buttons were a sign of rank in the serpent clan. Quetzalcoatl and Kukulcan had many buttons, more than anyone else in the clan. But to the trio of spy serpents, the last thing they wanted to do was issue a warning shake of their tail.

By the time they journeyed past the mountain known as Ute Mountain, where a tribe of native humans lived, one of the three serpents began to notice white fuzz growing on his scales. The serpent could no longer regulate it scales to stay invisible and the trembling in its tail was becoming more evident. The images it shared with Quetzalcoatl and Kukulcan was frightening. A Shaman was plunging bundles of fiery energy into the serpent's heart. His images became erratic then stopped altogether. When it finally died, it had no life force left to escape the body. Terrified, the other two serpents fled from the shaman's spell. They knew it was coming for them. In their panic to escape the shaman, it never occurred to them that they might become the vectors of a terrible disease; they were carriers of death returning to the nest of the serpent clan.

The serpents had already embedded spies among the foreign humans, in cities and towns all over the desert area of the continent. Once enough of the serpents had grown large and powerful enough, Quetzalcoatl and Kukulcan issued a war decree. They decided to practice war on the humans again. This time however, they would be more secretive about it. They would use the powers that the people themselves had used. They felt that if they could just cull the unwelcome newcomers they would be saved. They were afraid. After all, the newcomers did seem to possess terrible weapons, smallpox for example. It had killed nearly all the serpents at one time.

They met together and exchanged visions of capturing the minds of the humans and pitting them against each other. War was in the serpent's nature. They knew they could eventually conquer the humans. Their civilization would collapse, they would require a few hundred years and they would create another civilization. The cycle had repeated itself over and over like the climate patterns that El Nino created. They had a profound effect upon the humans. The human clan never learned to avoid the influence of the serpents. Humans easily adapted to war, it was in their nature.

War Stories

For a while, the serpents didn't actively engage in warfare with the humans, they simply planted ideas in the minds of the humans and watched to see what would happen. It was child's play for them and the many new serpents learned to manipulate humans well. In the end, the serpents decided to attack everywhere in small skirmishes, fighting a guerilla war like the native humans had often fought. The serpents relished the energy they would harvest.

In the small towns that dotted the San Juan River, humans began to do strange evil things again, but this time it also happened in other communities in another human nest. It was how the serpents caused the violence that was intriguing. The only common denominator was that in each case, a creature hid away and watched, hidden in plain sight camouflaged as a raven or any small animal, except for cats. The serpents had come to loathe cats.

Cats had an idiosyncrasy in that they could easily see the serpents. To them, the serpents were just another snake. Cats liked to play and torture snakes and other creatures that they capture. Unlike dogs, the serpents could not probe into a cat's mind. The cats would play with them anyway. Despite the obvious bite with a generous amount of venom that went into the cat, it took a while until the venom took effect. A cat can cause a lot of pain before they finally die. The serpent did not even relish the energy from the cat's death, certainly not like what they relished from the energy from a human death.

Finally, a signal was sent to all from Quetzalcoatl and Kukulcan. They had declared war on the humans, a long and protracted war. The result was that a long and dreadful series of mysterious tragedies occurred. Everyone took notice as reports began to pile up. The newspapers and television reporters picked up on the stories and soon everyone was wondering and talking about the mysterious occurrences that were happening all around them. The worst was in Albuquerque. Typical examples of what happened were in Albuquerque's northeast heights, in a neighborhood just off of Juan Tabo Avenue.

Jeremy Malone, a small boy discovered his father's gun hidden away in a closet. He then loaded it with shells, and put the gun in his small backpack. He casually walked out to the main road where he was normally not allowed to go, Juan Tabo Avenue. He sat his backpack down on the sidewalk, and casually reached into the pack and pulled out the gun. He then aimed it directly at the oncoming traffic and started shooting. Three of the six bullets found their targets. As several cars crashed into one another, a jogger ran upon the scene and seeing the boy was about to be struck by a careening car, tackled the tiny boy, carrying him several feet, saving his life. Immediately the boy started screaming at the top of his lungs. The gathering crowd asked him what was wrong and between sobs he would only say that something was hurting his head. He had no recollection of getting his father's gun or shooting at cars. He thought he was at home, in bed, having a dream. He thought he had wet the bed.

At several of the high schools in Albuquerque, general lockdowns occurred after a dozen or so students in each school began an all-out fight with anyone they could get close to. One of them was a petite little girl who was the top academic student at the school. Afterwards they all claimed to have been dreaming that they were humans who lived in a barbaric world, fighting with the enemy. They all imagined that they were in the middle of a death fight. Because of the savagery of the attacks, it only took one instance before the other students, who were not under a spell, realized that whatever was going on was deadly serious.

Eventually several encounters occurred, where a random student would be beaten to the ground. A crowd would gather and then the assailant would immediately begin hitting another student. Differences in size or sex meant nothing. It was a melee. Two teachers were severally hurt, one with a broken arm. Although a few of the students ran and hid as they were taught, there was always a larger group of students who would form a mob, they seemed to enjoy every detail.

In every situation, the teachers quickly realized that it would take several brave students to subdue each of the attackers. Three of the students who were under a spell were athletes who required amazing brutality to subdue. All three of them were seriously injured during the melee. Once subdued and calmed down, which took considerable time, all described a dream they were having.

In the South Valley, an unidentified lady was spotted wearing military gear walking between school buildings nonchalantly brandishing a machete. As she walked along, suddenly she stopped and appeared to be in some sort of altered state of mind. She turned to Ernesto Tafoya who was sitting on a bench munching on an apple and reading a book. She stepped to him and almost decapitated him with a powerful swing of the huge knife. She then took off, running as fast as she could run, cutting slabs of muscle off of fleeing students. The resource policeman finally had to use deadly force to stop her. She simply refused to stop trying to hurt someone. The machete lady was a parent of two honor students who attended the high school.

In Albuquerque, at the Heavenly Hills Home for seniors, Mrs. Marilyn Goldstein was an Alzheimer's patient. Thin, only a whisper of her former self, she liked to sit out on the porch watching the birds and other animals, sometimes for hours at a time. Then one evening she became secretive, while at dinner when no one was looking, she stealthily slipped a knife into the pocket of her housecoat and the bored lady who was serving the meals never noticed. Then, for a while Marilyn returned to her room.

On cool crisp days when only a shawl across a lap was all it took to stay comfortable, everyone liked to be rolled out on the patio where they could watch the lights come on in the city. They enjoyed watching for the occasional jet, landing at the nearby airport. Marilyn waited until everyone was comfortable outside before she suddenly started walking down the porch behind the other residents.

Mrs. Marilyn Goldstein had a clear memory appear in her brain. She remembered that she was a young woman living in Germany during the war, late in 1944. Marilyn was hiding behind the pseudo name of Marilyn Smits with forged papers. The Nazis were losing and like a cornered animal, they were looking for someone to blame, they were looking for victims. Everyone was looking for a way out of the war that raged around them and was about to fall in on them. She was living in abject fear. In the back of her mind she was always worried that someone might discover her Jewish ancestry. If someone discovered her secret, she would disappear like many others that she knew. The Nazi were still practicing the final solution for her people.

In her dream, she was working on the serving line, using a large forked serving tool to place large slabs of ham on the guests' plates. She knew that many of these very men that she was serving were responsible for the death of her family and many other families just like hers. She would have the opportunity of a lifetime, she could change history. She would place several pieces of ham on a serving plate and walk around behind the men and offer them more. When she got behind the most infamous general, she would stab him in the back of the head killing him instantly, then, quickly go to the next officer. As she tried to carry out this plan the second officer noticed what was happening and tried to protect himself, but she caught him in the eye, disabling him. By the time she had gotten to the third officer, the soldiers tackled her. She felt it was her duty to kill as many of the military elite as possible before they would undoubtedly kill her. It would be her contribution to the war effort.

When she awoke strapped to her bed, Marilyn had no idea that she had killed Mrs. Julius McKnight, who never changed her expression on her face; she smiled in death just as she had in life, and seriously wounded Mr. Edgar Thompson who was stabbed in the eye. Then she was tackled by the facility nurse. She just kept saying that she was doing her part to eliminate the ones who were trying to destroy her people.

In Albuquerque, numerous groups of young people suddenly got out of bed and dressed in whatever they had on when they went to bed and ran out into the streets in the middle of the night and gathered in a group. When enough of them got together, they ran down the street until they could find a home with an unlocked front door. They entered a random home and began stealing anything they could grab, when discovered by the occupants in their homes they mobbed them, eventually killing several of them. Often the occupants defended themselves; several of the teenagers were killed or badly injured. Then as suddenly as they came in to a house they would leave and find another one. When they were finally caught by the police they had no idea what they were doing. Often the girls and boys didn't even know each other. They had a memory of doing what they had done but they thought it was all part of a dream. One group of thirteen-year old children justified their actions by saying that they had a right to have money and things. When confronted with the fact that none of the victims had ever taken anything from them they said they had a right to it. Finally, one of them said "I am sure tired of this dream, when does it end?" Their demeanor instantly changed and suddenly they were just a scared bunch of confused kids. Neither they, nor the parents could explain what had happened. There were so many roving gangs of kids that the police could not keep up with all the reports.

It continued occasionally, on and off though the following day and into the following evening. Many people refused to sleep in fear that they would experience another terrifying dream. The second night, Albuquerque was on edge but not experiencing as many occurrences. The occurrences that did occur were not as intense or as deadly. The serpent warriors were on the move, as fast as wings could carry them. The following night, the main force met in Santa Fe and as expected, the following morning the city was paralyzed.

Many Santa Fe residents died in their beds, hiding from some unknown fear, they died in their dreams. Family tragedies occurred; the police could not keep up with the required reports that had to be filled out. A policeman who was directing traffic at an accident scene suddenly took out his weapon and started shooting at the passing cars. He stopped when he ran out of ammunition, then sat down and went to sleep. It was mass hysteria for a great reason. It was particularly difficult for those who realized that during a dream, they had done some horrible act. Afterwards, they couldn't set things straight in their minds; murder was not in their nature.

There were spy serpents scattered throughout the Rio Grande drainage. In almost every town that had a sign post as far north as Denver and as far west as Salt Lake City and parts between. Humans were killing humans for no practical reason.

In most communities along the Rio Grande drainage as well up on the San Juan, Schools were immediately closed, followed by businesses. But humans continued to die who stayed at home and hid from everyone. Family tragedies occurred. Jails overflowed with arrested citizens. When the jails filled, citizens were rounded up and held in guarded vacant fields.

Although beatings of solitary individuals were common, the number of guns being fired in every neighborhood spiked and then slowed as ammunition started to recede. Then other methods of death prevailed. The dreams continued until it was just getting light, then the sleepy serpents hid away, invisible.

The following day, as humans dared to leave their homes to sort things out they woke to the worst day of their lives. Nobody had any idea what had happened the previous night. As they spent the day examining house after house they determined that a death occurred in about fourteen percent of the houses in Santa Fe. Over one half of the population knew a friend or relative who had experienced terror personally. The sex, or the station a human held in life was irrelevant. A policeman was just as likely to do the shooting as a gangster. When awakened, no one could provide a logical reason other than they had found themselves in an intense dream where they believed the people they were shooting at were out to get them. They were all defending themselves.

Everything shut down. It was as if the entire southwest was in lock down. As the scope of the problem increased it became a national emergency and the men in the black government cars as well as helicopters could be seen again searching for a cause of an epidemic of death. All nonofficial use of roads was outlawed. Stores ran out of food and supplies, and then closed. It was anarchy again, just like the last time along the San Juan River.

Three Black Hawk Helicopters

The following day three Black Hawk helicopters landed on the open ground in front of the ranch house causing a panic among all the animals that lived in small buildings around the main house. Several men departed the helicopters but only two of them approached the front door. After the racket that the choppers had made, everyone was waiting for them at the door. They had expected them anyway.

After brief handshakes, they adjourned to the kitchen table which is where all family business meetings were conducted. We recognized Mr. Jones, who appeared to have prematurely aged, his hair was pure white and his face looked almost like an entirely different person than we remembered. With him was another military man a General Alfred Miller who began the conversation, "We wanted to consult with you before we react to what is going on here in New Mexico."

Jones says, Penny, you do realize that if you hadn't of released those serpents back in Farmington, we wouldn't be dealing with this problem"

Hidalgo stood up when he made the statement. "Sure you would," he countered. "You would just be dealing with a different Quetzalcoatl and Kukulcan.

You would be dealing with different royalty." Hidalgo sat down when the official didn't say anything else.

They talked for about an hour but found no answers to the problem. As they walked out the door, General Miller turned and looked at everyone for a moment. "You do realize that if the serpents will not work for us they will all need to be destroyed. But then," He paused, "I suspect that due to the efforts of General Armstrong that problem may have already been solved." With that said he turned and the three of them returned to the northern sky they had come from.

We all knew that General Armstrong had given up on weaponizing the serpents for his own diabolical uses. He decided instead that they would require extermination. We knew that he felt that if we couldn't use them as weapons, he didn't want anyone else to. The problem was, everyone knew that the serpents were at it again and there wasn't a thing in the world we could do about it. General Armstrong, the shaman had found a way to fling bundles of pure energy, cast like invisible fireballs into the hearts of the unknowing serpentine victims, killing them.

Visions of Death

It would take considerable time before the surviving two serpent spies had returned from the place of creation, where the migrations originated and from where they were forcibly marooned by the star people. Both serpents appeared before Quetzalcoatl and Kukulcan but only one could still communicate and only at times. The other one died in front of them. The remaining serpent was unable to make a full report to Quetzalcoatl and Kukulcan. His scales oozed a disagreeable smell, and there were little flecks of white stuff between them. He would be the one that would infect most of the rest of them. The serpent died from a spell that had been cast upon him by a great shaman, a ball of pure energy had enveloped his heart. Quetzalcoatl and Kukulcan would experience visions of death. In only a few days the nest was gutted. Only outlier spies survived the initial spell that was cast. In time, they nearly all died.

The war with the humans was suspended. Four percent of the human population had died. Ninety nine percent of the serpents had died from an unknown disease. The serpents won every battle, but a human shaman had won the war.

In the end, the biological weapons that General Armstrong's staff was developing and stockpiling were purposefully and specifically designed to infect and kill serpents. It was purposely allowed to escape into the wilds of Utah, where it began to spread like wildfire. A neurological disease, the serpents ended up with spongy brains; however as with all species that face a deadly pathogen, a few would escape and not die. But the survivors would live in terror of the disease.

Part 5

Dreams

The biggest adventure you can take is to live the life of your dreams.

—Oprah Winfrey

We all have dreams. Come into reality, it takes an awful lot of determination, dedication, self-discipline and effort.

—Jesse Owens

Ken Anderson's Vision

It was late in the night when the American submarine surfaced. With only a tiny sliver of moon visible, it was difficult to see your hand in front of your face but with a little effort Ken Anderson could just make out waves splashing in on a faraway beach. His rifle, which had a 10X scope attached to it, was sealed in a plastic bag that made it useless until he established himself on the island. In his sealed pack, he had combat rations and extra ammunition as well as a canteen of fresh water. The pack also contained a first aid kit with several morphine syringes, tablets in order to purify water, and insect repellant. Ken knew that if he encountered a problem there was little he could do but attempt to surrender which would only buy him a small amount of time. Non-conventional combatants were considered spies and usually shot on the spot.

The crew brought out a large net that had oddly shaped corks and tree branches tied into it. Once thrown into the water it would look just like another pile of flotsam. Then Ken put his gear on and dived into the water where he himself would disappear under the net becoming invisible. He hoped to make it to the island before morning but he had serious doubts. The island was too far away, it would take him several hours to swim there even without the bulky net and pack he was dragging with him and if he ran into a patrol boat he figured it might be another twenty-four hours before he could hide himself in the jungle and actually get to his job. He was under no delusion that he had to make fairly good time. Within thirty hours the navy would begin shelling the island and an invasion force would arrive as soon as the sun came up within two days. He began the long swim to the shore.

Ken was secure in his own mind despite the attitude he received by some soldiers. Some people thought that being a sniper was a cowardly way to fight in war. He thought to himself he had rather be a coward who actually accomplished something, and lived to tell about it, than to be cannon fodder. He thought back to the times when war was fought as an honorable venture. His mind focused on the Revolutionary War when King George's, British solders wore bright red uniforms and lined up in nice neat rows so that the dignity and bravery of the army could be displayed. Ever since the ages of Napoleon armies had fought that way. They also died that way.

During the War Between the States, the Civil War, thousands of Americans soldiers on both sides died while fighting in rows. The Napoleon method of fighting was still being used then. It was a dramatic waste of human life. Ken thought back to the last battle he had been in. He watched in horror as soldiers who upon first arriving at the scene of action, forgot their training and stood to aim their guns. They were usually killed before they could level their guns.

Now the idea of a combatant following arcane rules had long ago disappeared. During World War II, hitting below the waist was not only expected, it was encouraged by all sides. It was kill or be killed in its most simplistic form. Being a sniper meant that you were an expert in non-conventional warfare. But if he did his job right, if he could spot the Japanese snipers who tied themselves into the tops of palm trees and were expecting the Americans to unload out of landing barges within a few days, Ken knew that he could save hundreds of American lives.

It was a tiring job dragging the heavy net with all the brush and trash tied to it through the water but Ken knew that camouflage was his only defense as he closed on the shoreline that was getting closer by the hour. He could clearly see the waves crashing on the shore, followed by a long sandy beach that would require crossing until he could reach cover. Then he heard it before he spotted it. To his right was a patrol boat that was slowly making its way toward him. He did the only thing he could do and put his snorkel into his mouth and slid deep under the net. On the deck, the Japanese soldier, who was supposed to be spotting the enemy, was gazing past him into the ocean from where he had come. Passing only a few dozen yards from him, they ignored him. But he knew he would have to remain motionless for many more minutes until they were completely out of sight and now the sun was just making its arrival.

Ken had to decide what to do. He decided to motionlessly float in the water and let the waves carry him ashore. He knew that waves didn't really move objects until very close to shore but he had an entire day to kill before he dared to sprint across the beach into the trees. He worried about the patrol boat returning, sharks, jelly fish, and a number of other items over which he had absolutely no control.

As the sun rose the waves carried him on to the beach where all he could do was lay there as quiet and still as he possibly could. Within a few minutes his worst fear occurred. A Japanese soldier with his gun in hand, walked up to the flotsam that was floating in the surf. Ken fought off his instinct to jump up and tackle the soldier but over the screaming of his mind to attack the soldier he remained limp. The Japanese soldier took out a cigarette and lit it while looking over the horizon. Finishing the cigarette, he flipped it into the surf, right on top of Ken and walked away.

There were other soldiers who walked by, Ken knew that it would be several hours before he could make his move, but when darkness finally arrived he gathered up his gear and made a mad dash to the trees. He worried about the tracks he was leaving behind. They could be a dead giveaway but then there were many other tracks on the beach so he decided it didn't matter.

He slowly crawled into the jungle looking for a place to hide. It didn't take him long. Fox holes had been dug into the jungle by the Japanese so that they could shoot at any incoming forces. Finding one that was deserted he dropped down into it and unpacked his rifle attaching the silencer and scope.

He immediately began looking for enemy combatants but couldn't see anything moving. Then turning over on his back he decided to rest for a few minutes but just before he closed his eyes he noticed something strange in the palm tree a few yards away. He could just make out an enemy sniper who appeared to be tied into the top of the tree. Taking his time, he slowly focused in on the combatant and pulled the trigger. The soldier in the tree top immediately slumped over.

Even a with a silencer his rifle made considerable noise so he pulled himself down into the fox hole as far as he could and remained motionless for several minutes. Nothing happened. He was satisfied. The Japanese sniper would have killed many American soldiers the following morning if Ken had not shot him. Using his scoop, he examined every tree top he could see for more snipers but could not see any. Leaving his pack behind Ken slowly crawled down the water's edge for a hundred yards or so before he spotted another sniper tied in a tree.

The sniper was just starting to come down the tree when Ken's bullet ripped through his heart. He hit the ground with a loud thud, alarming Ken because now he was afraid that the enemy would spot him. He lay motionless for another twenty minutes and then he continued his slow crawl down the beach looking for more victims.

He shot two other soldiers who were just sitting on a log on the beach. They never knew what hit them. He waited a few minutes until he determined no one heard the shots and then dragged their bodies into the brush. He then turned around and began the slow crawl back to his original foxhole where he had hidden his pack with his combat rations. He was starving by the time he got back and it was starting to get dark. He knew that within a few hours the entire area would be lit up like a three-ring circus from incoming shells from navy ships. Dodging those incoming shells was a risk he was willing to take.

As soon as the American shells started coming in, the entire island was in turmoil. Everywhere, Japanese soldiers began to appear as they prepared for the invasion. Ken shot as many of them as he could; quickly losing count of how many he had shot when finally, he was spotted by a Japanese soldier. Ken never saw the soldier but he felt the bullet rip through his shoulder leaving a deep crease on his right clavicle. In an instant later his entire right side felt like it was on fire, as if someone had held up a red-hot branding iron and pressed it into his shoulder.

He slumped back down into his fox hole thinking that he would give himself a morphine shot, dress the wound somehow, and as soon as he could he would return to his job. As he picked up his pack, he was aware that there was something under it. A large snake appeared and immediately sunk its fangs into his calf muscle. It all happened so fast, and Ken was so distracted dodging bullets that he never even pulled his leg back. The snake quickly crawled out of the foxhole before Ken could even think about killing it. Besides, the ground around him was spitting up little puffs of dirt from bullets hitting the ground. Ken knew he was in serious trouble at that point and was fighting back panic when he noticed a Japanese soldier standing over him in the foxhole with his gun aimed directly at his face. He remembered the fire from the muzzle flash burning his face, then, covered in sweat; he awoke in his bed at the ranch at Serpientes.

June Anderson's Vision

June Anderson was one of the top archeologists in New Mexico and probably the entire Southwest. After spending years in the field getting her hands dirty, she joined the ranks of the academic world and was responsible for the documentation of Estancia Man, where she and the team from Serpiente discovered an Ice Age culture that lived in a cave on the shores of ancient Lake Estancia. The team was awarded the prestigious New Mexico Historical Society award for their efforts.

This year June found herself back at Chaco Canyon where a possible discovery had been made. Several miles from the monument area where the tourists actually visited the most mysterious ruins in the Southwest, she had been enlisted to explore a slot in the rock that had been completely covered over by blow sand. The sandstone rock that comprised the slot was completely covered by petroglyphs which brought up speculation that another sun dagger would be found. Actually, they had no idea what was there. The excitement was palpable among the archeologist, volunteer student workers, and park personnel who were working on the project.

The large sandstone cliff had been cracked at one time in the distant geological past leaving an eight-foot-wide opening at the base of the bluff. Other layers of sedimentary rock had capped the slot producing a cave which step by step was carefully being excavated by the troop of workers. It was a painfully slow job as each shovelful of sand required close inspection after screening. They were finding interesting objects in that sand. Pottery, often complete pots rather than just shards, bones, including many human bones and disarticulated snake bones were being found. They just assumed that the snake bones were deposited naturally.

Nests left by pack rats were also being discovered. The urine from the small animals cemented together the twigs and cactus pieces as well as many other interesting materials they carried into the nest leaving a record of all matter of evidence of what grew in the area at the time they lived. Artifacts were also being discovered mixed in with that material including macaw feathers and one broken arrow that still had feathers attached.

Having excavated several dozen feet back into the rock, the work crew were amazed at the number of petroglyphs that covered the inner walls. They were all classic Anasazi glyphs, including some head hunter glyphs much like the one found on the San Juan River.

Being late in the day, most of the crew had left, leaving only June and a couple of student workers there with tiny hand trowels to push into the back wall of the slot. Almost dark, June pushed her trowel into the sand and a tiny opening appeared. Excited that they were now digging into an open area she decided to go ahead and open the tiny hole so that they could at least see what was inside. Then she noticed something. There was movement inside the hole. Pulling the trowel back she wondered what could possibly be in the hole and finally curiosity overtook her. Plunging the trowel back into the hole she quickly dug out another trowel full of wet dirt. Then it suddenly happened; a rattlesnake appeared, sinking its fangs deeply into June's thumb. She jerked her hand back but as she did several more rattlesnakes spilled out of the opening, striking her several times. She screamed and tried to get away but more rattlesnakes just kept coming out of the opening, all of them seemingly dead set on attacking her.

She rose up and started to run. She found herself pulling snakes off of her but she was already feeling the effects of the venom. In her mind, she knew that she would most likely die from that many snake bites but she was determined to get away. She managed to take only a dozen or so steps before she realized that she was getting too dizzy to walk anywhere. She came down on her knees only to realize that the rattlesnakes had followed her and were striking her again. Her body started to convulse then she blacked out only to wake up in her bed with nothing wrong with her. She looked over at her husband Ken who was wide awake, covered in sweat and staring at her. They immediately hugged each other.

Corey Anderson's Vision

Corey was dreading it already. Sooner or later the prison guard would leave for some reason; to make a phone call, to eat a snack or to simply go to the bathroom and Chico would have time to walk over to him and kick him in the groin; again, or fake a kick and slug him in the stomach. All he knew was that life in a Mexican Prison was far worse than anything he could imagine. He was aware that in America there were low security prisons for inmates who had committed petty crimes such as DUI, Marijuana conviction, or petty thievery where they were put into community cells. Community cells are less expensive to operate, require fewer guards and if operated correctly are safe for the inmates.

In the jail that Corey had been thrown into only the *ricos* or the rich ones, those with political connections, got to be put into single cells. They were confined to their rooms but there were no restrictions on what they could have in their rooms. Often the wealthiest of them had a small refrigerator or even a television set inside of their cells. If they had money and were willing to pay the proper bribes they served their sentences safe and in relative comfort even enjoying an occasional delivery of contraband such as alcohol or drugs. Occasionally women could be seen visiting those cells. Everyone preferred private cells but few got them. In America the hard core convicts were put into private cells but without the creature comforts obtainable in Mexico.

Community cells in Mexico were extremely dangerous places to be. All manner of people was put into them from wife beaters to murderers. The clientele was mostly young; teenagers that were mostly thieves or gangsters who enjoyed inflicting pain. They were the hoodlums who would invade your home in the middle of the night stealing all your valuables, beat you within an inch of your life, rape any women in the house, and then brag to their friends about it. Killing someone meant nothing to them. It was a badge of honor to be able to kill others and get away with it. When caught, which seldom happened, they were put into the community cell at the prison where they had to prove their worth, their ability to be bad hombres all over again. In Mexico, the Anglo or non-Hispanic from the United States are on the lowest rung of the social ladder. People like Corey were an obvious target.

Chico had zeroed in from day one enjoying inflicting as much pain as he could to the naive gringo called Corey. As a result, Corey could never sleep more than a few minutes at a time. Often, he woke up to a sharp kick in the ribs when Chico caught him asleep. Once he woke up when he thought he was enjoying a spring shower only to discover that Chico was standing over him, urinating on him. It wasn't that Corey hadn't fought back. The first-time Chico tried to hurt him, Corey nailed him with a right cross which escalated into an all-out brawl that the guards eventually broke up. Unfortunately, Chico had many friends with him in the jail and the next encounter they held Corey's arms behind him while Chico beat him. It always happened so fast that either the single guard, who was afraid of the prisoners, couldn't signal for help in time or it was in a crowd where no one ever would see nor report a thing.

Corey's only hope was a bribe set up by his family in Serpiente, but at this point he hadn't heard anything for some time. The one thing he was sure of was that the drugs planted in his back pack didn't belong to him. The only drug he had ever indulged in was Hidalgo's coffee. At that moment, he would have given anything for a cup of Hidalgo's coffee. Strong and black, he tried to imagine what it would smell like.

It was late that evening after the tortilla and chili beans were served when there was a commotion along the chain link with razor wire strung over it. Corey ignored it, glad that something else was going on and he was being left alone. But then, after a short while he raised his head up and noticed a group of people standing in front of him. His stomach immediately began to churn as he expected a beating. Chico looked down at him and said for the first time in perfect English, a language in which Corey had never heard him speak, "I am going to kill you."

Corey replied, "You know that if you kill me, it will mean you could spend the rest of your life in here."

"That's true, but I am not the one who is actually going to kill you. My friend here is going to do it and you are going to die of natural causes."

"Then wouldn't your friend be in trouble," Corey asked?

Chico took a long pause before he answered, while pulling his hand out of a paper bag and holding a rattlesnake in it. "My friend here likes living in jail. Good bye gringo." At that moment, he tossed the rattlesnake on to Corey's neck where it immediately struck him on the jugular vein on the side of his neck. Death would occur in only a moment as the venom was fully injected into the vein that oxygenated the brain. Another moment passed until Corey found himself screaming at the top of his lungs. He was already sitting up in bed and it took him a full minute before he realized it had all been a dream.

Hidalgo's Vision

He certainly had a knack for talking people out of doing stupid things during intense moments such as during a robbery. Hidalgo was enjoying his dream about the days spent in Durango as a policeman. He was young and full of ambition. Sure, of himself in a very quiet way. He could easily have become an arrogant individual. On the police force, his work was that good. But arrogance was foreign to Hidalgo. Despite his upbringing on the Navaho reservation, he was actually better educated than most of the other policemen he worked with. He could thank his mother for that.

That thought made him think of his mother, a mental picture appearing. As a child, he was drilled by his mother for hours on end with school work. His mother, who worked as a school aide for the Shiprock School System, wanted her son to succeed where few others had ever dared to try. She believed in living by ways of being smart, not just doing hard physical labor. School never ended for Hidalgo just because school let out for the day. Every evening they practiced the daily lessons until Hidalgo had memorized everything that the teachers had talked about in the classrooms. He watched himself stand near the door of the Hogan. If he got the chance he would run out and play outside until his mother found him again. Around the Hogan they usually spoke in her native tongue of Navajo but his mother also made him learn how to speak English and Spanish. Hidalgo experienced a series of bright flashes of color in his dreams as if something was taking the dream over. He then heard someone cursing in Spanish.

Suddenly he found himself bent over, in a large field where thousands of adobes were in various stages of drying. He was pulling the wooden slip off of a wet adobe. Then he placed the adobe a few inches over. A line of workers carried mud on straw mats to wherever the wooden slip went. He knew he was the lucky one; the workers in the line had to continually run in order to keep up production. The pile of wet mud would need to dry in the sun for many days then be picked up and set with wet mud into the walls of the adobe garrison they were working on. Looking around he could see maybe a dozen other young Navajos and four others that he thought were pueblo people. Everyone had been captured by the Spanish and now they worked, all under the watchful eyes of the Spanish Masters they were serving.

As he toiled, he thought back to his capture, just outside of the newly founded city of what was to become Santa Fe. He had been starving. Unable to kill anything to eat except occasional cotton tailed rabbits. He had no salt and the thought of eating another rabbit made his stomach churn, eating the same thing all the time was not to his liking. He remembered thinking that if he could sneak close enough to the new hacienda that the outsiders were building; he might be able to steal onions, corn, chilies and salt. Not only would he be able to eat, his woman could eat. Once she had been pregnant but had lost the baby due to lack of food. He was deeply in love with her and was her protector. But for now, he had been reduced to being a slave.

The sergeant was getting angry at them for not working fast enough. The soldiers sat in the shade of a cottonwood tree while the slaves toiled out in the hot sun. Whenever a soldier decided that the slaves were not working hard or fast enough, he would step out of the shade and bring his whip across the center of someone's back. Everyone would work harder and faster for a few minutes. If they resisted the whip, he simply would take out his sword and start hacking at their flesh until they passed out for lack of blood. Sometimes it would take a long time for the slave to actually die. Everyone would feel grateful because work stopped, until the entire spectacle was over. Everyone stopped their work in order to watch the man die, the price for a few minutes of rest. Then it was more work for the remaining slaves who had to drag the dying man to an already dug grave, toss it in, and cover it over with dirt.

The work lasted from sunrise to sunset with a short break at noon when they would be allowed to drink water from the rain barrels. At least he was eating but he had no idea what it was he was eating. In the morning, they were fed a bowl of grainy grey stuff. Some kind of oats he guessed. In the evenings, they were fed better; a bowl of stew with venison meat in it. It was salted and Hidalgo relished it.

His mind meandered back to before he was captured. He and his new bride had lived in the back country, many miles from where he was captured. They had a large field of corn and squash and even a stolen peach tree that he had planted. More importantly he owned sheep that had been stolen from the area south of Santa Fe. He and another warrior had captured them and herded them all the way to his Hogan. Unfortunately, he had to divide the sheep with the other warrior, as well as his father in-law who expected his cut from any raids. But he lived in relative comfort, far better than most of the other members of the Dine.

Then one day the Spanish soldiers appeared. They drove their horses back and forth through the young corn fields and squash, killing them. Then they killed all the sheep. All Hidalgo and his woman could do was to hide and watch from the rocks that overlooked his fields. Fighting the soldiers was futile. The Spanish had won the battle but not the war. The war would go on forever as far as Navajo were concerned. They already were at war, coming together in groups in order to fight the Spanish. There was strength in numbers and outside of the garrison of Santa Fe the Spanish could, at times, be helpless.

Late that evening after the hot day in the cruel sun, a *carreta* as the Spanish called them, pulled by a single mule, arrived at the garrison. The wagon, with its huge wheels, had a large cage on it. Inside the cage were Indian women, but Hidalgo could not see them clear enough to identify any of them. That night he and all the captured Navajos listened to the screams of the women as the soldiers had their way with them. It was a humiliating experience for the slaves, locked in the building in which they spent their days making the walls even stronger for their sworn enemies. Then at night they would have to wonder what was happening to their women.

The next day Hidalgo just happened to be working in a place where he could see the women as they were loaded back on the *carreta* to be taken somewhere else. He watched as they were pushed and prodded like cattle to board the wagon, then he noticed his wife there. She was fighting one of the soldiers with all her might but after she managed to scratch his face he took out his sword and plunged it into her heart. Hidalgo ran as fast as he could to stop the soldier but couldn't get there in time. When he finally did get there all he could do was to lock on to the soldier's neck where he refused to let go until the soldier became limp. The other soldiers wrestled Hidalgo to the ground and then put chains on him. They dragged him to a tree pole that had been buried in the ground and then a soldier proceeded to whip him. This continued until Hidalgo blacked out from the pain.

He awoke with a start when a soldier threw a bucket full of water into his face. They wanted him to experience as much pain as possible. Unlocking his chains, they held him on the ground, and then they tied his hands in front of him and pushed a stick behind his back and through his elbows so he couldn't resist. They then lifted him off the ground and to his wobbly feet. Then they lead him to a deep hole that had been dug in the ground. Hidalgo wondered what it was made for. It looked somewhat like the many *kivas* he had seen around the country where Native Indians lived. But as he neared the edge of the hole he realized that the bottom of the hole was scattered with rattlesnakes. Fighting with all his might he could not help himself. He was tossed into the hole, landing face first. After hitting the floor of the hole, he raised his head up and watched as a snake struck him in the face, just below the eye. Being tied up there was nothing he could do but lie there in terror as the rattlesnakes bit him repeatedly. When he finally did open his eyes again, he could see the sun just showing through the window of his bedroom. He let out something of a war cry as the realization sunk in that he had just been dreaming.

Comparing Dreams

Everyone was terrified, except for me, Penny Anderson who apparently had had no dreams at all. I was mystified when Corey started grabbing at his neck and screaming in bed. She was also terrified when she heard Hidalgo let out a war cry only a few rooms away. Well before the sun was all the way up, everyone gathered at the kitchen table. June put on a pot of coffee and I served everyone as they just sat for a few minutes mulling over in their minds what had happened. Hidalgo seemed angry, Corey and Ken both put their heads on the table top. The experience was so intense that it left everyone, except me, with a dull headache. No one wanted to go back to sleep for fear that the dreams would return. Finally, I started the conversation with a simple, "What happened?"

For several minutes nobody answered me, they just all stared, wide eyed, into space. They had no idea that it was possible for a human to have such intense dreams with visions that produced agony. The realization that they had no control over their most private thoughts was frightening to everyone. Everyone's brain was on overload. It was as if lightning had struck and it was taking a while for their brains to recover from the overload.

I suggested that each of them recount their dreams. So, after a lot of prompting, each of them went through a detailed description about what they had dreamed.

Strangely, everyone but me was finding themselves dehydrated, after everyone took their turns at drinking several cups of coffee, Ken started the conversation by comparing his account of what actually happened on Macon Island to what was in the dream. "First of all, no submarine ever dropped me off. However, before I landed and in my mind, I visualized doing something like that. It was just a flash of a thought. Wouldn't that be a great way to get on the island and do some good before the main invasion occurs? For what it's worth, Special Forces units drop off operation soldiers that way, now days. I hit the beach along with all the other soldiers. But much of the remainder of the story was true. I was shot in the shoulder and I did see a snake on the island during combat but it didn't bother me and obviously, no Japanese soldier ever shot me in the face or I wouldn't be here now.

In what was almost a whisper, Hidalgo stated the obvious conclusion. "The serpents are at it again!"

June says, "After my experience at Zuni Pueblo as well as that horrible dream I had last night, I truly believe that those serpents are capable of far more than people realize. Needless to say, the serpents are playing on our fears, real or imagined. I have always been terrified at the thought of being trapped in a tight space with rattlesnakes. In fact, I have had many dreams in the past where I was killing rattlesnakes who somehow kept multiplying until there was not a place to step. The difference is, I simply woke up and usually had to urinate. The difference was, in the dream I had last night, everything seemed very real. I could feel the trowel in my hand, the sandy grit between my fingers. Last night's dream didn't come from within me; it was forced upon me from somewhere else."

Everyone looked at Hidalgo to see if he was going to say something but instead he just rocked forward and back in his chair. It was Corey's turn to recount his dream. "It was pretty much the way it was in the dream. Mexican prisons can be horrible and there was a Chico there that kept trying to pick a fight with me. We even traded a few punches, but as soon as he figured out that I would fight back he pretty much left me alone. I thought I had forgotten all about him and I certainly don't remember seeing a rattlesnake around the prison, certainly not a real rattlesnake, only humans who acted like rattlesnakes.

Everyone again turned to Hidalgo, who had already recounted his dream. This time, everyone was looking for more detail, was there anything he had forgotten? He added, "I am a little confused by my dream. Obviously, it took place in another time. Perhaps it is some sort of racial memory that occurred to one of my grandparents. The problem is, I don't know of any of my grandparents who were captured by the Spanish, although I had relatives killed in Canyon de Chelly."

"In 1863 Colonel Kit Carson sent troops to either end of the canyon to defeat the Dine population inside. They destroyed all the crops and cut down the peach trees that the people were growing and depended upon for sustenance. If it had not have been for scattered crops in well-hidden places, they all would have starved. Anyway, they were removed from their homes and force marched to Bosque Redondo. Several members of my family were killed in the conflict. However, as you all know, I have never been married."

I thought that by bringing up his relationship with the beautiful young lady who was an undercover policeman in Durango would lighten the conversation but everyone ignored me including Hidalgo who normally would have been overjoyed to participate in a tease.

Hidalgo only frowned at the interjection, "I'm sure that Navajos were held as slaves by the Spanish but they themselves held slaves. Everyone held slaves in those days and everyone did cruel and unjust things. That's just the way it was during that time in history. It was a rite of passage for young Navajos to steal horses, cattle, or anything with four legs on them. Stealing happened when you stole from a friend or another Navajo family. It just didn't happen. When you steal something from an enemy it was considered a badge of honor. A rite of passage, every young warrior lives for the day he will earn his honor capturing an enemy's cattle, sheep, or women, earning his *coup*."

"As far as the rattlesnake pit that I felt myself being pushed into, I don't remember anything like that actually happening except in pulp fiction novels."

Finally, everyone looked at me. I hadn't said much or even seemed too stressed. In fact, I had slept like a rock until Corey woke me. "What was your dream like?" asked Corey.

"I don't remember having any dreams last night. In fact, I don't even remember getting up during the night to use the bathroom."

June asked, "I don't understand it. We are all sitting in a house miles away from anything and several of us are visited by our little friends, the serpents. Who knows what they are trying to tell us." Turning and locking on to my eyes she implored me, "Why didn't you have a dream the way we did?"

I sat there at the table trying to understand what had happened. I was unable to answer the questions that I could see in everyone's eyes. Absent mindedly, I reached inside my blouse and flipped out the owl amulet that was tied around my neck. Flipping it back and forth in my fingers I realized that everyone was staring at the tiny amulet that was dangling from my fingers.

Hidalgo says, "I'll bet you were wearing that last night, weren't you?"

"Yes," I replied, looking down at it myself. I had forgotten all about it.

"How in the world did that tiny thing keep you from experiencing dreams like we did?" asked Ken.

"I don't know." I answered. "All I know is that I feel comfortable and safe when I'm wearing it."

June interjected, "We need to have that thing checked out. Are you sure it is an effigy of an owl, or could it be something else?"

"Well, I did think it was a strange looking owl," I answered, "but I agree, we should have it examined scientifically, by someone who has the right tools.

Aesop's Wisdom

Hidalgo was the one who stated the obvious conclusion. "The serpents are at it again but I don't understand what they are trying to tell us."

"Well one thing is obvious," says June, "Everyone had similar dreams, each involving angry snakes."

Hidalgo who was feeling better now that his headache was going away, and after realizing that he was certainly not the only one to have a bizarre dream, decided to share his thoughts, "My bet is, the serpents did not disappear they only dispersed. They have realized that there are very few places they can go without running into people and rather than living in a central nest, which they probably have done for thousands or even millions of years, they have decided to disperse throughout the Southwest as a survival strategy. Maybe they have tiny nests all over the place rather than one large one. I don't know, really, I'm just guessing but what else could they do? All wild animals now live on small biological islands."

Not new to brainstorming sessions, I added, "Bears do that in Tennessee. In Tennessee, small towns have grown into small cities making the range that bears live in, smaller and smaller. It is becoming more and more difficult for them to find safe places to live and find food. Even out in the country the human population has grown so much that bears are seldom found. It is also why the bears themselves have become pest in parks and large mountainous areas where they are protected. The sanctuaries they seek are overused when they finally find a safe place; they tend to make a nuisance of themselves. From a wild animal's point of view, we humans are a plague on the earth."

Corey added an interesting point, "Maybe there is more to it than what we know. Since it is obvious they can sense our innermost thoughts and even play with our dreams, maybe they sense that something is going to happen to them. I wouldn't put it past General Armstrong to be up to something. He may have wanted to placate everyone by going along with letting the serpents settle in the nest, and then now that no one suspected anything he may have thought about having the nest gassed, killing all of them when they least expect it. Maybe the serpents picked up on those thoughts, especially, his thoughts."

Hidalgo nodded his head and said, "Sounds just like something someone like him would do. There is hardly a single treaty that the government didn't break with the native peoples and as far as what they are telling us now, about what they are going to do, I don't trust them."

There was an awkward pause in the conversation as everyone thought about what had been said then I asked, "Why are they causing all of you to have such terrible dreams, and why have the serpents caused such horrible things to happen to humans?"

June answered my questions with an interesting story. "Have you ever heard about a fellow by the name of Aesop who was a Greek storyteller who lived in the year six hundred B.C.?"

Everyone had heard of the Greek but no one had any idea what she was getting at. "Let me tell you a story."

"One day, a scorpion looked around at the mountain where he lived and decided that he wanted a change, so he set out on a journey through the forest and hills. He climbed over rocks and under vines and kept going until he reached a river."

"The river was wide and swift, and the scorpion stopped to reconsider the situation. He couldn't see any way across. So, he ran upriver and then checked downriver, all the while thinking that he might have to turn back."

"Suddenly, the Scorpion saw a frog sitting in the rushes on the bank of the other side of the river. He decided to ask the frog for help getting across the river."

"Hello Mr. Frog!" called the scorpion across the water, 'Would you be so kind as to give me a ride on your back across the river?'

'Well now, Mr. Scorpion! How do I know that if I try to help you, you won't try to kill me?' asked the frog hesitantly.

'Because,' the scorpion replied, 'If I try to kill you, then I would die too, for you see I cannot swim!'

Now this seemed to make sense to the frog. But he asked. 'What about when I get close to the bank? You could still try to kill me and get back to the shore!'

'That is true,' agreed the scorpion, 'But then I wouldn't be able to get to the other side of the river!'

'All right then. How do I know you won't just wait till we get to the other side and then kill me?' said the frog.

'Ah'...crooned the scorpion, 'Because you see, once you've taken me to the other side of this river, I will be so grateful for your help, that it would hardly be fair to reward you with death, now would it?'

So, the frog agreed to take the scorpion across the river. He swam over to the bank and settled himself near the mud to pick up his passenger. The scorpion crawled onto the frog's back, his sharp claws prickling into the frog's hide, and the frog slid into the river. The muddy water swirled around them, but the frog stayed near the surface so the scorpion would not drown.

Halfway across the river, the frog suddenly felt a sharp sting in his back and, out of the corner of his eye, saw the scorpion remove his stinger from the frog's back. A deadening numbness began to creep into his limbs.

'You fool!' croaked the frog, 'Now we shall both die! Why on earth did you do that?'

The scorpion shrugged, and did a little jig on the drowning frog's back.

'I could not help myself. It is my nature.'

Then they both sank into the muddy waters of the swiftly flowing river."

"So, you are saying that it is in the nature of the serpent to do what they do," I responded?

"Sure, it is," answered June. "They are evil by nature, and actually cannot be reasoned with as humans think. We humans tend to think of other creatures as thinking like we do. But animals do not reason like we do, we tend to anthropomorphize when it comes to other animals. For example, when a human gets home from a hard day's work the dog comes out to greet him or her. Actually, the dog is just thinking, oh boy, here comes the provider of food. Humans do this all the time when it comes to animals; we tend to forget that each and every species of animal have brains that operate very differently from ours. Also, as a species we are culturally bound whereas most animals act by pure instinct."

But the mystery remained. Obviously, there were some of Quetzalcoatl and Kukulkan's relatives in the area or possibly Quetzalcoatl and Kukulkan themselves. They seemed grateful when I released them from their cage in Farmington, even doing their peculiar undulating dance before morphing into ravens and flying away. Why would they want to harm us now?

Over a breakfast that consisted of bowls of whole oats, pecans and peaches; nobody talked, nobody was hungry and what little they ate was done with mechanical motions. It would take a while before the effects of the dreams and the resulting headaches to completely go away.

Finally, Ken broke the ice by saying, "Obviously, the serpents are out there again. We need to make some preparations in case they return to their old ways and start killing animals around here again."

"That's true," countered Hidalgo, "But I think that they were singling us out for some reason. This family is the focus of their efforts to communicate even if the only way they know how is to use our memories to manipulate our dreams."

Corey finally entered the conversation with an idea, "Maybe we are the focal point of their efforts to communicate but we don't know that for a fact. For all we know there may be people all over New Mexico who are right now wondering if they are going crazy. The snakes could be mounting another attack against us humans everywhere. I think we had better get our facts straight. I think one of us should get on the phone and start making calls to see if anyone else is having strange dreams."

I laughed at that. "I can hear it now, Dr. Hartsell, or General Armstrong, Mr. Jones, how have your dreams been lately? If they have not had strange dreams they are going to think we are crazy. If they have had strange dreams they are going to know that we are crazy."

"I don't know," countered Hidalgo, "The only other person that I know of that has suffered through a personal experience in his dreams was John Luna, and we all know how that worked out for him."

Corey says, "I still think it would be a good idea to find out if we are the only people that the serpents are trying to communicate with, after all, they have had a longer relationship with us than anyone and at least we tried to work with them."

"Well I know one thing we can do right know that might give us a few answers," June got out of her chair and turned on the television first to the news station coming out of Albuquerque and then to CNN. As she listened, she called a short list of people who knew about the serpents. People she could trust. No one seemed to understand what she was talking about. Turning the television back off after listening to it for only a short while, she concluded that there was nothing in the news about people having terrifying dreams.

June called several of the local ranches surrounding Serpiente but after tactfully asking them if anything strange had recently happened all she got as an answer were stories about just about everything but dreams. In a short time, she realized she was wasting her time. Whatever the serpents were trying to say to them was directed at the family known as the Andersons living in a very isolated place called Serpiente.

Analyzing the Amulet

*N*obody felt like working that day, besides, most of the ranch work had been caught up and they always had Manuel and his family who watched over the ranch when they were away on business anyway. Everyone went except Ken, who wanted to ride around the ranch and see if he could spot anything that looked out of place. Everyone else loaded into the Jeep Cherokee and headed to Albuquerque where we hoped to could get some answers about the owl amulet, the only physical evidence they could investigate.

Due to the recent good weather, which meant good roads, they made good time and within two hours they were driving around the anthropology building at the university looking for a parking spot. Finding the parking spot was the most difficult part of the journey. June had spent considerable time in the building through her work as an archeologist and knew most of the professors that worked there. Directly in front of the building they pulled into a parking spot marked for William H. Conrad. June knew he was in Israel at the time. Following June, everyone managed to locate the person they were searching for.

Dr. Emory had a jolly disposition, an outgoing personality, and bushy white hair that made him look like Santa Claus at first glance. His hair was always unruly and the mischievous look on his face belayed his years as a serious scientist. An expert in Native American antiquities he had connections with other professors in the school of physics that were dating the artifacts that were brought to him. "What did you bring me this time?" he asked as June entered his office.

After introductions of everyone, I pulled the amulet from around my neck and handed it over to him. After brief explanations of where it had come from, he examined it.

Dr. Emory was fascinated by the amulet. "I have never seen anything quite like it."

"What do you mean?" asked June.

"Well before I answer that question, let's put it under a microscope. Why don't you folks follow me down the hallway?"

With the amulet in hand we all walked down to a laboratory where a special microscope was set up with a large screen set up so everyone could see what was being examined. Simply by putting the amulet under the microscope and displaying it on the screen, magnifying it to the size of the screen, it was obvious that the object was not that of an owl. The eyes were large like an owl but slanting and the ears were not ears; they were more like an exaggerated or raised coat collar. The amulet appeared to be wearing an amulet itself. A tiny red crystal appeared to be hanging at the bottom of the necklace that was made of tiny rings that appeared to be made of gold.

We returned their attention to the eyes for a closer look. They were yellow, with a vertical slit like a snake might have. Even without magnification it was obvious that what they were looking at was not an owl nor was it the product of some woodcarver's work. There was not a tool mark on it. The details were far too fine. At 10X magnification it was determined that the object was some kind of crystalline structure. At 100X we could make out what appeared to be the tiniest of scale markings, but we couldn't tell for sure. At 400X what we saw suggested cellular structure as if whatever it was made out of was alive at one time. At that magnification, we could make out several things that amazed us but we had no idea what we were looking at.

What we were examining appeared to be what would someday be called an integrated circuit. Electronic circuitry that had not, as of yet been invented. The parts of the circuit were all fused into a crystalline robotic structure.

We all starred at the creature on the screen for some time, dumfounded, not knowing what to say. Finally, Dr. Emory says, "I have never seen anything like it before in my life. It's obviously not anything a craftsman could make, it is far too detailed. It is as if we were looking at an insect under the scope. The closer you look the more detailed it becomes right down to the details in the individual cells. It is as if we were looking at a...well, an alien creature."

June asked, "Is there some way that we can find out more about it? Are there other test you can do?"

"Sure," answered Dr. Emory, "but it is going to take us a couple of days. I'll run it over to the physics building and see if we can determine a date for its age and composition. If they can't figure it out I know some folks out at Los Alamos Labs that will be able to provide some answers. I'll call you the minute we get the results."

"That's fine," says Hidalgo, "but we already know that the amulet acts as a protector to the wearer. I'm going to be concerned about Penny."

"I can take care of myself," I admonished them.

Corey hugged me and said, "Of all the people in the world, you would be the one who could most likely be able to take care of herself. But you didn't have those dreams like we did. Speaking for myself, I'm a little scared and worried about you. Let's hope that none of us have any more dreams involving snakes, serpents or monsters. I would prefer to have you in my dreams, as a matter of fact, I don't need to dream any more at all, all I have to do is open my eyes and there you are."

Penny's Vision

That night, I had several dreams. They were nothing out of the ordinary, just flashes of memory that I would normally disregard. Then on the second night without the amulet I had a serpentine visitor in my dreams. It all started out beautifully. In the dream, I was just starting high school and was living on the family farm in East Tennessee. I recounted the dream to the others the next morning. "I remember walking down the road, being careful where to step, walking in the tire ruts instead of the weeds. The weeds alongside the road were wet, and I didn't want to get my pants legs wet. It was a perfect day; the sun was out and I remember a slight breeze was blowing that kept me cool. I remember thinking that the fields were so beautiful. The fence line was covered in iris flowers that were blooming with brilliant blue and purple flowers. I paused to watch a hummingbird feed off of one of them. Then I noticed a red fox run across a field and disappear into the woods. I kept walking."

"Finally, away in the distance I could see some men loading hay onto a wagon that was pulled by a farm tractor. I remember that each and every one of my steps seemed very important. Each one had to be studied before I placed my foot. Then I looked up and I was closer to the men loading the wagon. They were hot and sweaty from the work they were doing. This time, one of them seemed vaguely familiar. I looked down and watched my feet carry me to where the men were working. Looking up I was surprised to see Corey throwing a bale of hay onto the wagon."

I paused and looked around the room at everyone and said, "No joke, he ignored me and reached for another bale of hay. I immediately spotted a copperhead coming out of the back of the bale. I tried to scream, to warn him, but nothing came out. He lifted it up in to his chest and the snake came over the top of the bale and bit him on the throat. I was frozen, unable to speak. I watched him immediately drop the bale of hay and reach down and slap the snake off of his neck."

Corey chuckled, "I'm sure tired of being the victim of all these snakebites. I don't think my neck can take many more bites, even if they are in dreams."

Well things got strange then. The muscle on the side of Corey's neck instantly turned black. Then it ruptured and seemed to turn itself inside out. I looked carefully inside the wound and it was filled with thousands of tiny black snakes. Then I woke up."

"When did the dream happen, last night?" asked Corey. "I don't remember you saying anything, and I don't remember having any dreams at all."

"Well, I think it was early on. You were all correct about how vivid the dreams are. I couldn't have imagined it. Anyway, I knew what was happening. I went back to sleep so I could have more crazy dreams."

"Well, what happened then," asked Hidalgo?

"Nothing, I don't remember any other dreams except the one that sleeps with me." I pointed at Corey who grinned.

Hidalgo says, "This is the first dream that someone has had in which someone else has the snake attack. Not the dreamer." Then Hidalgo let out a slight chuckle and said, "Corey ended up being snake bit twice. I'll have to work hard now to catch up!"

Electromagnetic Fields

After two days, we finally got a call from Dr. Emory who insisted that we come in to talk to him. He seemed secretive, as if he couldn't talk about the amulet over the phone. June decided to go in alone to talk to him so after another long drive into the city she confronted the professor.

"What did you find out," asked June?

"Well, we need to do some serious talking. I'm sure that you know that there are a limited number of tests that we can actually conduct on the amulet."

"Sure," answered June, "basically you can find out what it is made of and how old it is."

"That's right. Of course, we can look at it even deeper by using an electron microscope but I will have to wait a few days for the opportunity to use the one in the physics lab, it is booked until the end of the week by the biology department. Some botanist over there is discovering whole new worlds within flowers. But I will tell you right now that you have a very unusual amulet."

June asked, "Well let's start out with basics. What is it made out of? We have all been assuming that it was carved from some kind of bone."

"Well as you know, spectroscopy is a method of analyzing the properties of matter from their electromagnetic interactions. As a result of looking at the rainbow of colors as well as the spectral lines produced, we can tell what elements make up any substance or object. The bottom line is we tried every method that is at our disposal to determine what the amulet is made of."

"And it is made of?" June was getting impatient waiting for an answer.

"According to the results of the data we received it is made out of nothing." As Dr. Emory explained this, he had an incredulous look on his face. Obviously, he was very uncomfortable with his explanation.

"We tried to date it. It appears to be some kind of ceramic so we tried a new method called thermoluminescence dating, but again we drew a blank. It simply gave us no answers. We tried everything including optically stimulated dating but could not get a reading from it. It is as if it is made from a material that came from some other universe. We certainly don't have any material like that on earth, at least not that I am aware of."

"Have you tried any of the traditional methods such as radiocarbon, obsidian hydration dating, or potassium-argon dating?" June asked.

"Well, as you know we would need a tiny sample of it to be able to test it using those methods. To tell you the truth, after we got the negative result from the test we performed, I tried to drill a tiny sample from the tiny hole that the leather string goes through. The drill bit broke, so I tried another and it broke too. Those diamond tipped drill bits, are very expensive and very tuff but they didn't make a scratch on it. As far as I am concerned what you have is some kind of ceramic that is simply not from this earth. What I can tell you is that it seems to block any kind of electromagnetic field around it; it is some kind of device that is actually doing something. By the way I did get it over to the electron microscope for a few minutes. The closer we looked the more intricate and detailed it became. My guess is it is something electronic in nature. Again, I believe you have a piece of technology that is not from this earth. I will personally take it up to Los Alamos and see if they can determine anything.

Hidalgo's Anger

*D*espite the fact that everyone had always been very professional, dealing with a multitude of other people, we enjoyed our privacy. The privacy that the ranch had to offer us was important. We were simply independent people. But Hidalgo was getting angry just thinking about the snakes. What right did they have to enter our minds and interfere with our dreams? What right do they have probing our minds to discover our fears, to manipulate us? It seemed to him that we humans should have a few rights too! Then he began to think about it. Many Native peoples considered their dreams the real world and everyday life experiences as nothing but a conduit to the next dream. Then he thought about himself. He certainly didn't carry any real scars from the dream. Unlike others who had become insane when probed, he had, as far as he could tell, managed to keep his wits about him.

Yet he wondered, during his lifetime he had experienced many strange encounters with animals. Except for a few domesticated animals, all animals live on the edge of existence. Every meal has to be hunted. The signals animals give when cornered are always predictable. Perhaps this was the only way the serpents could communicate. Perhaps they wanted to scare us, but maybe this was the only way that they had of calling out for help.

Perhaps they were scared and were striking out in the only way they could get to us, in our dreams. All snakes will strike when they are scared. It is in their nature. Maybe they are scared of something that we don't know about. Maybe they think we are the only creatures that can help them? No, surely, they are trying to manipulate us. They want us to be scared. Or perhaps they are scared themselves and are trying to communicate their fear and displeasure. Hidalgo realized his worrying was becoming circular, he decided it was time to go to dinner.

Everyone met, as usual over dinner. It was the traditional family meeting time, everyone's chance to participate in the family business, whether ranching or detective work. Everyone enjoyed a green chili dish that Manuel's oldest daughter had prepared for them. At twelve, she was becoming as good a cook as her mother. She had taken ground beef and cooked it in a skillet. Then she lined a casserole dish with corn tortillas, pouring the meat over the tortillas, added a sprinkling of salt and a generous amount of peeled green chili, a can of celery and mushroom soups, and she flavored it all with cumin seeds. Followed with a generous sprinkling of more tortillas and cheese, she placed the casserole in the oven and went to help her mother who had spent the day there cleaning and working in the garden she tended.

The extended family talked and planned the order of ranch work making a list of things to do as well as lists of things to get the next time someone goes into town. They enjoyed the casserole with fresh tomatoes with cottage cheese. It was a great dinner. I particularly relished the chili dish because of the cumin seasoning.

It had also been two weeks since anyone had said anything about a strange dream, or at least one that they could remember. After the subject was broached, everyone stopped eating the instant Hidalgo announced that he had had another one of the serpent dreams.

"Well, it was a short, if not painful dream. It certainly was vivid, just like the other one. I dreamed that, as before, I was a person who lived a long time ago. A warrior I was, climbing through a large rock garden, just like in a western movie. Only like in the other dream, I could feel everything around me including the sand as it swished under my moccasins. I was being pursued by an Apache. He had seen me drinking water from the spring at the bottom of the canyon. There he shot an arrow at me, hitting the mud, between my fingers. As soon as the arrow hit I ran into the rocks trying not to leave any footprints, but it really didn't seem to matter. The Apache was closing on me and I didn't have any weapons. Just when I thought my lungs were going to burst I stopped and looked back to see if he was following me. Just then, his head popped up from behind a boulder, a short arrows flight away, and our eyes locked on to each other."

"I called out to him in Navajo, hoping he would understand some of my words. He acted like it only enraged him further. He jumped out from behind the rock and fired another arrow at me that smashed on the rock behind me."

"Again, I called out to him in my native tongue to stop, that I meant him no harm; that I was leaving. I also did sign language as I spoke so there would be no question of the Apache understanding me. Again, he stepped out from behind the rock and let loose another arrow. This time it ricocheted off the rock in front of my face and landed broken next to me. The Apache warrior was very good with a bow. If he gets a clear shot at me, I knew I would die."

"I scrambled up a rocky gully, stopping and looking back every few steps, expecting to see him just getting ready to shoot another arrow. Finally, I glanced back and there he was, as I expected he was already pulling on the string and instantaneously I saw the arrow being released. It flew dead center toward me but just then there was a shift in the wind and the arrow flew low and just slightly off course. Instead of killing me, the arrow cut deeply into the muscle on my left leg above the knee."

"I realized that I was almost at the top of the ridge I had been climbing and despite the agony of the imbedded arrow. I climbed the last few steps to the top. Another arrow flew past my face as I reach the top. Immediately I reached down and grabbed a rock and threw it at my attacker but it only slowed him down an instant. Reaching down again, I broke the arrow and pulled the shaft out of the leg. Then, using my headband, I made a tunicate over the hole the arrow made, to keep the blood from squirting out. I could hear the Apache running up the gully clearly now. It would just be an instant until he would be on top of me. Then my eyes focused on what was on the ground directly next to me. A rattlesnake lay there."

"Without even thinking I reached down and grabbed the snake and tossed it in the face of the warrior. It bit him several times before he realized what had happened."

"What happened then," I asked?

"Nothing, I woke up but decided not to stay up. I went back to sleep and had no more crazy dreams."

"What do you think the dream meant?" I asked.

"I don't know, but this time instead of the snakes killing me, they rescued me. But I have to tell you all, when that arrow hit me in the leg, it hurt! I was glad when I woke up and discovered my leg was not hurt."

Ken says, "All of the previous dreams were basically the same, that is, each of us were killed by snakes."

Corey put two fingers in the air. "Well one of us has been killed twice, but I'm not counting on it happening again. It certainly never affected my appetite" he said while loading a second helping onto his plate.

June says, "It's nice to know the serpents are helping us now, even if it is just in our dreams.

Rescue from the Mayan

That night both Corey and June had dreams. But I had no dreams despite the fact that I didn't have the amulet, and Ken slept well except for the part when June woke him up to tell him about her dream. She dreamed that she was in South America, in the jungle. She had been working on a site with another archeologist, a gentleman who believed they were about to discover the burial site of a local Mayan dignitary. They were both walking toward the excavation when suddenly two jungle warriors, dressed exactly like Mayan foot soldiers, obsidian axes and all, jumped into the road and challenged us.

"We couldn't run. I was frozen in fear, then I decided if it was my time to go, so be it. One of them stepped toward us and raised his obsidian blade over our heads. Then he lowered it, looking first at me and then the other fellow. He them pointed the ax at me then he brought it across the front of his throat. Then he did the same thing to my companion followed by putting his hands on his sides. The symbolism was graphic and clear. June immediately stepped forward. Perhaps it would shame him to kill a petite woman. But he started to raise his ax anyway then suddenly, he looked down.

Everyone focused on a large constrictor looking snake that poured into the road between us and the Mayans. It arose and faced the Mayan soldiers. Befuddled by the magic they were seeing, the soldiers turned and fled. Then the constrictor just slithered away, paying us no attention. I awoke, sitting up in bed looking at where I thought a constrictor had crawled away."

"Again, the serpents saved you. Do we have a pattern going on here," asked Ken?

June answered, "Maybe, but before we begin making assumptions about the meaning of these dreams, I want to hear Corey's story."

The Bear Attack

Corey had been very quiet, not saying anything until this moment. He seemed a little confused or distance to everything that had been said. We all realized that Corey obviously had something to tell us, how incredible a story we had no idea, we all thought to ourselves that anything as long as he wasn't bitten in the face again. Corey took his time, drinking almost a whole cup of coffee before he began his story. "I was listening to Mr. Owl, out in the forest. We were sitting on some rocks, to avoid ticks. We were next to the creek that I had almost fallen into, a couple of years ago. I remember we had an evening fire going, Mr. Owl was telling a non-sensible story, something about how skunks got their scents. I remember him saying, the skunk was once a larger animal than he is now, as large as a hill. But he became smaller and smaller and this caused him to worry. If I grow smaller and smaller, it thought, I will lose my strength. Then how can I hunt and kill my game and protect myself? And so, he thought and thought. I know, he thought, I will make a strong hunting medicine which will give me skill even when I am not as large as now."

"Then suddenly Mr. Owl stopped talking. He was silent for a moment or two then out of the blue, he began explaining to me in a different voice, what the amulet is."

"The amulet is a protective device star people used in order to keep invasive organisms like our serpents from probing into our minds. It is a basic tool that the star people use, among many. One of them was left here on earth during the transfer of the serpents."

"When the Star people arrived here," continued Mr. Owl in the dream. "There were no humans, only ice age animals that consumed other animals in a natural ecological procession. This place was picked because it would be a most unappealing yet livable place to imprison the serpents. Serpents are highly intelligent and social creatures yet are physically limited. Instinctually they built nest to live in, as they had done on their home planet, but they had evolved to parasitize other intelligent creatures. Secretly they would study and then enter into each society like invisible termites. By manipulating the conquered species or clan, the serpents live comfortably. Whole worlds are then farmed so that the indigenous creatures live only to provide life energy to the serpents. After they have absorbed all the nutrients available they search out and find another society. Like termites they eventually destroy nearly all that they come into contact with, leaving the society metaphorically like termite consumed wood. Often the natives became extinct before the serpents would leave for another place.

"The serpents naturally want to expand their influence thought out the universe. Instead they were long ago locked away here on this planet. When they were first placed here on earth, there was not a single living creature that could be manipulated and used as energy providers. Except for an occasional meal, the roaming Pleistocene fauna would be useless to the serpents. Just to the north of where they were marooned existed huge sheets of ice. The serpent would suffer just trying to stay warm. Again, the star people had little remorse about the sentence being served against them. Besides, it was warm enough in the summer so they could procreate. It wasn't considered a death sentence; it was considered a housecleaning of undesirable pest, much like cleaning out an infestation of lice from your home. Perhaps if the serpents had been a little more honest about their intentions the star people would have understood. Instead the serpents plotted against them..."

"Then there was a flash of bright light, swirling red colors forming intricate designs if I remember correctly, and I do. Something happened. It was as if the dream changed channels."

"When my eyes came back, I was focused on a commotion in the woods. Something large was moving through the brush, probably a bear. I looked back at Mr. Owl but he had vanished and suddenly the fire was threatening to go out. I remember thinking that it was amazing how fast Mr. Owl had disappeared. Had he actually run away or did he just vanish? I didn't know if he was real or just a figment of my imagination. I remember thinking that it seemed to me that what Mr. Owl had been saying didn't sound like anything the serpents would want to admit too. Serpents had never displayed a weakness. I wondered where the apparition had really come from. Was it from a phantom, a shaman, a *bruja* or a visitor from a different reality from a different plane, or Viracocha himself?"

Then I heard it again. There indeed was something large coming my way. It was a bear, and it seemed to have zeroed in on me. Everywhere I turned the bear seemed to be there before me. It was much quicker than I was.

I stopped running and the bear just sat there, staring at me, studying me, trying to figure me out. I took a dare step toward the bear. It didn't retreat. Instead it charged me, slapping me across the chest with its large claws. Hitting the rocky ground, rivulets of blood ran down my chest and I knew I was going to die. Then the bear suddenly looked distracted. A tiny snake crawled under the bear's massive paws. The bear seemed to forget about me, groping instead for the snake. I remained motionless for a moment and the bear slowly walked away with his nose following the snake. I turned over to crawl away and realized that I was crawling out of bed. I awoke, hard as I hit the floor."

Hidalgo was the first to say anything, "So they thought that they would be leaving them in stark isolation? That may have been the way earth was then but it certainly isn't the way it is now, I wonder what is going on in that collective consciousness?"

Dream Fragments

It would be a couple of more days until another round of strange dreams occurred. This time the dreams were more disjointed, even stranger. Hidalgo's was typical, only his dream occurred two nights later.

An evil human Shaman, looking like a Zuni *Kachina* but far more evil than a serpent, was casting spells. Flinging bundles of energy, cast like invisible fireballs that plunged into the hearts of the unknowing receivers.

Later he dreamed of walking through a field littered with dead snakes, including some that he thought had been serpents. He continued his walk to a rock outcrop where there were several serpentine creatures that seemed to be rolling around in pain, with their lighter colored stomachs appearing to turn over and over.

The serpent clan was the victim of a spell. A small trio of serpent spies journeyed to the place where they were originally sentenced to live on this planet. The inland sea was now nothing but a vast salt bed with mountains in the far distance. Humans had built a huge city close by and the serpents admired the way the humans had learned to fly in large metal tubes that looked like birds. Although they had images of the vast worlds in space, they had long ago cataloged the hieroglyphic memories of the world they had come from, even the librarian's world, but they knew how to instantly bring those memories back to life.

A journey was undertaken for the wishes of serpent royalty, to where their ancestors had first commenced their migrations. The trio of serpents was the first of the serpents to realize that something was terribly wrong. They found themselves wondering though a country where all the natural wildlife had died. Rattlesnakes, usually immune to most of the biological agents that cause death, were all being found dead. The dead rattlesnakes appeared to have decomposed from the inside out. They had died in an agonizing stupor, in pain yet unable to move.

The serpents had no idea what had killed the rattlesnakes. Despite their collective wisdom, they certainly had no idea why the rattlesnakes had died.

The family experienced several dream fragments, always short and disjointed:

Dream fragment: A trio of serpents entered a room where there are three little mice. The mice were perfect for eating; the serpents would not even need to waste venom on them. But as the serpents came close to the mice they suddenly grew in size and turned on the serpents, viciously chewing the serpents heads off.

Dream fragment: Quetzalcoatl and Kukulcan led a swarm of serpents that had collected next to what had once been a vast inland sea that was now nothing but a dry lake bed. After reaching their destination, Quetzalcoatl and Kukulcan began their unique undulating dance while they waited for the star ship to appear. The triangular shaped ship appeared, hovered over them for a short time, and then it disappeared back into the sky leaving the serpents disappointed again. They would not be released from their earthly prison.

Dream fragment: The cow just kept stepping on the serpent and rib after rib was crushed despite the venom that the serpent delivered. The cow didn't seem to notice the serpent.

Dream fragment: The cat held the serpent's head down under a paw, then, it slowly and casually chewed the serpent's head off.

Dream fragment: The Mayan didn't want to give his life force to the serpents, but as the warriors held him down he seemed to calm down, then just as the obsidian blade was to come crashing through his chest cavity, he suddenly found strength to turn away. The blade struck the stone where the victim had been and shattered. The shaman took it as a sign and released the captive who ran as fast as he could away. The serpent was terribly disappointed at the loss of the life energy.

Sitting around the kitchen table, the usual place for family planning and decision making everyone brainstormed. The conclusion that we came to was that the serpents had been calling out for help. At first they were angry at all humans and that is why the terrifying dreams. Their actions followed their visions they were causing, they would begin attacking the humans again to thin them out so they would not ever be bothered again. But there were too many humans to deal with. Besides, it was not humans that were attacking them. Eventually they realized that a pathogen was attacking them. The serpents would find themselves trying to communicate a need for help. They were asking for help with the only humans they trusted and had an association with.

Hidalgo suggested that they should attempt to communicate with the serpents but they gave up after they realized that they had no way to communicate with the serpents. They even argued among themselves that they really didn't want to save the serpents after all it was the serpents that seemed to be causing all the problems many humans were dealing with. In the end, they were helpless and decided they would just let it play out.

Piggy Back

It was a warm meeting at the Socorro restaurant and the same food was ordered. This time, Dr. Hartsell ate everything on her plate. After getting past the obvious question about how family members were doing, discussions about the pathogen topped the conversation. How did it work?

Dr. Hartsell thought about how to answer the question for a moment, then answers, "I think it is a piggy back, that is when chromosomes of two pathogens are combined and as a result, a new pathogen is created with characteristics of both. It takes a lot of research in order get the chromosomal combinations of genetic material that produces the result they are looking for."

"That is," I casually asked?

"A pathogen that is both virulent, that is, it spreads easily, and causes death. Those of us in the lab think that the general's scientists, piggy backed a fast spreading virulent pathogen with a disease that acts like mad cow disease. The serpents would have noticed nothing for a long time, and then a fever occurred followed by a few days of lethargy until the disease had time to spread through the brain and spinal cord. The creature starts to lose control over its bodily functions as brain tissue atrophies. Death is then immanent.

There were few other concerns discussed. Someone spoke up about

General Armstrong's scientist and staff. There was no accountability for what was being done now. There was no way of knowing whether or not others were still experimenting. Did he release other pathogenic agents? Most importantly we wanted more information about the pathogen that General Armstrong released upon the serpents. Could they eventually mutate and infect humans? No one knew the answer, only time would tell.

Dr. Hartsell set her fork down and waited until everyone was politely looking at her. She then said, "I talked it over with my sister. The pathogen that was released had a seventy-five percent probability to mutate into a form that will be dangerous to humans. I hope you realize that in only a short while it is possible that epidemics could break out. We all needed to avoid people and keep track of news reports.

The Great Dying

They were a different pair of serpents who assumed royalty but they still carried the collective consciousness of the clan and certainly the consciousness of the former royalty. Quetzalcoatl and Kukulcan were still alive. They had voluntarily isolating themselves, hiding deep among the rocks wary of any interaction with humans or even members of their own clan who may have possibly been infected. But the disease slowly ran its course killing nearly all of them. The survivors knew what had happened and could do little for now but wait, reproduce and make plans. Above all else they decided that an entirely new approach had to be tried when dealing with humans. War would not work, there was simply too many humans and their shamans were too powerful. The humans, they reasoned, could easily create even more deadly weapons that could destroy all of them.

For over a year, humans were unaware that anything was wrong, the entire world returned to normal. Then hospitals suddenly began to fill with people who were experiencing flu-like symptoms. The doctors at first treated the people as they would any viral infection. That is, they treated the symptoms. The humans would return home but would not be able to get over the illness. In time the patients would learn, that there was far more to their ailments than the flu. Although it was taking a long time to develop, something terrible was happening to everyone. Almost everyone appeared to be in various stages of mad cow disease. Dementia became the norm and as the humans lay in their beds wasting away they began to lose all control over their bodily functions and finally they starved to death. Eventually there was no one available to care for the sick. Thousands and then millions died causing a general panic. Anywhere people congregated, they shortly began to die. In time, they all died except for those who for some reason or another were completely isolated from the outside world.

In Serpiente, the humans had taken a calculated risk and constructed a double row of fences with locked gates across the main entryway. We knew what was going to happen and planned for it, unfortunately few members of our immediate families could be persuaded to leave their homes in time. Taking Dr. Hartsell with us, we isolated ourselves at the ranch and refused to mingle with other people. A tiny few of our friends moved to the isolated ranch and built homes for themselves on the grounds around the older ranch house. Among them was Jill Thompson, Hidalgo's friend, who had been living in Durango.

Jill did not want to leave her job and live at the ranch; in fact, she had to be duped into making the drive down to the ranch by June who told her that Hidalgo had been critically hurt and was asking for her on his deathbed. She showed up at the ranch after a long drive expecting Hidalgo to be in the grip of death. Instead Hidalgo was in perfect health. Initially this produced a flash of anger from Jill.

"Do you realize that I had to take emergency leave from my job just to come down here?" She exploded.

"I am trying to save your life," yelled Hidalgo.

"Have you all lost your minds?" Jill replied in angry disbelief. "What makes you think that I would be in danger of losing my life if I stay in Durango and do my job? There are superior doctors and hospitals there. If I get sick here, I will be in far more danger."

When Hidalgo told her of the pathogen she didn't believe him. Even after Dr. Hartsell explained the facts to her she thought everyone was working in collusion against her. She became extremely angry when she realized that she was being held there by Hidalgo who refused to let her return to her job and certain death.

The Durango police made inquiries concerning the disappearance of Jill but everyone claimed ignorance of her whereabouts. "Well, she never arrived here." June told them. They were lucky, only a day later the pathogen arrived in Durango but no one was aware of it for another few days and it would take several months before the profound effects began to show. By then all concerns of a missing detective vanished. But as the news of the plague finally hit the airways and television news programs and the world began to panic, Jill began to reevaluate Hidalgo's duplicity. In time, she was thankful to Hidalgo for kidnapping her even if it had seemed extreme in the beginning. Her attitude and feelings toward Hidalgo had been a roller coaster ride as first; then everything settled down. First, she loved him, then for a while she thought he was a criminal and finally as she became aware of the fate of humans all over the world she was eternally grateful to him. In time, they married and started their own family totally isolated from the rest of humanity. Unfortunately, only a tiny few people would make the journey to Serpiente and after the first reports of the pathogen appeared no one was allowed to enter the confines of the ranch for any reason.

Jenna Bear Anderson's Hieroglyphics

Grandma June and Grandpa Ken had long ago finished their meal, sitting back in their wooden rocking chairs watching the universe slowly slide around them. Everyone was satiated. Grilled steaks with corn on the cob and home grown fresh green chilies roosted over the grill and eaten outdoors with the family had always been one of our favorite meals. We had already bagged up the dirty dishes and everything was packed in the wheel barrow for the short walk back to the ranch house. It was already dark, the sun had set an hour ago, yet everyone sat and listened as I told the story of the history of the Serpent Clan. I had told it to the little girl many times before.

Sitting around and doing nothing, Hidalgo and Jill were getting drowsy. Corey had already prompted everyone that they needed to walk the hundred or so yards back to the ranch house before it got too late, and it was getting late. They had been listening to the story that I was telling my little girl, the story about us. The little girl kept asking questions. She was just like her mother when I was young, always moving, always inquisitive, always wanting to learn more. We were all sitting under the cottonwoods close to where I first met John Luna.

The men had constructed a table there with benches made out of lumber leftover from constructing a building, and using a little cement they had constructed a fire pit with a grill that was perfect to cook over. Using horses, they had dragged logs away so any bothersome rattlesnake or scorpion would not bother us. Eating outdoors in the cool fall weather had been a welcome treat, a respite from the summer's heat.

All little kids require constant entertainment, My little girl, Jenna Brook Anderson, was spoiled rotten by some very doting grandparents, not to mention a certain Uncle Hidalgo, a Navaho who had nicknamed her Jenna Bear. The little girl had never thought of the ambiguity of her uncle being a Navajo, nor had he. They were a constant source of comfort for each other. The family couldn't keep their eyes off the little girl who was a rolling circus of entertainment. Jenna Bear was getting bored. She wanted to hear the story again of a history of the Serpent Clan and she was in no hurry to return to the ranch house, which meant she would soon have to go to bed. But we were all tired; I had spent the entire evening telling the story already, a story told without the numerous deaths and destruction that occurred in reality. Rather the story was told more like a fairy tale, more appropriate for a child, but it was time to go to the ranch house.

Everyone felt a little sorry for Little Jenna Bear as there were many children at the ranch house but none of them were her age. They thought that she had no friends to play with other than the much older children of Manuel and of course the infants that had recently come.

Little Jenna Bear Anderson was always asking about the serpents. I would answer her, "I am certain that they are still around but they don't seem to want to bother us humans anymore. The contagion that General Armstrong released should have destroyed nearly all of them. Don't worry little precious one they will not bother you." As everyone started the short walk back to the ranch house, Jenna Bear asked, "Are serpents real or were they really talking about something else; a friendly creature who actually wanted to play with little girls?"

I would laugh and said no. Jenna was used to having stories read to her about mythological creatures, everything from talking bears to an animated mouse with large ears who wore little round buttons on his trousers. I reached down and grabbed her hand, directing her to the ranch house, and answered, "Well, a serpent is a serpent, let's hope that we do not have to deal with them for tonight."

A few days later, Jenna decided that she wanted to draw pictures with colored pencils and paper, while I painted an oil painting I had been working on for over a week. Leaning over the table the little girl entertained herself while I painted but Penny stopped her painting after a while and watched her little girl. A pencil had rolled away from the little girl, out of reach. Then to my amazement the pencil suddenly rolled back to the waiting hand of the little girl who casually reached for it to color in something. I knew that the pencil should not have become animated the way it did, after all, there were laws of physics involved and they had apparently been broken.

Little did I know that every conscience thought that I, as well as everyone else in the family, was being understood by a pair of creatures. Quetzalcoatl and Kukulcan were particularly interested in Jenna Bear. They were entering Jenna's dreams at night, playing with her, ever so gently. They kept her company in her dreams by playing games and teaching her all manner of things that only a serpent could understand, things that a doting human parent would never dream of.

June just happened to enter the study where I was working and Jenna Bear was drawing. I quickly signaled her over to see what the little girl was drawing. Expecting to see the usual stick figures of people and trees that looked like telephone poles with circular globs for the leaves, what we saw took our breath away. What little Jenna Bear Anderson was drawing were the same hieroglyphs that Grandma June instantly recognized as decorations on the walls of many Mayan temples. They were perfectly drawn with detail that no little girl should be able to accomplish. Jenna and her descendants were on their way to acquiring a whole new language and perception of the world. Little Jenna Bear could actually talk to the serpents that visited her dreams in their own unique language. A language made of symbols and visual diagrams that amazed her parents.

After the family got together to discuss the situation it was Jill Thompson, Hidalgo's new mate that finally said what everyone was thinking, the serpents had changed their approach to dealing with humans. They were now working with the humans, at least here in the small community of Serpiente in a whole new way than they had historically done. But the point begged many new questions such as would human survivors learn the ways of war and even human sacrifice. Had we changed our ways or was it now ingrained into our nature?

The serpents were certainly still here, studying us, plotting a way to change us and use us for their own means but the serpents indeed had decided to change their own way of dealing with humans. Instead of using us for the rush of energy that a death could provide, they believed the humans could become their partners to return to the stars and someday confront the ones who had imprisoned them here on this lonely planet. They couldn't do it by themselves, they needed the humans. They wouldn't wait for Viracocha to return, they would return to the stars with the help of the humans and confront Viracocha. They had decided that we humans who lived at Serpiente would provide them the means for that return to the stars, teaching them, manipulating them, one child at a time. Jenna Anderson had already proven to be their first success in programming the humans. In time, anything would be possible.

Readers Guide

1. According to the introduction in the preface, humans rarely identify the real dangers to their livelihood. What other dangers do humans ignore at their own peril that are not listed in the preface?

2. Why did the motel desk clerk in Bloomfield, New Mexico refuse to rent Hidalgo a room? When and where has this kind of discrimination occured before in American history?

3. According to astronomers there should be millions of planets in our own galaxy that have advanced civilizations on them. Yet there is no concrete evidence for alien contact. Why do you suppose we have not made contact with extraterrestrials?

4. There is much presumptive evidence of extraterrestrial contact on earth such as ancient stories, petroglyphs and ancient constructions that appear to have been influenced by extraterrestrials. What evidence is there of extraterrestrial contact?

5. What are auras? What is the life energy that is present in all living creatures?

6. Why is the author talking about food webs and other ecological relationships in nature?

7. Do you know characters like Dalton and Jackson? Why do you suppose that opposites in personality bond together?

8. Often people who fail in school or are arrested can only be embarrassed so much and then they fail to care. How did Dalton cope with being such a loser? Most people who are involved in crime often return to crime as soon as they are released from jail. Do you know people who have gone through this process? Is there a cure for this behavior?

9. Are you aware of any circumstances where teachers hae been dismissed due to students such as Jackson and Dolton?

10. The modern Navajo police take reports of skin walkers or shape shifters very seriously, why do you suppose this is so?

11. Corey interjected a though, "So the harder we fight or wage war, the stronger we make them. That could lead to our extinction." Why would a war with the serpents lead to the extinction of the humans?

12. Why did General Armstrong want to weaponize the serpents? Why did Penny release them from their glass cage?

13. In Hopi Prophecies, why did the Hopi representative, Mr. Hoyumptewa distrust Hidalgo?

14. Why do the Hopi as well as many modern Native Americans not want outsiders to view their religious ceremonies? What was the Pueblo Revolt?

15. Why were the stolen ceremonial objects being auctioned in France?

16. What are Kachinas? Why are they important to Native Americans? How are they similar to Christian representations of Biblical entities?

17. How did Mr. Hoyumptewa's prophecies come true?

18. While in France, why did the history detectives find it so hard to pretend that they were rich and arrogant Americans?

19. What was the real lesson that the art teacher was attempting to make when she turned the painting of the caricature of a court jester upside down and instructed the class to draw it that way? Why did she leave the classroom and allow the students to cheat?

20. Why are biological and chemical weapons used by some armies? Does the United States use such weapons? If so, why are they produced and stored by the military?

21. Why was Jim Wilkerson so secretive about where he lived? Why did June have so much trouble contacting him?

22. Ultimately, why is the only true value in the universe considered to be knowledge?

23. Why does the author trace the sequence of events such as the Norte Chico people until modern times? How did serpents effect theses cultures from an archeological perspective?

24. During the dream episodes, why were the history detectives having such unusual and prophetic dreams?

25. Why did June tell the story by the Greek storyteller Aesop? What was the moral of the story and why did it seem appropriate for what the history detectives were dealing with?

26. After the pathogen hit, most of humanity as well as the serpents were destroyed. How and why did the serpents change the way they were dealing with the remaining humans at Serpiente?

27. Why did the surviving serpents pick out Jenna Bear Anderson to communicate with?